Praise for Nicole Cushing's

"Noelle Cashman—I mean Nicol[e] . . .
shocking and satirical survey of the ranked . . . .
and its many horrifying discontents. *A Sick Gray Laugh*'s warts-
and-all metanarrative is reminiscent of such recent genre touch-
stones as Caitlin R. Kiernan's *The Red Tree* and Gemma Files's
Experimental Film, but told in a brutal and uncompromising
style that is all Cushing's own."

—Robert Levy, author of *The Glittering World*

Praise for Nicole Cushing's *Mr. Suicide*

"…a work of brutal and extreme horror… disturbingly graphic
content…"

—*Publishers Weekly*

"This tale of a damaged and murderous child is the most original horror novel I've read in years. Cushing's prose is rapid-
fire, grisly, and passionate."

—Poppy Z. Brite, author of *Exquisite Corpse* and *Lost Souls*

"Novels don't come much more transgressive than this one,
folks. Got a taboo? Watch Nicole Cushing grin while she danc-
es all over it. In other hands that might be reason enough for
the witty *Mr. Suicide* to exist. But this is more and better than
that—a truly nightmare world, richly imagined, told to us in
a canny, subversive second-person voice that makes you, the
reader, the hero of this tale, like it or not. That it also manages
to be ultimately life-affirming is yet another wonder."

—Jack Ketchum, award-winning author of
Off Season and *The Girl Next Door*

Praise for Nicole Cushing (continued)

"Nicole Cushing uses her sharp and confident prose like a surgical instrument to dissect both her characters and our emotions. *Mr. Suicide* is horrifying and harrowing, but just as much for the emotional devastation it causes in the reader as for the violence and depravity—as well as the twisted humor—it portrays. This is horror fiction that leaves marks."

—Ray Garton, author of
Live Girls and *Sex and Violence in Hollywood*

"The confidence and expertise so blatantly evident in Nicole Cushing's writing is astonishing."

—Thomas Ligotti

A
Sick
Gray
Laugh

A
SICK
GRAY
LAUGH

Nicole Cushing

WORD HORDE
PETALUMA, CA

First Edition

ISBN 978-1-939905-52-9

A Word Horde Book

To the memories of Witold Gombrowicz (1904-1969)
and Leonid Andreyev (1871-1919)

Part One: The Disease

1

When I started writing this book, I vowed to keep my madness out of it.

What, exactly, do I mean by that? Simply that all the books I wrote before this one were works of fiction inspired by my personal struggles with severe depression and anxiety, and that this approach was beginning to feel a little old. How many times can I write about characters on the brink of self-slaughter? How many times can I depict characters paralyzed by obsessive-compulsive disorder? How many times are you, constant reader, capable of indulging me in my habit of obnoxious repetition?

Maybe if I were still plagued by such ailments, I'd grit my teeth, suck it up, and find a way to be satisfied with the tried and true approach that has led my work to enjoy critical acclaim. After all, while madness has not been good for *me*, it's been awfully good for *my fiction*. Reviewers, academics, and awards juries have come to expect that I'll publish a steady flow of books with titles like *The Girl with the Gun in Her Mouth* and *Leather Noose*. Unrelenting nihilism, spiked with sadism, is the trademark of my work.

But therein lies the problem. You see, shortly before the publication of my last book (*The Breath Curse*) my madness became so severe that I was forced to seek the treatment of a psychiatrist. My OCD had morphed into something more akin to paranoid psychosis. After decades of fending it off on my own, I reached the breaking point and asked for help. I saw an old, wizened, mummy-like doctor of mixed German and Indian descent named Sherman Himmerahd-D'janni, M.D. He prescribed an oblong yellow pill. I take two each day. Since starting this medication, my ailments have gone into remission.

So even if I wasn't bored with the subject of madness, I no longer suffer from it. And because I no longer suffer from it, I no longer feel the urgency to vent my suffering onto the page. Make no mistake, I still wield the knife of pessimism. But instead of carrying it with me day in and day out, I often put it on the shelf for weeks on end. I no longer take the time to sharpen it against the whetstone of rumination.

This is good news to my friends and loved ones. Everyone close to me seems to appreciate the change. I've begun jogging and have lost seventy-five pounds. I am tan, healthy, and more mindful of cobbling together an attractive appearance (washed hair, brushed hair, brushed teeth, shaved legs). I play softball. I am able to become fully immersed in the drama of competition. I have joined with others to form a team. I am unashamed of having cast my lot with theirs. Unashamed of marching shoulder to shoulder with them, week after week.

This may astonish you, but it could even be said that—of all our players—I'm the least pessimistic. Even during our last at bat in the last game of our 0-18 season, even as we were losing twenty to eight, I believed that we'd be the recipients of a miracle and come away with a victory. And when our final batter grounded out, I spent five minutes in a daze wondering why the underdogs hadn't prevailed (the way they always do in the movies).

What's the point of this seemingly pointless anecdote about my athletic endeavors? Simply that, for the first time in many years, I'm capable of succumbing to Moronic Hope.

This, in and of itself, implies that I've been reabsorbed into humanity (the species that, to this day, remains the only known practitioner of Moronic Hope). But there were other signs of my reabsorption as well. I enjoy the company of my fellow man. Or, at the very least, the sea of humanity no longer makes me seasick. Or perhaps it still does, but the oblong yellow pills have an effect similar to Dramamine. In any event, to impress upon you just how far I've come in reacquainting myself with the human herd, I'll say this: I've even begun to listen to two (not one, but two!) local sports radio stations. This is, arguably, the most normal activity I've undertaken in many years.

In some ways, though, I regret all these changes. There's the real possibility that, already, they've disrupted my writing mojo. Yes, I have vowed to keep my madness out of this book. But my brain has always worked best when it's obsessively contemplating death. My spirit of creation is the spirit of decay. Corpse breath has always been the wind billowing my sails. Now I have to change? Find a way to maneuver my boat through a fresh coastal gale? This will surely have a negative impact on the artistic success of my writing endeavors.

Even worse, the positive changes in my life threaten to fuck up my *commercial success*. What I mean is, these changes could destroy my author brand.

You *do* understand what an "author brand" is, don't you? It's a concept that, in recent years, has become all the rage in conversations between writers. Just Google it and you'll find ten thousand and ninety-one blog posts emphasizing the necessity of having one. But let's assume, just for a moment, that you haven't heard of the concept and you're too lazy to Google it. How can I best describe it?

Well, as I understand it, an author brand is an author's unique identity, as perceived by bookstores, readers, and reviewers. An author's unique *commercial* identity, you might say. (And please note that by "unique commercial identity," I mean a unique identity as summed up in a single phrase that helps consumers and tastemakers get a sense of the *flavor* of a writer's products.)

So you can see my dilemma: if your author brand reeks of madness and squalor, as mine does, getting well creates problems. You can't proceed as you always have before: dipping a ladle into your own mental effluvium and distilling it into effective fiction. Pharmaceuticals have re-invented Noelle Cashman, the person. Therefore, it was inevitable that they'd also reinvent Noelle Cashman, the author.

This is why I've been forced to take a decidedly different tack with this book. In the past my work has been fueled by the aforementioned distilled introspection. It typically unfolded in the following fashion:

1. I experienced a fresh, jellyfish-like sting of mental torment (or the intrusion of wormy, mildewy, half-rotten memories of *past* torments).

2. The mental torment (or half-rotten memories) caused several strange disjointed images to flash before my mind's eye.

3. I took the most potent of the strange images and used it as the definitive image of a story; the image that held within it all the essential characters and plot points.

(Un?)fortunately, it has been too long since I've experienced mental torment. Therefore, my old tricks no longer work. So I am forced to change my writing habits. Since I can no longer depend on the strange disjointed images in my mind's eye, I've decided to switch to writing nonfiction. That way, I can write a book focused exclusively on the world *outside* my head.

But *which* world outside my head? There are so many to choose from these days. For example, there are the worlds of Twitter and Facebook. Sometimes I think of these as the worlds of moral exhibitionism (in which social networking accounts open their virtual raincoats and flash their social, political, religious, or anti-religious virtues in front of you, unbidden). Other times I think of these as the worlds of moral *pornography* (in which we voluntarily stare at the penetration of vice by virtue, and caress our own private parts—whatever they may be—in sync with the rhythm of the rutting).

Will I be writing about these worlds and their attendant moralizing?

No. I find social networking to be a dull obligation at best. (An obligation to push my author brand, that is.) At worst, it may be a tool of corporate and/or government surveillance. Furthermore, I will not get on a soapbox to endorse any social, political, religious, or anti-religious causes, even those that I privately champion. You see, I don't read a lot of polemical nonfiction, so why would I choose to write it?

But surely, you're thinking, *there are other worlds out there to explore in a work of nonfiction such as this. Worlds that afford a less stridently moralistic tone than that of Facebook and Twitter.*

Yes, of course. I know that. For example, there's the world of glossy sports magazines. The world of publishers dedicated to translating works of Russian, Czech, and Icelandic literary fiction into English. The world of lower-middlebrow American bestsellerdom. When I say I'll be writing about "the world outside my head," do I mean I'll be writing about any of these worlds?

Alas, no. While I've brushed against all these worlds, I don't feel very connected to any of them. I'm not a citizen of any of those worlds. I'm a tourist who has infrequently visited them.

I don't think I should write about worlds I know only from tourism (especially in this, my first work of nonfiction). Natives of such realms would rightly point out my superficial treatment of the subject. Better to write about something closer to home.

What about the world of twenty-first-century movies? Is that the "world outside my head" on which I'll be focusing?

No.

At the risk of sounding like an old fart who is out of touch with pop culture, I must confess that even now, during my upswell of mental health and tolerance of humanity, I seldom go to the movies. Even looking at the trailers makes me groan. There's too much CGI. Everything is a boilerplate kaleidoscope of pseudo-outrageous action in the manner of a video game. I say "pseudo-outrageous" because every 3D twist and stretch and explosion is there to serve reliably stale, melodramatic storytelling. (This, by the way, is an aesthetic judgment—not a moral one.)

What, then, about the world of twenty-first-century television? Surely *that's* the "world outside my head" that I'll be focusing on, right? Unlike the movies, broadcast television offers various *news* and *sports* programs presented in high-definition digital clarity. I consider myself to be a citizen of *that* world, don't I?

While I've watched several minutes of high-definition NFL broadcasts, I must hasten to add that I've never been able to finish an entire game. Something about high-definition digital video seems exaggerated. The world shown in such broadcasts doesn't look like the real world at all. It looks like the real world after it has been polished three days straight with Turtle Wax. How could I possibly write about such a world? It would be impossible. For starters, I don't have the necessary tools. To depict such a waxy world I'd have to rig my printer to use cartridges full of Turtle Wax instead of ink. Anyone who knows me well can tell you I'm not that mechanically inclined.

No, I decided to write about a world unmediated by any camera and/or display screen. It is simply the world as it appears outside the window of my home office.

At this point you may be thinking something like the following: *What do you see outside that window, Noelle? How can it possibly be worth writing about? If you limit yourself to a subject so prosaic, you'll sell yourself short. Don't go for the low-hanging fruit! Why do you even look out there anymore? What can you find in the world outside your window that can't be found a thousand times in a Google image search? How can you possibly claim that it's more deserving of my attention than MSNBC's coverage of the latest school shooting, or* The New York Times' *coverage of the National Book Awards? How can a nonfiction elaboration on this prosaic view possibly be worth our time?*

These are entirely reasonable questions. Be patient. All shall be revealed.

Allow me to set the stage.

I live in a small town in southern Indiana. Our population is just a little under fifty thousand.

My subdivision was built over fifty years ago. My neighbors work for factories, trucking companies, nursing homes, and the like. The houses here are smaller than those in most subdivisions, and show their age.

So when I look outside the window of my home office, I see modest lawns (maybe, on average, fifteen yards wide). I see red brick façades. Window shutters. Aluminum siding. I see a variety of landscaping styles (some minimalist and elegant, others a cluttered embarrassment of chipped-paint yard gnomes and one-winged angels). I see pickup trucks, jeeps, and Camaros, too. Many bear bumper stickers vowing allegiance to one or another of the local college basketball powerhouses. I see bumper stickers expressing pride in a child who's an honor student (or a football player, or a gymnast, or a marine). I see flags. Stars. Stripes.

But none of these are what I notice *first*, and it's this as-yet-unspecified first thing I see that makes the world outside my window worth writing about. Because the first thing I see captures the texture of life here in a way nothing else can.

The first thing I see outside my window each morning is—

Dare I even tell you about this? If I do, you may think I'm nuts (and not in a sexy, self-destructive, sophisticated Sylvia Plath sort of way, but in a foul, fetid, fiendish bag lady sort of way). And what about my vow to keep my madness out of this book? Here I am, only a few pages later, paralyzed by nervousness!

The thing is, there will be no book if I don't force myself to push past the inertia that wants me to leave well enough alone. Any book worth reading is born from a writer's courage to finally confess that she's seen something she doesn't want to admit she's seen. So there's no getting around the revelation I'm about to make.

That first thing I see when I look outside my office window is…well…how do I even begin to tell you this?

It's…

…an overwhelming Grayness that's slathered over everything like a thick coat of snot.

Does that make any sense?

It doesn't, does it?

You don't think this revelation lives up to all the hype I set up for it, do you?

This is too abrupt a transition, isn't it? I've just introduced a speed bump—this ambiguous concept of Grayness. Now the natural flow of this book will be interrupted while I take time to explain what I mean by "an overwhelming Grayness that's slathered over everything like a thick coat of snot."

ahem

What I mean is: when I look out my window, the green of the grass and leaves is a *muted* green. It's a green that's been contaminated (by the Grayness of faded, cracked asphalt; by the Grayness of the cloud-stained sky). The Gray *dominates* the green; seeps into it and snottily saturates it until the *Spirit* of Grayness replaces the *spirit* of the green. Nature is no match for it.

Neither is humanity. My neighbors and I represent various different races and backgrounds (African-Americans, Caucasians, Latinos, Muslims); and yet, there's no zest to be found in this diversity. The faces may be colorful, but they aren't Colorful. Everyone is connected to one another all right, but only in the sense that we're mutually attached by a network of thick strands of Gray soul-snot.

As a result, my neighborhood has taken on the burden of a boring, coiled-up heaviness. It's as though the Gray Air has congealed around everyone and everything, like chilled animal fat, thus making people, animals, and objects move in slow motion. The only things my neighbors ever scream at are their children and sports teams. No one screams at the Grayness. No one screams at the unfairness of it all. No one screams at funerals. No one screams into the mirror. No one screams at morons. No one screams simply for the sake of screaming.

In Gray Towns, life is something less than life, but everyone has found a way to adjust. I have to think that my more sophisticated neighbors probably suspect they've been cheated— handed a life that's worth only sixty cents on the dollar. But they never speak of their suspicions. Instead, they endeavor to decrease their intelligence, by contorting themselves to fit some political or religious orthodoxy. That way, their suspicions don't ignite in their heads too often. There isn't enough mental oxygen in the cramped space of orthodoxy to fuel mental fires.

Or perhaps they sublimate their thirst for adventure by taking the family on a vacation to one of the theme parks owned and operated by media conglomerates (or a theme park for adults, like the Vegas Strip). Or they go on Twitter and shake their fists at their supervisors (or their employees), Democrats (or Republicans), Scientologists (or Terrorists).

Meanwhile, my less sophisticated neighbors revel in the architectural clutter of my town's main drag. The grease-stained limestone. The dented aluminum gutters. The poorly zoned clutter of dollar stores, churches, and dive bars. They visit the payday loan rackets and rent-to-own establishments. Or they go on Twitter and shake their fists at their supervisors (or their employees), Democrats (or Republicans), Scientologists (or Terrorists).

The thick, sick Grayness—that's what I see outside my window. It corrodes life until all that remains is rust. It corrodes rust until all that remains is dust. It's the *genius loci* of unsafe factories, shady nursing homes, overdose funerals, abandoned railroad tracks, and grubby little strip-mall churches. There. That's it. I said it. *That's* what I see outside. Every. Single. Day.

Of course, I'm the not first writer of bleak, transgressive texts to notice the Grayness. In *The Confusions of Young Törless*, the early twentieth-century Austrian writer Robert Musil not only mentions "the sea of grey sensations that crowded around… day after day," but goes on to describe gloomy rural mist as being like "a slimy trail" that "clung to the newly ploughed land and lead-grey turnip fields."

Nor, for that matter, am I the first writer from the Midwestern United States to notice the Grayness. Essayist and short story writer Susan Neville has opined (somewhat whimsically) that "[i]t's well known that midwesterners have over one hundred words for gray."

William H. Gass's short story "In the Heart of the Heart of the Country" takes a more severe approach. Gass deploys the word "gray" eleven times in a single paragraph to describe a desperate little Indiana town. Here's a partial sample, so you know I'm not just making this part up.

> Streets, sidewalks, faces, feelings—they are gray. Speech is gray, and the grass where it shows…. Everything is gray: hair, eyes, window glass, the hawkers' bills and touters' posters, lips, teeth, poles, and metal signs—they're gray, quite gray…. Horses, sheep, and cows, cats killed in the road, squirrels in the same way …. all are gray, everything is gray, and everyone is out of luck who lives here.

You may be saying to yourself: *Now, Noelle, given that other writers have already written about Grayness, why don't you pick another subject? Is there anything more to be said about it?*

There is, indeed. You see, Musil, Neville, and Gass did nothing more than simply acknowledge the existence of Grayness. I suppose they deserve a thimbleful of praise, but that's it. When the history of Grayness Studies is written, they will no doubt be seen as the first crude explorers of the subject, whereas I will loom large.

I say this because they seem to be of the belief that Grayness is relatively mundane in origin—the result of a nasty confluence of meteorological, socioeconomic, and psychological factors. It never occurred to any of them that Grayness is, in fact, soul-snot that's slathered over everything, saturating everything. It never occurred to any of them that it's a DISEASE. (To be clear, I don't mean that it's a *mental* disease; no, I mean something far worse. Grayness is a disease *afflicting the souls of the land and all those who inhabit it.*)

And what an Epic Disease it is! When I look outside my window, things don't merely look "gray," they look Gray. The capitalization is necessary to convey the ominous nature of the infection. If I gaze out that window for too long, *I* feel infected. I get itchy. Nausea seizes hold of my stomach and esophagus. I feel as though the Grayness wants to grab me out of my chair and slam me through the window. It wants me outdoors, so I will commune with it. It wants to assimilate me.

2

You may be wondering why I don't just lower my office mini-blinds so I don't have to look at the world outside my window. Well, you see, I have a cat that has destroyed the mini-blinds to such an extent that they no longer lower. Come to think of it, she's a *gray* tabby cat. Could it be that she's secretly in cahoots with the *Grayness?* That she destroys the blinds intentionally so I have no choice but to gaze at the Grayness slathered like snot over the world outside my window? This is a silly idea, of course. Just a joke. I'm fully aware my cat is *not* conspiring against me.

The fact is that, even if I *was* able to lower the blinds in my office and block that particular vantage point, I'd occasionally have to venture outside to go to the grocery store or to the doctor or to a bookstore or even just to a softball game. And then I'd have no choice but to look at the awful Grayness firsthand, without even my office window to buffer its assault.

So what can I do? I simply resist the pull of this oppressive Grayness with all my heart, soul, and mind. I've built up tough mental defenses against it—defenses constructed throughout my childhood years, when I intuited that there was a malevolent force in my desperate little town that saturated both Nature and Industry; a force committed to suffocating my soul and the souls of everyone I knew. I envision these defenses as a series of shells around my brain, protecting it like a multi-layered hull. They resist assimilation. They make living in a Gray Town bearable.

You see, despite the wanderlust I felt as a teenager (dreams of seeing the pyramids, dreams of backpacking through Europe), I've never traveled too far from the sort of desperate little American towns most susceptible to The Gray Influence. From my earliest years I've seen it coughing out of corroded exhaust pipes and ejaculating from smokestacks. I've seen it staining the hair of anyone over thirty and churning in the eyes of their children. I've seen it on Main Streets, in long-abandoned concrete storefronts. In forests, on the bark of dying trees. At cut-rate funerals, on the faces of corpses that have been given only minimal aesthetic preparation before being displayed.

However, this most recent window-gazing spell was the first time it dawned on me that it is a disease, and the first time I realized it could possibly serve as the inspiration for a book. I should have considered it well before now. My work has always been driven by my obsessions, and you can no doubt tell that I'm obsessed with the Grayness outside my window. Moreover, the fact that Grayness is a disease implies that, through hard work, I might be able to discover a *cure*. The search for this cure would provide a solid, easily understandable narrative structure for me (and the reader) to follow.

That being said, I didn't just dive right into things. I had to overcome a couple of doubts first. As you might imagine, I wasn't at all sure the Grayness would be a sufficiently strong commercial hook upon which to hang a work of nonfiction. I mean, it's too vague a nemesis, right? What's the worst it can do? Mute the colors of trees and grass? Inflict an ambiguous sickness (a boring, coiled-up heaviness) on certain Midwestern towns?

These are not the ingredients of a bestseller.

A bestseller—even a nonfiction bestseller, about a medical discovery—requires action-packed, aesthetically simple story-telling. The narrative must be adjusted ever so slightly, like a bonsai, to bring out its beauty. There must be heroes, villains, good, evil, stylized sex, stylized violence, high stakes, and a clear idea of what constitutes victory and defeat. This is why so many authors have been called out for embellishing their memoirs to the point that they cease to be memoirs. You know, James Frey's *A Million Little Pieces* and all that. People want melodramas, preferably set in New York, L.A., or Chicago.

They don't want introspection, or swampiness, or rumination on what it's like for a writer like myself (who has, for most of her career, only been published by small presses) to look out her office window at a blue-collar subdivision in southern Indiana and see a snot-like Grayness slathered over everything, congealing over everything, permeating everything.

But I eventually got past that concern. I remembered that, after all, I'm no stranger to forging ahead with books written for a cult audience of Giggling, Grimacing Outcasts. So it's not like I'm James Patterson impulsively deciding to go slumming in the aesthetic of Henry Miller. Buying my books has *always* entailed walking into the sketchier neighborhoods of Amazon.

There, you'll find me shivering on a street corner, selling my wares. A Cincinnati Reds cap rests supine on a grimy sidewalk—barely escaping ensnarement in a wad of gum. Readers plunk their hard-earned cash into that hat. In return, I guide them past the litter of used syringes, rubbers, and whiskey bottles and into an old canvas tent that reeks of mothballs. (I've set it up on a nearby vacant lot.) In this tent, I whisper stories into their ears and thus hypnotize them into feeling intense discomfort. I am compelled to be such a hypnotist, and my readers are compelled to undergo such hypnosis.

This is the kind of writer I am. This is the kind of writer I've always been. Why should my switch to nonfiction change that? The story of Grayness is indeed factual (not fictional), but it is nonetheless one of intense discomfort.

Why am I committed to making you, constant reader, feel intense discomfort? Am I a literary dominatrix? Do I want this discomfort to be so intense that it triggers your own personal descent into madness and squalor? Am I being intentionally cruel?

No. Not at all. It's just that the most intense moments of my life have been absolutely marinated in madness and squalor. (Honest madness, not the typical pulp horror fiction *stereotype* of madness. Honest squalor, not some JT LeRoy *hoax* of squalor.)

How, then, would I describe myself? I am a literary drug dealer. As I see it, this is a far more ethical calling than that of the literary dominatrix. A dominatrix endeavors to create fresh pain in her victim. I, on the other hand, use words to *wake up the pain* already sleeping in the reader's psyche.

No. Wait. I misspoke.

I'm not waking up pain. Or at least, what I wake up isn't *confined* to pain. There is, of course, madness and squalor, too. Not to mention the oddness of the outcast. The giggling. The grimacing. Let's sum it all up by saying that my drugs (books) wake up the latent Foulness (both physical and mental) already lurking inside my readers.

Foulness will never be a bestselling theme, but it's the only drug I'm capable of creating. And this isn't, in my opinion, such a bad thing. By focusing exclusively on Foulness, I can corner the market on Foulness addicts. Who knows? With the right publicity, I could become renowned throughout all literary history as "Miss Foulness," the Foul writer of Foul books for Foul readers.

Yes, there's a unique kinship between myself and my readers that the James Pattersons and Bill O'Reillys and Jennifer Weiners of the world will never have with theirs. They don't have to meet their readers on the filthy backstreets of Amazon. They don't have to set up a smelly old canvas tent in a vacant lot. They don't have to help their readers negotiate the path between used rubbers, syringes, and whiskey bottles. As you might imagine, this shared time together creates a connection. I get to know my readers, but—more importantly—my readers get to know me.

You see, after coming to patronize my tent on the vacant lot multiple times, my readers inuit that I, too, am a giggling, grimacing outcast. If anything, a rational, market-driven adherence to my author brand (which is, if you haven't already guessed, Miss Foulness) *requires* that my books continue to serve as mad, squalid carnivals where you, constant reader, can giggle and grimace along with me.

Therefore, the fear of commercial limitations didn't stand for very long as an impediment to the completion of this book.

No, what gave me greater pause was something far more visceral: the aforementioned fear that this obsession with Grayness proved I wasn't as far along in my mental health treatment as I'd originally believed. Yes, I'm no longer suicidal. That much is true. But what if my perceptions of the world are doomed to be forever stained by morbidity and a weird sort of civic hypochondria? (By which I mean an irrational, implacable fear that desperate little towns such as my own suffer from an irrational, implacable disease.) Carrying such strangely dark notions around in your head, decade after decade—is that any kind of life at all?

Let's be frank. What kind of person peeks out her window and reports that the first thing she sees (the *first thing!*) is "an overwhelming Grayness that's slathered over everything like a thick coat of snot"? Especially right after publicly disavowing the tactic of "dipping a ladle into your own mental effluvium and distilling it into [a book]"?

What if the problem isn't with the world outside my window? What if the problem is with my own sick brain, which insists on superimposing nasty bodily fluids over harmless— some might even say "wholesome"—scenery? What if the Grayness is a snotty discharge *from my own psyche?* What if my continued championing of madness and squalor isn't an indication of rational, market-driven devotion to my author brand? What if, instead, I'm so mentally ill that madness and squalor are the only things I'm able to see (and therefore, the only things I'm able to depict)?

For many months, such worries incapacitated me. I began to look on all my books (past, present, and future) as the deceptively alluring blooms of a poisonous flower named Foulness. I worried that my mental illnesses had forced blinders onto me, and that these blinders concealed all that is pleasant, kind, and beautiful from view. By writing fiction, I was foisting this poison on my readers, inflicting the same blinders on them. I was enabling them to worship at the altar of Foulness.

And yet I could find no other topic to write about. Every day I glanced outside my office window and saw how Grayness contaminated all that should have seemed healthy and bright. That foul, fucking Grayness! Neither solid or liquid, but a snotty state in between; dripping onto leaves and soaking through leaves and crusting over leaves until my eyes became so revolted they bulged ever so slightly out of their sockets (as if trying to escape). How could I possibly ignore this phenomenon, which shook my nerves more than any sexual titillation, political upheaval, or publishing industry kerfuffle ever could? How could I *not* write about it?

Of course, you already know that I moved ahead with the project. You're holding it in your hand. I decided that, even if the Gray obsession was a sign of madness, the fact that I was tackling it in a *nonfiction* project meant I'd be forced to remain clear-headed. After all, I'd be relying on the relatively objective tools of memoir and (even better) systematic academic analysis. Even if some measure of Foulness would be involved in the project, the use of rigorous, objective research techniques would curb its excesses.

So the book you hold in your hands is a work of history (both personal and regional). Even more so, it's a work of civic epidemiology—that is, an objective description of the incidence, distribution, and possible control of Grayness. (At least, that's what *I* think. I understand that you may leave unconvinced of the reality of Grayness, and therefore believe that any objective study of it is impossible. You may come to the conclusion that this notion of Grayness is a delusion fomented by my still not-quite-well brain.)

Perhaps it all boils down to one question: "Am I sick, or is the world outside my window sick?"

As I wrote that last sentence I felt a quiver down my spine, as though I had accidentally grazed against one of the great themes of literature. (Which has a greater claim to sanity: the individual or society?) Such a theme seems to ooze gravitas from its very pores.

But now, upon further reflection, I'm mortified I wrote it.

It's a navel-gazing sentence and—even worse—a meaningless and inconsequential one. "Am I sick, or is the world outside my window sick?"

What difference does it make? In either case, these pages will be marinated in disorder, pestilence, and blight.

3

What, exactly, makes a town vulnerable to Grayness? Earlier I said that desperate little towns were "most susceptible to The Gray Influence." Why would that be the case? This is the most important question of all, pregnant with consequences for both theory and practice. If we know the causes of Grayness, we can begin to find a cure.

Surely, isolation is one key factor. Just as a wolf is cunning enough to target the sheep that's farthest from the center of the herd, so too does Grayness most frequently strike isolated towns. Some would say this explains everything.

But the world is seldom as simple as that. If Grayness comes about from isolation, we then must ask: "How does isolation comes about?" After all, it's rare to find an isolated town that was *intended* to be isolated, from the moment of its founding and forever after. Few people actively *seek* to live far away from hubs of commerce and the comforts that often accompany them. Even Thoreau's famous cabin on Walden Pond was only two miles from Concord. Some even say he went home from time to time so his mother could do his laundry.

Maybe towns end up isolated because they have a dormant seed of Grayness present, even at their founding. Maybe, for those towns, Grayness is congenital.

That's a tempting theory, but an ultimately dissatisfying one. For starters, it doesn't answer anything. If isolation comes from a dormant seed of Grayness, we then must ask: "Where does *the dormant seed of Grayness* come from?" There's another problem, too. If we say that Grayness comes from isolation, which in turn comes from *the dormant seed of Grayness*, we've stumbled into a tautology.

So pure logic can only take us so far. If we try to apply it to Grayness, it soon begins to feel as if we're trying to untangle a clump of a hundred wire coat hangers. To answer these questions, we must get out of our heads and into the real world that surrounds us. We must bravely stare into the abyss of clouds, concrete, truck exhaust, and prematurely gray hair. We mustn't flinch from the sight of sullen desperation whirling in the dull eyes of jaded children. We must *observe*. We must, in fact, undertake an empirical case study. And if we're going to undertake an empirical case study, we should probably focus our attention on the Grayest of all Gray Towns.

Based on my travels across the U.S., I'd say this dubious distinction falls on a town about an hour west of my house: Naumpton, Indiana (population 3,695). It may even be ground zero of the Grayness epidemic. I find that any time I drive within fifteen miles of it, waves of vertigo and mental quicksand assault me with such ferocity that I have to turn the car around. I've never experienced anything like that with a Gray Town before. It's as if the Grayness radiates out from it. Or, rather, rapidly *sneezes out from it,* sending drops of contagious snot falling in all directions.

You'd think that, given its malignancy, Naumpton would be well known. But if you Google it, you'll find that it doesn't even have much of a Wikipedia page; just a stub that lists its population, latitude, longitude, and a written description of its location. ("It rests across the Ohio River from the small Kentucky village of Cirot; roughly halfway between Evansville and Louisville.")

Before I go any further, let me address the geographical whiplash you might be experiencing right now. Many of you will be surprised to learn that Kentucky and Indiana share a border. The former seems quintessentially Southern, and the average American imagines that it's tucked somewhere down around Mississippi or Alabama. The latter seems quintessentially Midwestern and is often confused with Idaho and Iowa. (When I was traveling in Southern California a few months ago, a chatty taxi driver asked where I was from. When I said "Indiana," he said "The potato state?")

So the juxtaposition of Kentucky against Indiana often strikes visitors as abnormal; perhaps even slightly malevolent. The mass media has done such a thorough job of defining Americans' perceptions of regional identity that even well-educated travelers feel an uncanny sensation when they cross the narrow bridge connecting Cirot to Naumpton; a sensation far more intense than mere cognitive dissonance. Maybe the right phrase to sum it up is "cognitive *dizziness*"—that is, the sense that a mighty wind blown from the mouth of the primeval demiurge ripped towns (and states, and worlds, and words) up from their foundations and rearranged them in the wrong order.

I suspect it's not an accident that the Grayest of all Gray Towns can be found on this particular state line. As a resident of this so-called "Kentuckiana" region, I know that when you belong to an area defined by such an improbable (some might even say freakish) border, you belong to nothing but confusion. And, from what I've observed, confusion can be a gateway to Grayness (for confusion is a sticky-brained sort of feeling).

That said, the border situation can't explain *everything* about how Grayness came to be so severe in Naumpton. I think it merely suppressed the town's immune reaction. If we want to know the exact point when it was infected, we must take a look at Naumpton's past. For you see, Naumpton wasn't always so Gray, nauseating, and congealed. Life there was not always less than life. That much is clear. After doing only two hours of investigating online, I've discovered that the town was originally settled by quite a Colorful group of utopian cultists. Would-be revolutionaries! Why, how, and under what circumstances did Grayness sneak in? What changed, and who changed it? If we want to find out, we must proceed with epidemiological precision.

You may have noticed that, already, I've shifted into a more scholarly tone. This is intentional. I want to exhibit a certain amount of mannered stodginess as a counterbalance against my (at times) feverish enthusiasm. While it's true that my ability to research Naumpton is limited by my inability to stomach the town's geyser of Grayness and visit in person, there are plenty of research materials available at a distance (websites, books, and the like). I'll be making extensive use of them.

However, longtime readers needn't fear that this book will constitute a complete departure from the style they've come to love. Rest assured that any stodginess I strategically deploy for this book will be the maddest and most squalid stodginess possible. I will play the part of an academic, yes. But my performance of the role will be a madly squalid one (or, should I say, squalidly mad).

Part Two:
The Case Study

1

Allow me to start this history of Naumpton by stating the obvious: there used to be many Indians in Indiana. In the southern part of the state, the so-called "Mound Builder" peoples thrived from roughly 1000–1650 A.D. They established footholds along the Ohio River, near the modern cities of Evansville (in southwest Indiana) and Jeffersonville (in the southeast). However, there were no permanent settlements along the stretch of riverbank halfway in between those two sites—the stretch of south-central riverbank that came to be known as Naumpton. Archaeologists who study the Mound Builders think this may be due to the area's unpleasant geological anomalies.

You see, most of Indiana is flat and has rich soil, because it was made so by the advance and retreat of prehistoric glaciers. But little Naumpton is located in an area the glaciers never reached. Historian James H. Madison refers to this region as "the unglaciated triangle." Even the Ice Age wanted nothing to do with it! This is why Naumpton's river valley only extends for a quarter-mile before rising up into hills and crags that are difficult to plow.

If you till the soil there, you may even now find that it is littered with scattered hunks of limestone. In that limestone,

one can find a vast array of well-preserved fossils from the Devonian period. Corals mostly, along with a handful of trilobites; traces of life that inhabited the ancient ocean that once engulfed this area hundreds of millions of years ago. The scientific value of such fossils was little appreciated at the time of settlement. They were seen only as obstacles to farming. One can't eat a fossil.

Thus, while Indiana was granted statehood in 1816, Naumpton wasn't settled until 1868. You might well be wondering why it was settled at all. Why not let it lie uninhabited (as other parts of the unglaciated triangle remain even to this day)? When glaciers (motherfuckin' *glaciers*) are too timid to tread on a swath of land, humanity should perhaps take heed from their example. Why didn't the Europeans figure out that if the Indians hadn't settled there it was probably for a good reason? Why did they insist on trying something that should've never been tried?

The answer has to do with a strange combination of industrialization and religion.

By 1868, the steamboat was enjoying its heyday and agriculture no longer had to be the lynchpin of a new settlement. The Ohio promised to bring a steady flow of customers to any trader who built his homestead along its banks. The area surrounding Naumpton was home to vast oak forests. If a man really knew what he was doing he could make a small fortune manufacturing furniture, shipping it out west on the Ohio and then taking it down the Mississippi, where it could offer a resting place for the buttocks of a South in the process of Reconstruction.

Sadly, the founder of Naumpton was not a man who really knew what he was doing. He didn't care about the nuts and bolts of building a new town from scratch. He didn't know what he didn't know.

To him, the Platonic Forms of things were more important than their material emanations. Possibilities were more exciting than realities. He was an advocate of communal living, and a utopian dreamer. He was also an advocate of aggressively increasing the pace of industrialization. He saw no conflict between these two stances.

He sailed over from England, undertook a scouting expedition of the area in question, appreciated its virgin landscape, and saw an opportunity to put into practice his dogma involving the *redemption* of industrialization—a lovely, poetic vision of industrialization being rendered not only humane, but spontaneously affectionate.

In the 1858 pamphlet *The Righteous Factory,* he elaborated on such theories: "I have seen it written that the blessings of the steam engine are no blessings at all. I have even seen it written that the new, *mechanical* way of work and its attendant demands are a corruption of human nature wrought by Satan; a second Fall of Man to an even deeper abyss of depravity. It is at this point that I must paraphrase the Bard and say this: the fault, dear Englishmen, is not in our manufactories but in ourselves.

"There is nothing *inherently* evil in the new, mechanized work. I daresay there's much to its credit: it brings a worker together with his fellows in pursuit of a common goal (viz., the creation of a necessity or comfort that will improve the lot of unseen thousands). It removes the bane of idleness and bestows upon a man the dignity of honest sweat upon his brow. Was not Our Lord the son of a carpenter? Is it not probable that, in his youth, he was apprenticed as one Himself? Is it not likely that He and Joseph were employed in some variety of *manufacture?* (Of a chair? A bowl? A wagon?) How, then, can the gathering of many for the completion of such tasks be evil?

If undertaken in the correct spirit—that is to say, the spirit of Our Lord's Grace and Truth—industry could be a Peaceable Kingdom wherein the men who are lions join together in harmonious action with the men who are lambs.

"Any evil in our factories stems from a lack of *moral joy* in both the proprietors *and* their charges. Truly, both are corrupted by human frailty. Neither the robber barons nor the workers know happiness or virtue. Each is a cause of chaos rather than harmony, but sees only the defects of his enemy. Would that more men could see their way through to obeying the admonition of Christ: 'Ye have heard that it hath been said, An eye for an eye, and a tooth for a tooth: But I say unto you, That ye resist not evil: but whosoever shall smite thee on thy right cheek, turn to him the other also.'

"Hear ye this Word given me by God! Close not your ears to His wisdom!

"There are many who have taken up the cause of pacifism in the affairs of one nation against another, and make much of their avowal never to take up arms on the field of battle. But is not the removal of hatred from the factory of far greater importance to our daily lives and the happiness we wish to nurture therein? Is not *the factory* the first place we should redeem? Shall we not first proceed to rectify the errors of fallen human nature in *that* limited arena—where good Christian men relate one to another each day—before we seek to establish a grand peace among all nations? And does not the relative ease with which such an arena might be rendered heavenly suggest a *pre-existing tendency* toward sanctity? Far from being wrought by Satan, is it not likely that our manufactories are gifts from God? Is it not true that every new thing which arises in the affairs of Man does so because it is a manifestation of God's will? Could it be that Our Redeemer brought forth the manufactories so that they might serve as stepping stones to His Second Coming in Glory? Could it be that, once properly inoculated with *moral joy*, the factories will cleanse the souls of all Men to such a degree that Our Lord will deem us ready for the Joyous Judgment foretold in the scriptures?"

This may strike you as a strange philosophy. For starters, it implies that the Second Coming will not occur until humankind—or at least, a sufficient segment thereof—reaches a state of perfection. Thus, it assumes the Second Coming is something humankind can trigger by its own actions. This is, of course, a striking contrast to the way the Second Coming is viewed by present-day fundamentalists who take quite the opposite view: that Jesus will come as soon as he's good and ready, regardless of the actions of man.

The chutzpah doesn't stop there. This pamphlet manages to romanticize physical labor to an extent the world wouldn't see again until the advent of Socialist Realism, while at the same time pooh-poohing the need for class struggle. It invokes the phrase "moral joy" as a panacea, but doesn't bother defining it. It turns a blind eye to the power differential between labor and management, and refuses to acknowledge the existence of *justifiable* anger. It seems to advocate a serenity built on spinelessness and invokes the single most idiotic saying of Jesus. (Who among us honestly would offer our right cheek to someone who has already thwapped us hard on the left? Who among us would honestly wish for our children to behave in such a cowardly manner?)

But, at the same time, the preceding quote is not entirely naive. It recognizes that there is little hope of establishing immediate peace between all nations. It seems to imply that the peaceable kingdom must first manifest itself in our quotidian affairs before it can blossom into a planetary state of being. In my opinion, the juxtaposition of this sort of practical realism against the dewy-eyed utopianism of the rest of the pamphlet makes it all the stranger. The strangest part of all, though, is that the author of the pamphlet never revealed his true identity. *The Righteous Factory* was published under the byline "The New Moses."

Ah yes, a pseudonym. And, you must be thinking, *an especially pompous and grandiose one at that.*

Well, yes and no. To understand such audacity, we must place it in its proper historical context. We must understand that this was a less cynical time. I don't mean that people were merely more credulous regarding the literal truth of the Bible (although that was certainly the case). I mean that people were also more open to the grand ambitions of do-gooders who split away from the government-sanctioned churches of Europe to preach their own truth. Their minds were far more open to the idea of sweeping all conventions aside, even if it meant radically restructuring the way they were paid for their work. They were *less docile* toward lifeless, droning institutions such as parliament, the nobility, the Crown, and the capitalists. They were *more docile* toward eloquent individuals who presented themselves as a cut above the rest (either due to their grave, more-simple-than-thou piety or their feverish, tremulous fits of more-unearthly-than-thou divine inspiration).

We must also understand that, in the nineteenth century, this restlessness had an unprecedented outlet. I speak of the vast stretches of land west of the Appalachians. Small utopian settlements were all the rage in the nineteenth century, and the unsettled Midwest was one of their favorite proving grounds. For religious fanatics of all stripes this constituted a blank slate, a chance to do away with the greed and hypocrisy afflicting both the Roman Catholic Church and conventional Protestantism. A chance to revive True Christianity as originally practiced in the first century by the Apostles (who, according to the New Testament's Book of Acts, lived communally, "sharing all things in common," so that no one among them was needy).

While we can scoff at The New Moses for thinking he could build Utopia, we should realize that Utopia may have been a more feasible project in times and places (such as the days of the American frontier) where there was little pre-existing order to be supplanted. In the Wilderness of Indiana, The New Moses' endeavors would have breathing room. His followers would not have to rub elbows with unsympathetic neighbors who remained tied to convention.

And so, when you consider that this man wanted to *lead his charges out of the slavery of conventional labor, with its attendant hardships and strife*, and *into a veritable promised land*, it only follows that he would think of himself as The New Moses. For all we know, he didn't even come up with the pen name himself. Maybe a wide-eyed disciple christened him as such. Or maybe, just maybe, God bestowed the name on him in a dream.

Finally, I feel compelled to point out that The New Moses wasn't the first utopian leader to take on a lofty title. Nearly a century before him, in New England, a sixteen-year-old girl named Jemima Wilkinson slipped into a coma. When she awoke, she claimed that the coma was no mere coma at all, but that she had in fact died and her soul had gone to heaven. Historian Mark Holloway, in his book *Utopian Communities in America, 1680–1880*, discusses Wilkinson in some detail. According to Holloway, she asserted that her body "was now inhabited by the 'Spirit of Life' which came from God to warn a lost and guilty world to flee from the wrath to come." Eventually, she was to insist on being referred to only as "The

Public Universal Friend." And, when she demanded expensive gifts from her subjects, she excused her greed by invoking the phrase: "The Friend hath need of these things."

So the title "The New Moses" really isn't as strange as it might seem from our own modern (or, should I say, postmodern) perspective. However, what is strange is that—unlike The Public Universal Friend—we don't have any idea of The New Moses' legal name.

Moreover, the mystery goes into far more essential and bizarre territory. You see, we haven't even a clear idea of what he looked like. In a gesture reminiscent of Hawthorne's Reverend Hooper, this leader always wore a black veil over his face and encouraged every settler who traveled with him to do the same.

Why resort to such theatrics? Was it a case of overzealous modesty, a way of nullifying male and female beauty alike in the interest of chastity?

No.

Was it meant as a gesture of bereavement? (Perhaps over the supposed fall from grace humanity suffered in the Garden of Eden? Or even mourning the fact that he was separated from God, marooned here on Earth, still awaiting Heaven?)

This is closer to the truth, but still not quite there.

No, The New Moses (shall we call him T.N.M. for short?) was inspired, instead, by various Bible verses that present the power dynamics between God and Man as a zero-sum game. He asked himself the following questions. If the rise of "manufactories" was instigated by God's will, why had we not already seen a *Righteous* Factory come to fruition? More generally, why had all previous attempts at harmonious living always ended in fractiousness? Then he arrived at this conclusion: it's impossible for the power of God to completely manifest itself while the ego of Man is in the way. At first glance this may seem like a relatively innocuous belief, not at all extreme and consistent with the ideology of even the most amiable, twenty-first-century, NPR-listening Episcopalian.

But T.N.M. was inspired by a far more vicious, absolute shade of this belief. He held that the relationship between God's power and Man's ego was not just inverse, but also proportionate. (Meaning that in order for the Kingdom of God to *fully* assert itself on Earth, one hundred percent, Man had to become an *ego-less puppet* animated by God's strings. Only then, with Man's own willfulness yanked away like weeds, could God's Will grow unhindered. Only then, with the pomp and arrogance of Man defeated, could the full Glory of God be revealed in all its splendor. Only then would the conditions be right for the Second Coming of Our Lord.)

The half-measure of gentle humility had been tried for centuries and found wanting. Only absolute 24/7 enslavement to God would yield results.

But what has any of this to do with veils?

Well, where is the true home of the ego? The seat of human pride? For T.N.M., it wasn't the brain or the heart or even the soul. It was the face. After all, it's the way men *look* that truly sets them apart from one another. And of all physical characteristics, the face—more than any other—is the home of treasured individuality. Therefore *it* was the aspect of Man that had to be erased.

No doubt T.N.M. thought that by taking the time to carefully describe his beliefs (proceeding smoothly from premise to observation, from observation to conclusion, in the mode of a geometry proof or logical syllogism), he would attract a huge following among the well-educated.

In retrospect, we can see how T.N.M.'s logic was—for lack of a better word—goofy. It fails to give the face its due. It sees it only as the wellspring of ego. But life is always more complicated than religious fanatics (or political fanatics, or artistic fanatics) would have us believe. The face has many facets, several of which are beneficial.

It is not only a joy to look at faces, it's a necessity. And I don't mean just the comely ones, either. *Anytime* we look across a room and see the familiar, symmetrical pattern of eyes, nose, and mouth, we know that we are not alone. The need to look upon faces is a deep-seated one, stretching back to our infant self's need to see the faces of its caregivers. Try to go an entire day without seeing another human face, without seeing an image of one captured by a camera, without looking at one in a painted portrait, without reading the description of one in a book, or without remembering one from your past. Try all these things for several weeks and take note of the toll they exact on your sanity.

This may be one reason people imagine that they see the man in the moon, or the Virgin Mary in a taco shell. We are social mammals and need to surround ourselves with other social mammals. Our need for faces is so intense that, when there are no faces around us (such as in the case of poor Tom Hanks in *Cast Away*), we invent them. So it is that no man or woman worth their salt would agree to live without them.

We need to see faces so we can feel surrounded by our fellow humans, and we need to see faces so that we can deduce something about the nature of their owners. Is this person a man or a woman? If a woman, does she choose to wear makeup or go without it? If a man, does he wear a beard or shave? Are the eyes unfocused and weary? Stoned? Fully engaged or apathetic? Tearful?

The New Moses expected well-educated people to agree to live in a world without any such data. He thought they would be won over by logic and cast aside their longstanding emotional attachments to eyes, noses, and mouths. He thought his logic would prove *so* convincing that they would walk away from their professions, take a pay cut, and humbly labor in a Righteous Factory (where they could toil and experience moral joy). But this was not the case.

Let us pretend that T.N.M. had constructed a different logical syllogism to make his point, one untainted by even a whiff of goofiness. Even *it* would not have persuaded the well-educated, because logic is rarely a major factor in the making of life-changing decisions. Man, like all beasts, is motivated by the short-term satisfaction of his appetites. Bourgeois professionals weren't immune to this limitation. The tug of a logical argument against their neurons proved to be no match for the tug of coins against their pockets.

This was the first failure for The New Moses. Had he just given up, both he and everyone else would have probably been better off. Naumpton would never have been founded. The location would have remained a wasteland. This book (as it is currently structured) would not exist. You would not be reading these words.

But religious fanatics are stubborn. When you believe that your freshly minted dogma can eliminate the woes of the entire world, you feel a moral responsibility to persevere. As the appeals to logic failed to win over the well-educated, one of T.N.M.'s most enthusiastic disciples, a defrocked Anglican priest by the name of Samuel Terry, realized the need to disengage from that tactic and instead buttress "The Doctrine of the Veil" (as it had come to be known) with *scriptural* support.

Terry astutely realized that the bourgeois professionals were a lost cause, and that therefore the settlement needed to market itself to the pious simple folk instead. To this end, his unimaginatively titled essay "An Exegesis of the Doctrine of the Veil" cited John 3:30 as the key Bible verse supporting T.N.M.'s dogma. This is the passage in which John the Baptist says: "He [Jesus] must increase and I must decrease." Terry also cited Luke 20:17–18 (in which Jesus compares himself to a boulder that will crush people "into powder"). "The pulverization spoken of by Our Lord shall not be a literal, physical demolition, but rather a demolition of the ego, which must commence with the abolition of the face."

This effort failed as well. For starters, Terry chose a poor medium to reach out to these pious ones, as the vast majority couldn't even read. And even those who could read couldn't understand the connection between scriptures endorsing self-effacement (on the one hand) and literally hiding one's face behind a veil (on the other). This is the problem with cooking up justifications to support a doctrine *after* it has already been preached and put into practice. It comes across as insincere and forced.

It takes real ineptitude to fail in the religion business. Usually such an enterprise—no matter how strange—can find at least a dozen credulous souls to become its first adherents. And with any luck, the religion will take such feverish possession over these disciples that they'll become enthusiastic proselytizers themselves. If each of the twelve disciples brings twelve others into the fold, and if the process repeats itself only a few more times, there will be a following sizeable enough to subsidize the founder of the faith in any lifestyle he or she desires.

Unfortunately, it would appear that very few of those who traveled to Indiana with T.N.M. were true believers with visions of *righteous factories* and *moral joy* dancing in their heads. Thus, the cards were stacked against The New Moses from the very start.

At this point you may well be wondering how an aspiring utopian society could attract anyone besides true believers. Who else would voluntarily take on the peril of travel by ship, boat, wagon, and foot? Who else would submit to all the deprivations of decent food and shelter that such voyages, by necessity, entail? Who else would voluntarily bow to the will of The New Moses and cover his or her entire face with a veil?

Well, who would have something to gain by living in a society where everyone wears a black veil over their face? Take just a moment to ponder this question.

Yes, that's right! Criminal fugitives. The horribly disfigured. Dangerous lunatics who'd escaped from asylums. Benign, free-range lunatics with paranoid delusions of persecution. And perhaps, most interestingly, nineteenth-century transgender individuals who wanted to hide their masculine features under a black veil the better to pass as women (or hide their feminine features the better to pass as men). In short, my kind of people! The Giggling, Grimacing, Outcasts of their time!

In fact, I must confess that I was less than honest with you in the first several pages of this case study. I fell into using the pronouns "he" and "his" to refer to T.N.M., simply out of convenience. But it's never been confirmed that T.N.M. was male, and there seems to have been confusion on this issue during T.N.M.'s lifetime. So please indulge me in switching now to using the gender-neutral pronoun "they" to refer to this enigmatic figure.

Contemporary accounts offer varying guesses about the gender of T.N.M. Some claimed to have gotten a momentary glimpse behind the veil in a windstorm, and say they saw an effeminate man underneath, a proto-Decadent dandy whose face was adorned with a waxed handlebar mustache. Others swear The New Moses' voice, wide hips, and narrow shoulders could only be those of a woman (albeit a masculine one).

What are we to make of all this? Was The New Moses male, female, intersexed, nonbinary, or a manifestation of some other phenomenon not yet understood? Was the veil intended to hide said phenomenon? Was all this chatter about the veil's role in the obliteration of the ego a sham? For that matter, is it possible T.N.M. was horribly disfigured? That they were a fugitive from justice? That they were a fugitive from an asylum? That they were a benign, free-range lunatic with delusions of persecution?

Here's another possibility: perhaps The New Moses consciously cultivated a reputation for androgyny because it granted them a desirable aura of the unearthly. While present-day Midwesterners have a reputation for intolerance for the gender variant, the region wasn't always so narrow-minded. This is made clear in Professor William E. Wilson's 1964 book *The Angel and the Serpent: The Story of New Harmony.* In that volume, Wilson states that George Rapp (the early nineteenth-century leader of southwestern Indiana's utopian New Harmony community) preached that God was a hermaphrodite, and that Adam was originally created as one, too. He further taught that the creation of Eve from Adam's rib was essentially the splitting off of Adam's female aspect into a separate entity, and that this separation constituted a punishment against Adam.

Could it be that The New Moses was familiar with Rapp's teachings? Could it be that they cut that specific article out of the Harmonists' dogma and pasted it into their own? Could it be that they were (Theory #1) genuinely moved by Rapp's notions and consciously sought to modify their appearance toward androgyny? Or perhaps that they were (Theory #2) merely lazy and recycled this heresy because they knew it had been effective settler-bait in the past? After all, Rapp's settlement preceded the rise of The New Moses by nearly fifty years, and was located on a tract of land only eighty-seven miles to the west of T.N.M.'s.

For either theory to be true, T.N.M. would've had to have been aware of Rapp's teachings before their departure from England. (The wearing of the veil and the accusations of androgyny predate their arrival in America.) This isn't completely out of the question. Rapp had become famous enough to earn a reference in Lord Byron's satirical poem *Don Juan*.

Moreover, it's entirely possible that—even before learning of Rapp's praise of androgyny—T.N.M. was introduced to the idea via the Shakers. They'd already embraced an eerily similar belief in the late eighteenth century.

All of these conjectures seem credible, and I wish I could sit here in my blue-collar subdivision, look you in the eye, and say: "I have determined exactly which one is correct."

But, alas, I can make no such claim. In my defense, I can only say this: I am at a distinct disadvantage. There are no scholarly summaries of Naumpton's founding for me to use as a launching pad for my own historical scholarship. I am the only researcher who has taken the time to look into the matter with any degree of objectivity. By which I mean, I'm not driven by the genealogist's need to make her ancestors look good, nor by the Chamber of Commerce's need to sand all the rough weirdness and ambiguity out of the town's history.

That said, I'm not a proper historian. I'm merely a novelist moonlighting as one. But alas, Indiana's professional class of historians have bigger fish to fry. If nineteenth-century utopian movements are their thing, they'll try to find something new to say about Father Rapp and his secular successor, Robert Owen. New Harmony has been talked to death, but somehow it has managed to retain a certain gravitas when it comes to these matters; a gravitas that has thus far eluded little Naumpton. New Harmony, after all, has its museums, its restaurants, its hotel and conference center, its public sculptures, and a gently eccentric vibe redolent of Upper Middle Class American Buddhism, David Sedaris, and *Utne Reader*.

Naumpton has none of these things. The few photos I can find of it online suggest a sullen place full of pained expressions and scabby rust. The little bit of economic and demographic data obtainable via census records is no more encouraging.

No sane academic wants to forage through the sociological detritus of such a town in hopes of finding something interesting. It is not sufficiently sexy. So the story of Naumpton's founding has been abandoned to whoever seizes it.

This has often not gone well. While the primary sources all agree that The New Moses wore a veil over their face and that, furthermore, this example was followed by their followers, local historians (the genealogist types, the town booster types) have bent over backwards to reinterpret this testimony into something far more palatable to the sensibilities of present-day Naumptonians.

Perhaps the most egregious example of this sort of 'scholarship' is the booklet *Naumpton: Then and Now*. In that publication, one Marian Steele boldly proclaims: "It's almost certainly the case that the 'veil' spoken of by The New Moses' contemporaries was figurative in nature. When they say 'These New Israelites wore black veils,' they merely meant that 'They were known for all having impenetrable poker faces.' That was a common expression of the time. The primary sources' comments about the wideness of The New Moses' hips and the narrowness of his shoulders can be explained by noting that such warped proportions often afflicted men who fell from their horses, or who suffered vitamin deficiencies while cross-ing the Atlantic."

To be clear, Steele offers no actual *facts* to support any of these assertions. She cites no sources to prove her case. We're asked to simply accept these assertions on faith. Well, I hope you'll join me in finding them unconvincing. (Whoever heard of the phrase "they wore black veils" being used to describe a group of people who were universally stoic? Or of a man's shoulders narrowing and hips widening as a result of a horse riding accident? Or of scurvy likewise twisting bones into la-dylike dimensions?)

Nonetheless, Ms. Steele's work succeeded in transforming Naumpton's founder and his followers into an easily digestible commodity. In fact, according to several *Naumpton City News* articles I found online, she was the town's official liaison to Wayne LaGrange—the sculptor who created a granite statue commemorating T.N.M. (The most comprehensive of these articles, "A Solid Hero in Solid Stone," appeared in the June 27, 1991 edition of the *City News*.)

The figure stands some twenty feet tall, dominating the mid-dle of Pioneers Park. It depicts a man in a frock coat and top hat. The expression on the face is inscrutable, though the head is undeniably masculine. It reminds me of a photograph I've seen of the composer Richard Wagner.

2

The mystery of a black-veiled cult dedicated to the merger of Christianity and Industry. (Christi-Industry!) Insanity, criminality, and the hint of gender transgression. Someone could probably spend three hundred pages just covering these intriguing aspects of Naumpton's history.

But that is not my goal. My goal is to discover the exact moment when Naumpton succumbed to Grayness, and to use this information to arrive at a hypothesis for how it might be cured. Let's start by widening the scope of our inquiry beyond the charismatic leader. Let's spend more time focusing on the others who made the trip from England to America.

As I've said, these settlers were the pariahs of Victorian society. Many were inclined to criminality and madness even before the treacherous voyage across the Atlantic in their ship (a clipper registered as the *Albion* but apparently referred to as the *Bulrush Ark* by the early Naumptonians). Once separated from civilization and cast into the vertiginous expanse of the hungry ocean, their transgressive natures came into full bloom.

Bartholomew Hanson, an old sea captain who had been making the transatlantic journey for some forty years out of the port of Plymouth, was so appalled by the scene that he took the unusual step of writing a letter to Indiana governor Conrad Baker, warning him of the burden his state had just taken on and exhorting him to immediately whisk the entire group to an asylum.

I discovered this letter preserved in the microfiche archives of Indiana University, but as far as I know this is the first time it has ever been published.

Hanson writes: "I was sent a message from their leader, requesting passage for himself and his 'associates' to Philadelphia, as he was bound to America to 'carve out, from the unholy wilderness of this New World, an even Newer World of Moral Joy.' The letter was signed, simply, 'The New Moses,' and this appellation—along with the stated ambition of remaking the world—provided the first clues that I was dealing with a reformer of the sort I had not infrequently met during my many years at sea. On one or two occasions I conducted such settlers, their possessions, and ambitions to America, only to sail them back to England a few years later when their utopian plans came to naught. On these return trips, their baggage was much lighter and their eyes much darker. The only ambitions I could detect in these returning, prodigal sons was a desire to refrain from speaking of their adventures in America, and a yearning to reconnect with their families (and, indeed, the Greater Family of Civilization) in the land of their birth.

"I make mention of such details as these, sir, so that you will understand I have no pre-existing animus against such passengers. I may look at their activities with more skepticism than the average man, owing to the fact that I have seen such failures, but I have never encountered any such group that was disruptive to my crew. To the contrary, the earnestness and quiet piety of these groups often led me to grieve their losses in America. I once sailed a group of Shaking Quakers to Virginia, and even *they* kept their conniptions to a minimum during our voyage and made no general nuisance of themselves.

"And so I gladly agreed to provide passage to this 'New Moses' and company because I was given to understand that while they had, perhaps, their own queer interpretation of the gospels, they were nonetheless in the main good Christian men and women.

"How grievous was this error! For it became clear, even before they boarded, that these settlers were better suited for strait-jackets than clerical garb! As they removed themselves from their wagons and strode onto the docks, they summoned gasps and guffaws from observers. Drunken sailors rubbed their eyes, as if trying to wipe away rum-dreams. Young ladies fainted into the arms of their husbands. In general, there was much chatter and excitement at the sight of them. This was all in reaction to their bizarre appearance—for each one of them wore a black veil that allowed not even so much as a glimpse of an inch of the face underneath.

"Presently, a figure of small stature emerged from among the veiled ones and approached me. In addition to the black veil (which was made of lace), this person wore silk pantaloons (white), a collarless silk shirt (also white), and a silk cape (black, with a white lace trim). I was given to understand that this was 'The New Moses' who had arranged the party's passage and who wished to make certain that all the pecuniary arrangements between us were satisfied.

"I was made much uneasy by the fact that, in addition to the strangeness of the veil, I could not ascertain if this 'New Moses' was not in fact a Zipporah! The figure before me was utterly epicene. The hands seemed too large, bony, and covered with hair to be those of a woman, but the voice seemed too sweet and melodious to be that of a man. I did not allow my eye to dwell long on the bosom of this creature, for if it were a lady I would not wish to give the impression that I was a cad. Furthermore, I don't believe any such inspection would have resulted in a solution to the mystery. For the costume adorning this individual was ill-fitting, as a five-pound potato sack would appear, if worn as an infant's baptismal gown! And thus, even if such female attributes were present, there would be no proof of them. The hair was long, brown, and curly but not styled in any of the typical fashions of the female sex. Thus it was of no assistance whatsoever in making the needed determination. (Just because the style was not that of a traditional lady, one shouldn't infer that, by default, it belonged to a man. I reckon that it could have been the hair of a 'lady' who had unsexed herself and taken on the manners of a man.)

"When I asked this leader of the settlers to remove the veil, so that I might be assured that I was not placing my crew in proximity to lepers, I was given a letter of introduction written by one Dr. William Copeland of Devonshire. Said letter vouched for the health of the settlers and attested that, while their customs involving the veils might indeed seem odd, they were a reflection of sincerely held religious beliefs and in no way constituted an attempt to conceal an infectious disease.

"Once I had finished reading the letter, 'The New Moses' attempted to explain the 'religious necessity' of veil-wearing. What followed was a sermon of such excitation and strangeness that it was nigh unto the ravings of Bedlam. I was informed that theirs was ultimately to be a manufacturing colony and that the greatest error made in the conduct of manufactories was the resentment that divided owners, foremen, and workers from one another. For this division was founded in the sin of pride, which manifests itself chiefly in the esteem held toward the human face. With the face restrained under the cover of the veil, I was told, it could not draw the sinful self-esteem of its bearer (in the manner of Narcissus), nor would it attract the lustful or envious gaze of onlookers. Veils, I was told, would pave the way for the eventual erasure of all distinctions between workers, foremen, and owners. And only in *this* way would 'moral joy' be allowed to prevail in the establishment of a 'manufactory of righteousness,' and from there on to the 'redemption of every industry, in every country, of the world.'

"Then this 'New Moses' presented me with some dozen black lace veils and directed me to don the first at once, and to distribute the rest to my crew. When I balked, I was further reminded that faces were 'icons of individuality' and therefore a distraction from the unity of their society. I was told that faces were also 'false idols,' 'veritable golden calves' that receive the worship and admiration that belong to God. I was told that, by looking upon the unveiled faces of my crew, the believers might grow envious of the free license given them and want to show off their own faces, and that this would prove disastrous to the success of their mission in the American wilderness.

"For, you see, this person speaking to me insisted that the ship should be a 'half-way house,' in which the conditions of Utopia would not yet be firmly established but the temptations of the world would be minimal. No sooner was this initial volley of madness uttered than it was joined by a second wave. For I was instructed to 'refrain forevermore' from referring to my ship as the *Albion* and to immediately re-christen it the *Bulrush Ark*, 'so that when this ocean passage is recorded in future volumes of history and scripture, the faithful will more easily associate this new incarnation of my spirit with the previous one—which led the children of Israel to the promised land. Such as this, the Lord commands. For He hath spoken to me at length about it.'

"As you might well imagine, sir, I did not take well to such a presumptuous command from a person more deserving of ridicule than respect! I told this insolent creature that the Lord had seen fit to keep the *Albion* afloat during many a storm and swell, and that this was proof enough that He took no offense to her name. I then explained that I alone command my men, and that they would at no time be encumbered in their duties by the wearing of a veil. I further exhorted him to reconsider the wisdom of wearing such a costume while on the high seas, as gales were not uncommon and the faces of anyone on deck (or even below decks, near a porthole) would not be concealed under such conditions.

"This strange person thanked me for the warning about the wind, and said that—in light of such conditions (which he had foolishly not anticipated)—all members of the society would remain sequestered in the steerage for the entirety of the voyage. In those 'holy chambers,' they 'would wait out the journey, like Jonah in the belly of the beast.' Down there, they would soon conduct their own private ceremony re-christening the ship in the manner previously described. Thus, 'in the registry of the Kingdom of Heaven, if not that of Her Majesty the Queen, it shall be correctly named.' I was told, also, that this retreat to below decks would prevent the society from being exposed to my face and the faces of the crew, and thus their 'half-way house' would remain unpolluted by the sinful world.

"In this manner, the *'Bulrush Ark'* would serve as an 'incubator for holiness.' This, the leader said, would have been important under any circumstances, but was doubly so in consideration of the fact that one of their number was with child. 'This is the true miracle of our settlement, for it will allow this child full immersion in a world without faces from the moment of birth and forever after. And in so providing this blessing of

Moral Joy unto the babe, we shall also be able to show any doubters the tangible results of Righteous Manufacture. For I have no doubt that any child raised in our system cannot help but take on the virtues of piety, hard work, and co-operation with the utmost alacrity and therefore prove superior in all functions to any child born into the reigning system of Sinful Manufacture and Immoral Despair.'

"This news of a coming baby made me even more disturbed. I inquired about how soon the child was expected, simply to have an idea as to whether it might have to enter the world in the lightless steerage. The 'New Moses' replied, with great irritation, that this was the society's own business, and none of mine.

"The subject was then quickly changed to the practical handling of the society's isolation during the voyage. Regarding victuals and other such necessities, the leader suggested the following arrangement: a daily ration of food, wine, and lamp oil was to be left at the bottom of the stairs descending to their compartments, with fair warning bellowed down to them 'no less than three minutes before the crewman's descent' that an outsider was en route, so they could avert their eyes (or, better yet, turn about so their eyes were placed against the plain, dark hull).

"I pleaded with this lunatic to reconsider, as it was my custom to permit any travelers in the steerage to come onto the deck for a little while, during the day, for light and air. Seeing as this society was already quite deranged, I did not feel it wise for them to take greater burdens onto their nerves. Their leader, however, would not yield an inch, and in fact said that he felt he had already endangered the society's principles by permitting me and the crew to flaunt our 'fleshy-idols' on the 'Bulrush Ark.'

"The gall of this uncouth figure greatly unsettled me. I felt it unwise to commit myself to three weeks at sea with them and had nearly a mind to return their passage fees and tell them to find another ship. But a man of my age can ill afford to indulge in such caprice.

"And so they boarded, nearly three score in all. My crew and I attempted to collect the information required for the completion of a passenger manifest, but nearly all the names given were utter gibberish. As if The New Moses wasn't bizarre enough, one of the followers stated his name was Bo Lorne Abrumble. The passenger next in line said that her name was Colora Crumble. The one after that claimed the name Dull Oswald Drumble. Thus the line proceeded through the alphabet, all the way to Z, after which time a new set of rhyming monikers began with the letter A, and so on. To complete the manifest, we had to record each passenger's sex. I went on the assumption that 'Bo' was male, 'Colora' female, 'Dull Oswald' male, etc., but my confidence in such assumptions was minimal, as they often seemed to contradict inferences founded on the passenger's height, shape, and manner of speech.

"The only one of their number who reported an ordinary name was The New Moses' aide, one Mr. Samuel Terry.

"Furthermore, nearly every traveler reported he was twenty-five years old (even those with the creaking voices of grandmothers), and they all listed their occupation as 'Industrial Pilgrim.'

"The only one of their number who broke ranks with this ruse was, once again, Mr. Terry, who reported his age as thirty-seven and his occupation as 'author and gentleman.'

"How sad there were no other gentlemen among these passengers! Though I could not see the rabble's faces, I saw their deeds. Their manic gesticulations, speech impediments, fondling of one another, and slovenly posture exposed them as a collection of fiends; a flock of cripples, cretins, and inverts. I was utterly bewildered by Terry's association with them. I was revolted at the notion that persons such as these were engaged in procreation.

"Besides being morally and physically misshapen, these settlers were also indigent. Few of them had brought along personal baggage. The society's cargo consisted mainly of such rudimentary tools as were needed to clear the wilderness and build simple half-camps and log cabins before winter. Beyond that, they brought along with them a single crate filled with such literature as the society had been able to print to promote their plans and six large canvas bags that held sundry jewels, bars of gold, and silver coins (some, I was told, dating back to Roman times). These latter articles would be exchanged in American port towns for such food, drink, medicine, and industrial machines as they would require.

"I should point out to you that when I inquired of their leader what *sort* of manufactory they intended to establish, I was told that the Lord had thus far been silent on the matter, but that there was great confidence the answer would be heard soon—surely no later than the first day of spring.

"It was at this point that I began to comprehend that their plans were quite general in nature and showed little promise of arriving at the degree of specificity necessary for such a venture to prosper. For while I have faith in the Guiding Hand of God, it is my experience that He does not keep company with the careless. So I began to anticipate that I might find myself— perhaps before the year was out—sailing some of these loonies back to England on a disappointed return trip. I imagined that their veils would be discarded, then (or perhaps repurposed as handkerchiefs to soak up a gallon of tears).

"And, upon the flow of such thoughts, I felt an odd resurgence of confidence. For mixed together with my scorn was no small portion of pity—and I suppose that it is difficult to feel intense fear toward such a group of passengers while at the same time feeling intense pity. I began to ruminate on their similarity to all the other groups of reformers I'd carried to America. Certainly their peculiarities were more pronounced than those of their predecessors, but what of it? Is it not the nature of the world to grow ever more peculiar in the eyes of an aging man? Do not the fashions and manners of each passing year drift ever further from the anchor of an old man's expectations? Will that anchor-chain not, at some point, break? When a man begins to fade away, is it not to be expected that the fashions and manners of his youth should also begin to fade away? That the *world*—as he once knew it—should begin to fade away and be replaced by a new one beyond his comprehension? Just as the steam liners are replacing sailing vessels? Thus I commenced our journey and reassured myself that I had been making too much of a small matter.

"I was wrong. For, as soon as the coast began to fade from sight, I heard rumblings from underneath. (My first mate, Mr. Harold Lindsey, who listened with his ear to the deck, informed me that this was the so-called 're-christening' ceremony. He said the leader bellowed in a voice like a shrieking wife: 'What name ye this craft, in accordance to the wishes of the Lord?' And the lackeys shouted in response: 'The *Bulrush Ark!* Swift as a shark! The *Bulrush Ark!* Swift as a shark!' And they continued that chant for many hours.)

"I, on the main deck, was not so agile as Mr. Lindsey and was no longer in condition to bend my ear to the wood, as he had. But even without such assistance, I could discern the dull whirring of their chant's repetitive rhythm:

The *Bulrush Ark!* Swift as a shark!
The *Bulrush Ark!* Swift as a shark!
The *Bulrush Ark!* Swift as a shark!

"Muffled as it was by its distance and coming as it did from the steerage, this rhythm sounded like the churning of a steam engine. Now, sir, the *Albion* bears no such mechanism within her hull. She is an old sailing ship, and I her old captain, and I suppose there will be coming soon a day when both of us shall settle into ruin. But for the duration of the society's chanting, the *Albion* glided through the sea at thrice the speed I could ordinarily coax from her—even with optimal winds. (And the winds that summer afternoon were far from optimal.) So it was that these New Israelites were able to get the *Albion* to move like a steamship, simply by mimicking the churning rhythm of a steam engine with their chant!

"I must confess, Governor, that I am at a disadvantage now, as I do not know what variety of the Christian faith you profess. You may be inclined to interpret what I have just told you as a case of miraculous divine intervention, intended to speed these pilgrims along in their progress. But, if this be your inclination, sir, I ask that you forestall the making of any conclusions until I complete my account and demonstrate how this society of reformers showed signs of an aberration that can only be diabolical in nature. I believe that, after achieving an awareness of all these disturbing facts, you will come to recognize this sudden onset of rapid speed as the work of black magic, and not that of God.

"Even before discovering the most disturbing aspects of their conduct, I had an intuition that they were witches. This, as you might imagine, led me to tremble and pray as I never had before. I could not kneel, but I folded my hands and bowed my head and kissed my Bible and asked Almighty God to deliver me and my men from the evil that I had foolishly allowed on board.

"I commenced to fear that they might be worse than witches. Perhaps they were demons in the midst of a grave act of spiritual (and material) piracy. Perhaps this was why they wore black veils: to conceal the horns and snouts and that would reveal them to be Satan's acolytes. Perhaps they had absconded to the steerage so that they might plot, in secret, against me.

"After praying, I went to Lindsey and told him to instruct all the men of the danger before us; to inform them that their lives and their very souls might well be imperiled, and that they should sharpen their daggers and load their pistols in the event such armaments were needed for defense against a mutiny. While I had no doubt my crew was far stronger, more quick-witted, and agile than the cult in the steerage, they outnumbered us four to one.

"Lindsey did as he was told, but I am not convinced he was able to impart to the men the severity of the threat against us. For their mood was lighthearted—as if they were grateful this queer threat introduced novelty into a trip that would have otherwise proven monotonous. Even Lindsey himself was swept up in the merriment. The men wanted a fight and thought the passengers to be an easy conquest.

"I was not so optimistic, as I saw that the roots of this society reached down to the lowest bowels of Hell. For, although food and drink had been brought down to them daily in the manner heretofore described and was by all appearances consumed, the chanting (the rhythm, the whirring) went on constantly, not even interrupted for the sake of taking a meal!

"What explanation can be offered for this other than that

of Satanic power? I have heard it said, among those who have seen much more of the world than even I have, that there is a class of demons who bear two mouths—one in front of the head and one in back, which remains hidden by a thick growth of hair. The front mouth does not eat, but only speaks or sings, and the rear mouth does not speak or sing, but only eats. This rear mouth is jagged-toothed and voracious, and is fed by way of tentacles forming from the demon's hair.

"This may seem extraordinary to you, sir. But I beg of you, for the sake of God, to withhold judgement until I have completed this tale of woe.

"On the second day of our voyage, as we continued to travel far faster than merited by the wind, Lindsey once again came to me. This time there was no sign of jaunty bravado. Rather, he looked as though he finally shared my conviction that the *Albion* was possessed of the Devil. He said that as one of the crew endeavored to deliver a fresh supply of victuals to the society, he lost hold of the supplies and sent them crashing down to their recipients. For the boy heard issuing forth from the steerage such womanly screams as are the stuff of nightmares. 'The congregation still recite the same poem,' the crewman (a lad all of thirteen years of age, named Henry) said. 'But now their recitation has grown quick and hushed, and in their whispers they sound like hissing cobras! Now the scream is the loudest noise from the steerage.'

"The lad described the screaming as ragged, wordless, and guttural. 'It was the sound of pig slaughter,' he said. 'The sound of a mauled cat.' It was, I gathered, a sound resonant not only with pain, but also with shock and sorrow—like the cry of the Virgin watching her son bleed on the cross or the cry of Caesar feeling the first dagger in his back.

"I recalled the leader's statements about the woman in the

group who was with child. I did not know if Henry had overheard the birth pains of this woman, or if the howling was an indication of some violence taking place. In any event, I arrived at the conclusion that the extreme circumstances compelled me to negate the agreement I had forged with 'The New Moses.' I would send a group of no less than five armed crewmen, under the direction of Lindsey, to investigate the steerage by lamplight to confirm it wasn't the site of murder, human sacrifice, or rape.

"The very moment I gave that order, however, we were beset by yet another catastrophe. Without warning, we found ourselves suddenly thrown into a tempest the like of which I had not seen in all my years at sea. Though the *Albion* was indeed shaken from side to side, the most violent action of the waves cast us first heavenward, and then lightning-fast down toward the abyss. So repetitive and nigh unto predictable were the ship's gesticulations that it was almost as if it were wildly dancing in the arms of a drunken Leviathan. Inspection of the steerage would be impossible in such conditions. Even the most seasoned of us felt the assaults of vertigo. I myself stumbled and caromed about with the clumsy rigidity of a corpse! Indeed, it's a wonder I did not end up in such a state. More than once my skull nearly collided with a bulkhead. I can only attribute my lack of injury to the Grace of God, who in His mercy intervened so I could survive at least long enough to write you with this warning.

"And yet even Our Lord's mercy had its limits. I shouted a prayer to Him, asking that He calm the sea as he did once in Galilee for the disciples. But this was not His will, for He did not appear on the bridge and shout to the Atlantic: 'Peace, be still!' I could not believe that Christ had surrendered before the might of Satan, so I prayed longer, with greater urgency, but to no avail.

"Perhaps the fault was mine. In the gospels, Jesus took steps to save his disciples, but looking back onto my life at sea and at port and back again, I came to realize I'd been a poor disciple of the Lord, and that this was without doubt why I didn't find myself as well cared for as they had been.

"I must confess that I cannot reckon how many days the storm lasted, for the skies were so afflicted with dark clouds that day was not much brighter than night. Nor, for that matter, could I even speak to the crew, as the storm raged with such ferocity that its howling swallowed up both their cries and my own. This deprivation of my senses was nearly as vexing as the rattling of the ship, as it created a vertigo of the mind that only reinforced that of the body. I found myself untethered from space and time, whirling through both without any hope of coming to rest.

"But come to rest we eventually did. And when it happened, it was like waking from a nightmare. Upon composing ourselves, the men and I left the bridge to examine the damage. I saw then that the Lord had indeed not abandoned us. We miraculously emerged from the tempest with no harm to either sail or mast. More shocking still, a distant dot of land rose before us like a wart on the skin of the sea: the port of Philadelphia. Also, the chanting in the steerage had stopped.

"Once docked, I told Lindsey to do all in his power to expedite the disembarking of the passengers. I myself had reached my limits in dealing with these evildoers and had no desire to speak with them again. And thus the next aspect of this tale comes to me second-hand (but is nonetheless credible, as I can vouch for Lindsey's soundness of mind). Lindsey told me that when he opened the hatch and called down to them, he started as if to vomit. A fetid odor rushed up out of the steerage. Not just the smell of sweat or chamber pots, but the smell every seaman comes to fear most: that smell redolent of rotting fruit and rotting meat; which is to say, the smell of death.

"The New Moses was, as might be expected, the first to climb out on to the main deck. And he spared Lindsey no reproof, stating that our exposed faces had tainted the 'Bulrush Ark' with blasphemy, and this 'infection of sin' was what led to one of his followers dying in childbirth, and to the stillbirth of the infant itself.

"Then the leader gave Lindsey a harangue about how *we* were impious demons, and how the society had wanted to hide from us that deaths had occurred, for fear we would forcibly remove the bodies and bury them at sea (where their veils might be swept off their faces by currents or scavenging fish, with the result that their humility and equality would be destroyed). The New Moses then went on to explain how the removal of a veil from a corpse was a mutilation, just as savage as if someone had taken a knife and carved off the scalp, or cut away the head and shrank it, in the manner of certain Peruvian tribes.

"Lindsey then left the hatch to find the lad, Henry, so that he might order him to fetch such materials as might be appropriate to enshroud the dead at least temporarily. And then he joined me on the bridge, to tell me of all that had just transpired.

"So it fell to young Henry to relate the final act of this tragedy. The lad came on to the bridge in a state of excitable confusion. He said that he had planned to take spare bed linens to the cult, but that when he reached the hatch down to the steerage the passengers were already marching away from the dock—in the manner of a funeral procession—with members of the 'congregation' raising the bodies (free of any cover) over their heads, allowing those worms that accompany the corruption of the flesh to rain down on them!

"Such worms littered the main deck of the ship, giving credence to the lad's description. Thus it was that, seized by great horror at the whole series of events, I retreated to my quarters to sleep.

"I found no respite. For sleep brought on a hideous dream in which my face had been monstrously deformed. It had been turned into clay. A potter's hand reached down and twisted it ninety degrees, so that the corner of my mouth now resided where my eye used to be. Somehow I ascertained that this was done for no other purpose than the potter's mischievous entertainment. Then I felt myself cast into a kiln, where my face baked so that it might be preserved in that grotesque expression for all eternity.

"I woke with a start. My face still burned. I peered into the looking glass and saw that it had taken on an uneven, infected shade of red. For a few moments it even appeared to me that it had become deformed, as it had in my nightmare. This impression lingered with me for some time, then abated, and then returned. And thus it has continued to afflict me, sporadically, whenever I see my face in a looking-glass, or in the reflection of still water.

"Therefore I do entreat you, dear sir, to do all in your power to incarcerate these witches and warlocks so that their settlement in your State cannot be used as Satan's foothold in the New World. Bad enough it is that I carried them onto American shores. Let them not be allowed to reside in peace, where they might gather their strength for a full-out assault against Christ and Christendom!

"Very truly yours,

in all Sincerity,

Bartholomew Hanson, Captain of the *Albion*"

***

We don't know, exactly, what Governor Baker thought when presented with this missive. He does not make mention of it in his personal diaries, nor do any of his staff in theirs. We do know this, however: there's no documentation (at least, no *extant* documentation) suggesting anyone in Indiana State Government took Captain Hanson's letter seriously.

Remember, Hanson was an unknown quantity. All Baker would have had to go on was the reputation of Hanson's profession, which is not the best when it comes to reporting events factually and abstaining from excursions into fantasy. The captain's age was probably also used against him, as no sea captains were thought to be as prone to exaggeration as *old* sea captains were.

It's also possible that Baker—a longtime resident of Evansville—knew about the utopian communes that had settled in the southwestern corner of the state many years before. Two groups, in rapid succession, had brought strange ideas to a nearby village on the banks of the Wabash River that eventually came to be known as New Harmony.

The first were German Pietists under the direction of the aforementioned George Rapp (and therefore often referred to as Rappites). They were opponents of the established Lutheran Church in their native country, and had split off to form a community that eventually came to practice celibacy, alchemy, and the ritualistic walking of a garden labyrinth. They believed in the imminent arrival of the Millennium foretold in the Book of Revelation. This group spent ten years in Indiana before eventually moving back east and selling their land to the second group.

The second group (led by a man named Robert Owen, and therefore dubbed the Owenites) was wholly secular and far from celibate, but possessed its own reputation for oddity, owing to the motley group of eccentrics who joined the commune, and to their outrageous ambitions. (They felt that the example set by their socialistic community would prove so inspiring that it would be quickly adopted by the rest of the world, thus freeing it from the scourge of inequality. In fact, the experiment floundered until it was put to a merciful end a mere two years after its founding.)

Both groups were viewed by neighbors as strange, but rarely malicious and certainly not Satanic. Given that his older neighbors' impressions likely influenced Baker's own, he may have taken Captain Hanson's account as an overreaction and misunderstanding. Perhaps he attributed the account to a fit of drunkenness, or even to a fever. (Hanson's own description of his upsetting dreams, and the burning sensation he felt on his face upon awakening from them, would seem to support this interpretation.) Moreover, we know Baker was an early advocate of women's suffrage, and thus a reformer in his own right. While he must have surely found the description of The New Moses to be bizarre, he probably sympathized with any attempt to cure the ills of industrial capitalism—regardless of how strange the underlying theological motivation. Thus, he may have declined to act on Hanson's warning because he saw it as knee-jerk and reactionary, with no actual substance behind it.

3

Despite its occasional lapse into the realm of superstition, we can be grateful for Captain Hanson's correspondence. Delusional though it may be, it alone gives us some idea of the harrowing circumstances aboard the *Bulrush Ark* (to use the society's preferred nomenclature).

After relating the haunting, epic grandeur of an ocean voyage, it would be tempting to breeze over the society's relatively prosaic inland journey from Philadelphia to southern Indiana. Moreover, it may seem to some of you that I'm spending too much time on these preliminary matters, when I should be cutting to the chase and telling you exactly how everything I've discussed so far touches on the matter of Grayness. After all, here I am, saying that this book is about Naumpton (the Grayest of all Gray towns), and I haven't yet gotten around to describing the settlers' arrival and how it contributed to the rise of this foulest of all diseases.

So I'll try to keep this aspect of the story concise.

When they first landed in Philadelphia, the society had to deal with a morbid duty: the burial of those who hadn't survived the voyage. We do not know the name of the mother. The child, obviously, hadn't even been baptized yet. We don't even know if it was a girl or a boy.

65

That said, a fascinating legend continues to pass through the hills and hollows of southern Indiana regarding how The New Moses ended up disposing of the bodies. Since this legend appears in none of the histories of the society (and did not appear in print at all until it was catalogued in William Pehl's 1982 *Hoosier Folklore*), its accuracy is suspect. We are all familiar with the child's game of "telephone," in which a single sentence is whispered repeatedly around a circle (and, by the end of its trip, ends up quite altered from its original version). We can only assume the gossip around The New Moses evolved in a similar way. So take the following with a grain of salt.

The story goes something like this. Upon arriving in Philadelphia, The New Moses took some coins out of the treasury and paid a local undertaker for two coffins and burial plots (one large, one small, befitting the relative sizes of the deceased). However, one condition of the arrangement was that The New Moses and their right-hand man, Samuel Terry, would personally handle the gravedigging duties. They did this under the cover of a cloudy night, and it is said that while the bodies of these would-be settlers were indeed so interred, their heads were cut off, so that their veils would never be tattered by the decay of the grave. Some of the more involved variations of this tale say that T.N.M. placed each head in a velvet bag and that they carried the mother's while Samuel Terry carried the child's, all the way through the long trip to southern Indiana.

Furthermore, it's said that each night they would offer, as a sacrifice to the heads, a few shreds of smoked pork. They would reach under the veils and insert the meat into the decaying mouths. After the food eventually rotted away, T.N.M. would claim that it had been miraculously devoured by the dead.

Supposedly, the heads expressed their gratitude for the offerings by passing on helpful prophecies. (It was claimed that the souls of the mother and infant were undoubtedly with the Lord in Heaven and therefore had knowledge of all things. As part of the 'communion of saints,' they were eager to use this information to assist their brothers and sisters still on Earth. When their dead tongues spoke, the ears of the living took heed.)

Setting folk legends aside, the only documentary evidence we have of the remainder of the journey comes from the pen of Samuel Terry, who sent a letter to one of the society's benefactors, Enoch Cardwell III, dated September 2, 1868.

"My Dear, Kind Sir:—

"This letter is sent to inform you of the progress the Crusade for Moral Joy makes as we commence to-wards the third part of our journey, on the Ohio River.

"I am certain that you will be pleased at how events have transpired since your servants saw us off at Portsmouth. It is one thing to receive from the Lord a message that the world must change. It is yet another to have such confidence in the revelation as to publish its contents for the edification of all those literate. It is most holy of all, though, to leave one's homeland, one's kin, and one's face behind and dedicate oneself wholly to the success of such Godly Enterprise as is described in *The Righteous Factory*.

"At this time, I am told we are still in the American state of Pennsylvania, although how this can be the case I do not know. It is a vast country, and even though we have traveled by wagon for nigh unto a week, we have only now come to the point where we can expect to soon reach the river.

"Roads here can be desolate. Our supplies, while adequate, must be rationed quite strictly if they are to last until our arrival at the borough of Latrobe, where we shall eat the first hot meals we have had in a while, and where I shall mail this letter. We are led to believe that from Latrobe it is only a short distance to the great Ohio River. This is the relief for which we so desperately yearn, as this river journey shall take us directly to the New Promised Land. Moses says that the steamboats on the Ohio do not toss one about, as ocean-crossing ships do. Moses says that this is but the beginning of their advantages.

"In fact, Moses has spent a great deal of time speaking to the Lord about steamboats and has been granted a singular insight that is now being shared amongst us. As our patron, you deserve to be included in the dispensation of this wisdom. So attend ye to the following, as told by Our Lord to Moses, and immediately thereafter told by Moses to me!

"The Lord has said unto Moses: 'That which is fueled by steam is fueled by the Holy Spirit. For when I led you, many centuries ago, out of Egypt, did I not place a pillar of cloud ahead of you, to guide you on your daily travails? What is a pillar of cloud if not a pillar of *steam*? What I placed ahead of you in those days of yore, Moses, was a vision of a mighty smokestack—such as would be fitting for a grand Righteous Factory. But, in those ancient days, the time was not right for you to understand such a revelation.'

"The Lord went on to explain to Moses the further evidence of this fact. To wit, that the Red Indians (a people who must have existed for thousands of years) had not yet invented the steam engine. This was undoubtedly because, being heathens, they were not filled with the Holy Spirit. This gift was only granted to the followers of Christ, as the final fulfillment of the sign granted during the Exodus. For just as the Old Incarnation of Moses led the Jews out from slavery in Egypt, so too will the New Moses lead the Veiled out from the slavery of the face! (Out, even, from the Greater Slavery of joyless toil.)

"Steam power, then, is God Power, Sanctified and Holy. Its growing abundance, as seen in the manufactory smokestacks of the English cities, is an indication that the Holy Spirit is on the move and that the factories shall be the instruments of humanity's salvation. All that needs to happen is for them to be operated by men and women in veils, with a commitment to harmonious action, so that all distinctions might be erased. The subsequent surge of Moral Joy will show Christ that we are indeed prepared for that long-awaited Millennium, during which the Old Serpent, which is the Devil, shall be detained in the Mouth of a Mountain after which a peaceable kingdom shall flourish.

"This new dispensation of wisdom gives us great encouragement, raises our spirits, and makes all the suffering of the journey tolerable. More than tolerable. Indeed, it is a sufficient cause for celebration! Moses reminds us that since we, the Veiled, are the New Israelites, it only makes sense that the Lord would have us sojourn in the wilderness before reaching the Promised Land. There is, of course, great wisdom in these words. And I take solace in the mercy of Our Lord, who has seen fit not to afflict us with pursuers like unto those who vexed our predecessors as they fled Egypt.

"Now, Dear Mister Cardwell, Moses has asked me to instruct you not to repeat The Revelation of the Holy Steam to those not already committed to the proliferation of Moral Joy. Moses says this is an advanced teaching, and that the Lord was not even certain that we, the Veiled, were well-enough prepared for its dispensation. Those with no preparation in our doctrine cannot even begin to understand it, and may not feel obliged to give it a fair hearing before twisting it into something far less sensible than it actually is. Instead, Moses has come to a conclusion that there should be a new pamphlet published on the matter, to explain fully the connection between the smokestacks and the 'pillar of cloud' in Exodus, with all the Biblical references clearly identified with footnotes and—if possible—clarified with illustrations. Moses says that this pamphlet may need to be more voluminous than the last—perhaps even growing to the size of a book. Moses says this increase is necessary so that, after the description of the Revelation itself, a second section can be added that identifies the likely arguments against it and then counters each in turn. This book is to be a tool of great evangelism, and it is hoped that many lives will be made better and many souls saved by its publication.

"So you can see that, even while we experience the hardship of an American wagon journey, we are planning all such necessary steps as will be needed to save the world. That said, I am not yet certain how we shall accomplish the task the Lord has set before us. At present we have no typesetting implements, and the costs of renting the use of one in some city will undoubtedly be prohibitive as we focus our small treasury on meeting those expenses necessary for the establishment of The Righteous Factory (which is to be that rarest of places, where splendor and efficiency shall walk hand in hand).

"Moses has asked me to forestall mentioning the need for a new publication to you, as your abundant generosity has already proven itself to be an integral part of God's plan for humanity. Moses does not wish you to part with any such fraction of your fortune as could prove, in time, injurious. Nor do we wish to draw the ire of your family, who as apostates will not understand the urgency of the matter. However, I feel Our Lord commanding me as I write this, to speak to you of all these things. I believe God has a special role for you in the unfurling of this new epoch, and that one day you will perhaps find yourself venerated like unto the saints. Please search your heart and pray for guidance, inquiring what God's Will is for your treasure.

"But enough of such matters. Let me tell you of what I have seen on this leg of the journey. First, I will speak of the land. Proceeding northwest out of Philadelphia, one soon enough encounters a series of lush green hills (each of which, it seems, hosts its own wood frame house, its own barn, and its own herd of cattle). Such hills are mild in their inclination, and there are roads aplenty by which the rarely encountered severe ascent may be surmounted.

"The air in this countryside was so warm and heavy that inhaling it weighed down our lungs. Dragonflies flew under our veils, some of them causing minor (but annoying) injuries with their bite. However, it was harvest time, and upon approaching one of the farms, we felt the lingering *frisson* of recent celebration. We could smell sweet cider. Little children giggled and screamed as they heard our approach. Likewise, the women could be heard muttering excitedly and the men called out greetings.

"I believe they mistook us for expected visitors, which made things all the more awkward when they saw our veiled faces. Moses commanded me to approach the farmers with kindness and thus allay their fears. We had not resupplied in Philadelphia, as Moses believed the prices there to be outrageous. Therefore, we hoped that the farmers might sell us corn, fresh water, smoked pork, and bread.

"These efforts, I'm sad to say, did not initially meet with success. I approached a few young men engaged in the watering of horses near a well. Their jaws went agape and I saw—even from a distance—a variety of fear so extreme that I had never witnessed it before. It was fear seasoned with disgust.

"Instead of understanding our voyage to be ordained by Almighty God, they appeared to think we had clawed our way up from the bowels of Hell. Instead of expecting us to fatten their cash tills, they thought we were harbingers of utter calamity, and would not speak to us—but rather abandoned their plows in the fields and did not emerge from their houses until after we started up again to leave.

"Such incidents were not uncommon, and it was only with great difficulty that we were able to purchase a few staples from a farm near the village of Lancaster. There, a poor beggar, seeing that we were perhaps even more bedraggled than himself, took pity on us, spoke to us, and determined that we were no menace at all, but rather a group of good Christians on a Crusade. This beggar agreed to play the role of go-between. Once he explained our society to the villagers, we were at last able to resupply.

"You will recall that, when we mapped out our journey in your study, we were to reach the city of Pittsburgh, and from there board a steamship to travel the remainder of the way west, to our land. However, Moses has commanded that we are to embark from another port, not too far from Pittsburgh. In that place, Moses says, there are settled the followers of a certain Father Rapp—a reformer of sorts, who did inculcate in his sheep the spirit of the early church, in which all property was held in common. While this man (now deceased) was undoubtedly a false prophet, Moses thinks there could still be some value in hearing the experience of those who followed after him, as we share with the Rappites the intention of bringing some measure of Heaven down to Earth. While we know their doctrine to miss the mark, Moses hopes to learn such practical lessons in community living as these Rappites may be willing to share. At the same time, it is hoped that some of their number might be persuaded to leave the path of false-hood and take on the path of Truth. For if they are living apart from the world, in a community focused on the sharing of property and of duties, then they are half-way converted to the Doctrine of the Veil already.

"The place we are to visit is called Economy, in honor of the Rappites' frugal habits, and there we hope to enjoy such meagre comforts as can be provided in the wilderness. Moses is eager to meet with the current directors of the communi-ty, Messrs. Henrici and Lenz, and also to see the grave of the founder. It is rumored that the sect maintains a garden ar-ranged as a labyrinth, and that there are many other wonders to behold.

"In closing, I shall inform you that we did have the sad oc-casion of burying two of our number who did not survive the sea journey. You will be pleased to know, however, that neither was a person with whom you were acquainted, and you can be assured that their passing—though, of course, highly unfortu-nate—will grant us ears in Heaven, and lips to whisper such prophecies as will prove a blessing to the Veiled.

Yours, in all sincerity,
Samuel Terry"

Cardwell, incidentally, is a colorful enough character that he deserves a book of his own, and it's difficult to mention him without tracing at least a general outline of his eccentricities.

He was the scion of one of England's wealthiest families, and a confirmed bachelor to boot. At the time Samuel Terry wrote to him, Cardwell was forty years old. He had a reputation for tossing money around to various utopian schemes with indis-criminate zeal. For example, the younger Cardwell dispensed huge sums to both the polyamorous, eugenics-obsessed Oneida community and the celibate, longevity-obsessed Brotherhood at Brocton.

It's as if he wanted his *money* to travel where he *himself* never would. Although he maintained a romantic view of the New World and its possibilities, he declined all invitations to make the voyage himself. In fact, it's said that, once he turned thirty, he never left the family estate near Glastonbury. His father, who at the advanced age of seventy still managed the affairs of his various enterprises with a fervor that would today be called workaholic, must have been appalled by his son's willingness to fritter away his time reading the latest radical literature by the fireside. Perhaps he only indulged his son's pursuit of Heaven-on-Earth because he thought it might grant both of them admission beyond the pearly gates. (Such motivations for philanthropy are not uncommon, even in our own times.)

In any event, the elder Cardwell may have been particularly pleased with his son's interest in The New Moses and his followers, as their dogma seemed, upon first glance, infinitely agreeable when compared to the more revolutionary rumblings of other groups. Much of the fervor surrounding the publication of *The Righteous Factory* stemmed from capitalist excitement over its approval of industry and the emphasis placed on perfecting it.

4

The Rappites kept excellent documentation of their membership. No record exists of any defections from their number after The New Moses' visit. Based on what we know of them, this isn't unusual. They were an ethnically homogeneous and insular group and the majority of their members only spoke German. While they were undoubtedly happy to take the Veiled Ones' coins in exchange for food, supplies, and rooms at their tavern, they would not have tolerated attempts at conversion.

We can presume, then, that when the New Israelites boarded the steamboat *Elizabeth Suiter* at the port of Economy, their bodies were nourished but their evangelistic goals were left unsatisfied. If the story of the two disembodied heads is true, it could be that the Rappites stumbled onto them and found the retention of such relics to be deal-breakers. Or it could be that, for all their courage in leaving behind convention, they were just as taken aback by the veils as any worldly passerby would be.

We can suspect that The New Moses had a talk with the captain of the *Elizabeth Suiter,* in which requests were made similar to those made of the *Albion*'s Captain Hanson. We can assume that the *Elizabeth Suiter*'s captain (one Alexander

Corrigan) offered some of the same objections to them. But we have no record of him sending a letter to Governor Baker. We have no evidence that the riverboat captain vented his outrage to *anyone*.

Perhaps those who navigate rivers are less convinced that life is a cosmic, Manichean struggle than their brethren who navigate oceans. A riverboat captain must follow a narrow, twisting path. It's a claustrophobic job, a job all about threading the needle. On the other hand, they who steer ocean-going vessels risk being swallowed up by the great expanse of liquid blackness beneath them. They may even fear being swallowed up by the celestial blackness above—where ghostly stars look down from their pedestals and mock human ambitions. Ocean captains walk on a grander stage, and so it only makes sense that they would imagine grander stakes involved with their journeys. It only makes sense that they would believe angels and demons were always afoot, sowing miracles and mischief wherever they tread.

We might expect the steamboat journey to be documented in letters from Terry to Cardwell, but this is unfortunately not the case. Terry wrote few letters to Cardwell after the one written in Latrobe, and their contents are far less interesting. In them, Terry takes a surprisingly scolding tone and accuses Cardwell of "backsliding" and "suffering the corruption of the soul which always results from keeping the company of unbelievers."

What are we to make of this? As a medical historian, I am limited by the fact that the only record extant is that of Terry's correspondence to Cardwell (we do not have Cardwell's responses). However, it's fair to conjecture that Terry's dismay was a response to Cardwell tightening his purse strings.

A question: why would Cardwell have suddenly turned stingy?

It's entirely possible that Cardwell-the-elder read Terry's letters and was appalled by the respect he granted the Rappites for their interest in communal living. If this were the case, the father would have almost certainly put a tighter leash on the son's philanthropic activities, as he would not want to fund any project that carried even the faintest perfume of animus against the free market. Or perhaps Cardwell-the-younger was savvier than historians generally give him credit for and felt the "dispensation of wisdom" regarding smokestacks and the Biblical pillar of cloud was too looney even for his tastes.

It wasn't unusual for Cardwell to give heavily to one utopian project and swear his lifelong allegiance to it, only to switch gears shortly thereafter and direct his attention elsewhere.

And now, constant reader, it is time for an essential digression. I have an important question to ask you: with which figure in Naumptonian history do you identify?

If you're older, British, male, fascinated by the occult, and have maritime interests, you may identify with Captain Hanson. If you're a teenager, perhaps you identify with Henry. (One might say he's the closest thing to a Wesley Crusher aboard the *Albion*.) If you're a middle manager attending to all the details of a project while your boss remains isolated in self-delusion, you probably see yourself in Samuel Terry. If people describe you as "shadowy" or "a riddle wrapped in a mystery inside an enigma" (or, for that matter, "unstable"), then you probably identify with The New Moses.

You may be wondering which figure I identify with.

Well, I see quite a bit of myself in Enoch Cardwell III. When I was young, I too waffled in regard to my ideological commitments. In my twenties alone, I pinballed between atheism and Christianity, between Christianity and Buddhism, between

Buddhism and alcoholism, between alcoholism and the Green
Party, between the Green Party and clove cigarettes, between
cloves and the Republican Party, between the Republican Party
and the Libertarians, between the Libertarians and the Unitarians, between Unitarians and my boyfriend's Ambien, and
so on, and so on, until I finally came to understand that I'm
incapable of devotion to *any* ideology or addiction.

Each time I pinballed away from one fixation to another, I'd
be slightly embarrassed by my about-face. I felt it signalled my
inability to come to terms with adulthood, as adults tend to
have at least one or two firm fixations upon which they build
their lives.

But this sense of failure didn't plague me for too long. I gave
myself pep talks. Told myself that there was no real shame in
such flightiness. To the contrary, I thought it was a virtue. By
easily casting aside fixations I'd once held dear, I was demonstrating my ability to grow. I was showing that I lived on a
higher plane of existence, unmoved by simple tribal loyalty to
the atheists, drunks, Christians, smokers, Greens, Libertarians,
socialists, pillheads, and Republicans I had called friends. I
wasn't subject to the need that so many people have to stay entrenched in a habit or belief system, no matter how ridiculous,
simply out of a need to save face.

And maybe I wasn't even lying to myself when I thought such
things. Maybe I really was developing my capacity for critical
thinking by discarding, in turn, each of the balms available to
me. That said, it's also entirely possible that my embrace and
subsequent dismissal of cures was the result of a constitutional
incapacity to stick with things and see them through. It could
be a sign of a sort of malignant immaturity that made me always open to flirtation with the latest ideological (or addictive)
crush, without ever feeling the weight of commitment.

Anyway, the point is that I find it impossible to judge Cardwell-the-younger too harshly. I have been in his shoes. Hell—even now, I'm suspicious of any and all commitments. I am a free agent. Although I am an atheist, I am not chomping at the bit to overthrow the current Christian hegemony. I know that some Christians are better people than some atheists, and I have recently had strange experiences that are difficult to explain without reference to the supernatural. Although I've been clean, sober, and tobacco-free for well over a decade, I occasionally have nightmares in which I succumb to the lure of gin and a menthol. Although I loathe Trump and voted for Hillary Clinton, I am not so naive as to think she was without her own sins.

Our current age is one that hungers for moral simplicity. If we declare ourselves virtuous and our enemies vicious, the world begins to make sense. But maybe the world isn't supposed to make sense. Maybe my role as a historian is to describe the past from a perspective that's utterly bereft of values. Maybe the only legitimate role for a historian is to describe the past as a series of physical and emotional *textures*. Maybe history should be handed down as a slideshow (or, better yet, *side*show) of impressions, progressing along the continuum of time but otherwise untethered to any sense of order. Maybe we should stop trying to pass it off as a meaningful, well-choreographed dance of causes and effects. Maybe it's time to declare bluntly that history isn't a samba, but a seizure. Maybe it's time to present history to schoolchildren as a billion disordered, melting stars, entangled in one another like coat hangers. Such a curriculum would do a fine job of preparing young people for the world they will face in adulthood. At least, it would do a far better job than any course offered today. Children need to learn that sometimes there are no causes to events. Sometimes events just happen.

Let's apply this approach to Enoch Cardwell III's abandonment of the The New Israelites. Maybe there was no actual, logical *reason* for it. We need to consider this as a distinct possibility—maybe even a likelihood.

There's something about the historian's craft that makes them blind to the workings of chaos. They believe history falls into easily understood patterns, and that we can find the right answers to our current dilemmas by cracking the code of analogies.

The Republicans say Trump is like Andrew Jackson and should be lauded as such. The Democrats say Trump is like Nixon and should be subject to similar congressional investigations. The radicals say Trump is like Hitler and should be deposed by any means necessary. I understand why the Republicans would find the notion of a Jacksonian Trump alluring (for it recasts the man's foolishness as a sort of rugged, take-no-bullshit machismo with a presidential precedent). I can understand why the Democrats would find the notion of a Nixonian Trump alluring (for it suggests that although Trump is indeed toxic to democracy, he can be neutered by the same constitutional mechanisms that forced Nixon's resignation, and this is reassuring). I can understand why radicals would find the notion of a Hitlerian Trump alluring (for by rebelling against absolute evil they implicitly take on the mantle of absolute good).

But are any of these comparisons entirely accurate? When someone looks at Trump and sees Jackson or Nixon or Hitler, doesn't one stop seeing Trump for Trump? We want to find Trump in historical precedent, but he is a weed that could only have grown out of the soil of early twenty-first-century America. He is warped in a way that Jackson, Nixon, and Hitler could never be warped. The soil of this century is more twisted and bizarre than that of the past, and so it only makes sense that it grows stranger weeds.

The human species is often known to have skewed perceptions. For example, there is the phenomenon of pareidolia—in which we perceive patterns that are not really there. This is the perceptual hiccup that leads us to see animals in the clouds and the face of the Virgin Mary in a taco shell. We will subconsciously shoehorn meaning into the meaningless. We want the world to be writhing with patterns, symbols, analogies, equivalences, Plutarchian parallel lives, etc. We want this because it gives us some handholds in the universe. It helps us avoid the vertigo of total ignorance and makes the world seem more predictable, and therefore safer.

But Trump has no precedent. Just as Captain Hanson, Enoch Cardwell III, and Samuel Terry had no precedents. Just as The New Moses had no precedent (despite all his self-serving claims of reincarnation, despite any similarities between him and Father Rapp).

People don't exist to be precedents for future people. Places don't exist to be precedents for future places. Decades don't exist to be precedents for future decades. Like the Buddhist mandalas, they are colorful while they last but sooner or later find themselves totally wiped away and discarded.

5

The New Israelites came to America without an idea of the specific industry they would engage in, but this didn't stop them from drawing up elaborate plans for the building that would house their efforts. They didn't hire an architect. Instead, T.N.M. themselves assumed the job and poured their wildest imaginings onto a deerskin scroll that now resides in one of the dustier archives of the Indiana Pioneer Heritage Museum, up in Indianapolis.

I have taken the time to examine T.N.M.'s drawing (really little more than a crude sketch), along with the handwritten notes sloppily scrawled next to it. It is every bit as grandiose and impractical as you might imagine. Rather than building several different structures (houses, an armory, a church, a factory, a town hall), T.N.M. imagined one single, giant, seven-story tower that would encompass all five functions at once.

I should pause here to mention that other nineteenth-century utopian communities were similarly beguiled by such architectural dreams. Take, for example, architect Stedman Whitwell's ambitious design for a mammoth, square-shaped building that would house the entire Owenite Community in New Harmony, or Victor Considérant's concept of U-shaped "phalanstères" for the Fourierist communities.

Why this obsession with keeping everyone under one enormous roof? The reasons are not all that difficult to discern. By uniting the entire community in a single structure, each member of the community would have far less privacy than they would if housed alone or in small groups. All eyes, ears, and hearts would be turned toward the common goal (in the case of The New Israelites, the much-vaunted "moral joy"). The community would be less likely to engage in side conversations, gossip, and dissension. A community that is dispersed is far more difficult to control than one that shares a single space.

The other attraction, I think, is that an architectural plan—however impractical—shows an intent to transform a philosophy (the stuff of thought and words) into something tangible (the stuff of stone and mortar). And is not that alchemical project the very core of utopianism?

One cannot aspire to remake the world without reinventing the world's aesthetic sensibilities. And the easiest gesture one can make toward reinventing the world's aesthetic sensibilities is to propose an architectural plan radically changing the way "church" and "factory" and "town hall" and "armory" and "home" look.

If anyone *had* challenged T.N.M. for being impractical, T.N.M. could've responded by saying that all the Lord's works had been impractical. That their first incarnation's plan to escape the bondage of Egypt had been "impractical." That Christ's casting out demons, turning water into wine, and raising Lazarus from the dead had been "impractical." That the Divine Plan for God to send His only-begotten offspring to suffer on Earth to atone for mankind's sins was "impractical," and so on!

Thus, the inability to limit oneself to the feasible becomes a badge of honor, rather than a vice. God is an audacious God, not shackled to any set of rules. Thus (the reasoning goes) as God's people, a utopian community should feel free to follow its most extravagant whims.

So follow them The New Moses did. In spades. Their design was the most eccentric of any such community. And yet, even though the drawings are available for any researcher to look over, present-day Naumpton likes to pretend they don't exist. Weirdness is Colorful, and a town afflicted with Thick Grayness cannot long abide it. The local historians in Naumpton refer to it as "a quaint first draft, the modern equivalent of a napkin sketch." And they leave it at that, without entertaining the notion that, even if such an assertion were true, the plans nonetheless say something disturbing about T.N.M.'s state of mind.

It is for this reason that I must briefly describe them.

Stained-glass windows, each about as tall and wide as a man, were to somehow peacefully coexist with the rattling and rumbling of working gears. T.N.M. didn't know exactly which sort of manufacturing the settlement would undertake, but nonetheless seemed to have been fixated on the image of huge, intermeshed gears being at the heart of the effort. In the drawing, there's no apparent purpose for the gears. And yet, there they are, running throughout each of the Righteous Factory's seven stories. There are even a couple of arrows drawn next to the gears to show the direction in which they would be moving. Their churning minuet never actually materialized in Naumpton, but the mere idea of them seems to have inflamed T.N.M.'s mind. It's as if the vivid daydream of working gears affected them the way a vivid daydream of whirling dervishes (or a mesmerist's swinging pocket watch) would affect you or me.

Each story of the tower was to be dedicated to a different era in the history of the world (as understood by nineteenth-century Christians). The first floor, for example, was to be called "The Tabernacle of Creation," the second, "The Tabernacle of the Exodus," and so on through floors dedicated to "The Prophets," "The Incarnation," "The Crucifixion, Death, and Resurrection of Christ," "Pentecost," and "The Apocalypse."

The Tabernacle of Creation was to feature three windows. The first would depict "the forming of Adam from mud." The second, "the grievous separation of the female part from the intended whole" (i.e., the creation of Eve). The third was to illustrate "the original sin and original veil."

A note scrawled in the margin appears to indicate that this is where the settlers would "fabricate gears." Another says that the floor would be constructed in such a way as to leave a circular mud pit in the middle. ("A soft bed of earth upon which babies shall be manufactured and under which they shall, if necessary, be buried.")

The "Tabernacle of the Exodus" was to feature two windows. The first was titled "THE HOLY RELEASE" and would've depicted a wrathful Jochebed as she spurns the infant Moses from her presence, in a bulrush ark, to an uncertain fate. The second ("THE HOLY CAPTURE") would've illustrated a scene in which a wrathful God chains Moses' neck to Mount Sinai, so that he will always be tethered to it and never enter the Promised Land.

From there, the notes on the scroll become more fragmented. It's as though T.N.M. realized that, in their excitement, they had written far too copiously about the first two stories and that there was not enough room on the scroll to go into the same amount of detail with the remaining five. Yes, that may be why the descriptions for the The Tabernacle of the Prophets consist of only two phrases: "Where the departed shall appear to us with oracles" and "Where the foremen shall gather to plan each day's work." Next to The Tabernacle of the Incarnation, they scrawled: "Where children are to be sent when they are naughty." Next to The Tabernacle of the Crucifixion, Death, and Resurrection, they dashed off a line that looks as though it may say "Judgement" (although it could also be read as "Judas men"). Next to The Tabernacle of the Pentecost, they wrote: "The only place where there shall be fire." And next to the Tabernacle of the Apocalypse, they wrote just one word: "Telescope." At least, I believe that's what it says. The handwriting on this part of the scroll is more gnarled, wiry, and distorted than elsewhere. It might also read: "The Escape."

6

In her novel *O Pioneers!*, Willa Cather writes: "A pioneer should have imagination, should be able to enjoy the idea of things more than the things themselves." If we apply Cather's approach to the case of The New Moses (and the fanciful designs for a Righteous Factory), we may come to the conclusion that these plans were not only harmless but actually productive; that for pioneers to end up prosperous, they must be audacious; that audacity is blessed not only by Almighty God, but also by the Almighty Dollar.

Certainly, in Cather's novel such imagination pays off. Alexandra (the plucky heroine) endures much suffering out on the Great Plains, but imagines a day when her family's efforts will be successful. Through decades of hard work (and the shrewd application of her superior intellect), she is able to coerce the land to give up its treasure of vegetables and wheat.

It's a fascinating novel, for its opening pages depict 1880s Nebraska as a place saturated with Grayness. (The word "gray" appears four times over the first two pages alone. One sentence reads: "A mist of fine snowflakes was curling and eddying about the cluster of low drab buildings huddled on the gray prairie, under a gray sky." Even when the word "gray" itself is not used, it is implied in phrases such as "the leaden sky.")

For Cather, however, Grayness only plagues the first generation of settlers. By the last page of the novel, it has been
replaced by "the evening star," "yellow wheat," "rustling corn,"
and "the shining eyes of youth." Surely, the heroine's journey
has been bittersweet—with tragic losses along the way. In the
end, though, she cherishes a sense of mature contentment with
the world and her place in it.

This sense of mature contentment resonates with readers
who on the one hand don't consider themselves naive, but on
the other hand can't summon up the gumption to embrace
full-throated pessimism. This is probably why the book proved
so successful. If Alexandra's little patch of Nebraska had started
Gray and ended Gray, and if Alexandra had spent much of the
book railing against Grayness and discussing the futility of her
various attempts to defeat it, *O Pioneers!* would not still be
with us today. It would've faded into obscurity.

Nobody likes a whiner, especially when the whining rings
true.

Of course, Alexandra's contentment becomes less convincing
when one learns that Cather herself got out of Nebraska in her
early twenties. She escaped first to Pittsburgh and then to New
York City, where she worked for popular magazines until she
became confident enough to begin work as a novelist. She died
in Manhattan and is buried in New Hampshire, of all places!
One imagines that, if Cather knew a real life Alexandra, she
would've pitied rather than praised her.

So I do not think we can accept Cather as the final word on
all things Midwestern. Don't get me wrong, I don't *hate* Cather. Her prose has literally taken my breath away. It is magical.
(No, strike that. It's not truly *magical*—but is rather *the work
of an illusionist*, and that's the rub. She employs her awe-inspir-
ing prose in the vulgar task of depicting outcomes that are not

wholly convincing, and thus cheapens it.)

I find Sherwood Anderson far more realistic. For here is a man who did not move out of the Midwest until he was forty-eight, and whose escape landed him not in Manhattan but first in New Orleans and then in rural Virginia. (Freeing himself from Ohio's desperate little towns only to end up buried in a desperate little Southern one.)

Anderson's book of interconnected short stories, *Winesburg, Ohio*, may not use language to the same entrancing effect as Cather does in *O Pioneers!*, but this is because Anderson's Midwest is not a place for romantic lyricism (or exclamation marks). Cather can afford such flourishes, as hers is ultimately the poetry of hope. Anderson's is the poetry of false hope. (Let's be even more blunt and call it what it is—Moronic Hope.)

People came to desperate little Winesburg because they were fleeing from trouble they'd gotten into on the East Coast. They *stayed* in Winesburg because they convinced themselves that they'd *succeeded* in fleeing it. Or, in other cases, they came to Winesburg because they yearned for something, and stayed because they convinced themselves that they'd found it.

Had they *actually* succeeded in fleeing trouble? Had they *actually* succeeded in finding the object of their heart's deepest yearning? No, and that is the crux of the town's desperation. Winesburg is a town riddled with misunderstanding. The townsfolk misunderstand their neighbors, yes. More tragically, however, they misunderstand themselves.

What is most poignant about the whole thing is how the Winesburgers (Winesburgians?) *need* to misunderstand themselves. Many of the townspeople are unhappy, but those with even a scintilla of happiness obtain it only because they have the capacity to keep the harsh truth of their situations at bay.

***

When T.N.M. arrived at his Hoosier land claim, he found himself betrayed. He almost succeeded in convincing himself that this betrayal fit into God's plan; that it was parallel to a betrayal experienced by the first Moses at the hands of the original Israelites. But unlike the residents of Winesburg, he was unable to completely delude himself into a bearable facsimile of happiness.

We know all this because Samuel Terry was one of T.N.M.'s betrayers and wrote his account of the whole ordeal in a pamphlet titled *A Repudiation of the Doctrine of the Veil.* This essay appears to have been motivated by Terry's need to publicly dissociate himself from this odd little cult and thus improve his chances for mainstream business success.

It's important to keep Terry's motives in mind. His account of the settlement's activities upon landing in Indiana are no doubt polluted by his own agenda. Ever since I stumbled upon his letter to Enoch Cardwell III, I sniffed in Terry something of the huckster (that slimy asking-but-not-asking for money, that ingratiating manner). Unfortunately, Terry's version of events is the only one extant. History is written by the victors, and if anyone can be considered to have emerged victorious from The New Israelites, it was The New Moses' right-hand man.

With that caveat in mind, here is an excerpt from Terry's *Repudiation*:

"This is the most difficult essay I have ever commenced to write. I am only able to bear the memory of this misadventure by reminding myself that I was but a callow youth in those days, and that my appalling association with the Cult of the Veil was a manifestation of an earnest wish to see the world redeemed.

"What folly! Had I only listened to my father (and to Father God, who speaks through His Holy Church and Scriptures), I would have realized that the full measure of Man's redemption is already available to him through the sacrifice of Christ Crucified. But, being still inexperienced in the world, I saw only the outward mask of the workers' suffering—the tears and toil of laboring children, the whimpers of complaint from callused old men, the grimace of an emaciated young girl limping her way through filthy streets each night in the hope of finding customers for sin (the only item she has to sell).

"I did not yet understand that the matter was far more involved than all this. Though my schooling had been an excellent one, it was focused too narrowly on the works of Greeks and Romans and fine English poets and not enough on the study of heredity, physiognomy, and phrenology. For it is only by the empiricism of these advanced sciences that a thorough understanding of the plight of the poor can be achieved.

"Had I been as well-read in Haeckel as I was in Herodotus, I would have realized the poor were congenitally indolent and plagued, as well, by inherited idiocy and insanity. My tutors, however, were slow to accept the reading of our present scientists as essential to the formation of young minds. There is much irony to be found in such stodginess. In their focus on the Greco-Roman world, the professors seem to have intuited the superiority of Caucasian civilization over all others; but in their unwillingness to teach the science of race, they blinded themselves to reality of *why* Caucasian civilization was so superior!

"So it was that I languished in relative ignorance and found much to admire in the siren song of this self-proclaimed 'new incarnation of Moses.' What young man can resist a call to organize with a group of peers, to found a New Society in the

New World—one free of the social maladies that had grown up on England like so many ugly barnacles? What young man could not be taken in by the simplicity of the cure? ('Moral Joy!' this and 'Moral Joy!' that.) What young man could not feel himself mesmerized by the dramatic gesture of veil-wearing and by the defiance with which it said to the world: 'We do not need faces, and neither do you!'

"But once we actually arrived in Indiana and got down to the business of settlement, my blind faith in the Progress of the Poor came to loggerheads with the sight of the chaos that erupted when they were unleashed from the yoke of supervision.

"I had expected that, once we had landed on the parcel that was to be our new home, this 'Moses' might offer some blessing, or at the very least make a speech commemorating the occasion. Instead, our leader whisked off, without explanation, toward a wooded hilltop some two hundred yards or so farther inland. When I gave chase, Moses screamed at me, saying that I was to wait with the others by the landing and begin to look about for food.

"I tried my best to follow this command, as I had with all commands from Moses. (For I'd thought them to be like unto the commands of God Himself.) However, upon returning to the shore, I discovered some of our charges moaning and drooling and thrashing their heads about as they sang filthy lyrics to the tune of 'Amazing Grace.' Others splashed about the river shallows, dancing tremulous jigs.

"When I raised my voice to remind these would-be settlers that we were on a holy mission and that blasphemy would doom us to failure, I was reminded in turn that ours was a society of equals and told that *I* was the blasphemer for rejecting one of the key articles of the Doctrine of the Veil.

"'Wh-wh-wh-wherefore art thou so wrathful?' one of the dullards said as she dunked another follower's veiled head under water. Her arms were far hairier and more muscular than those of any woman I'd seen before. A brown crust clung to her veil, smelling of vomit and excrement.

"I immediately went to rescue the poor old wretch whom she was drowning, only to be rebuked by him for interfering. 'I asked her to do it, and now you've ruined everything. I asked her to do it! I asked her!'

"While I was thus distracted, I heard—off in the distance— a familiar jingling. A jangling. A *chink-a-chink-a* chinking. When I was finally assured of the old man's safety, I turned around so I could discern that which had created the noise and found a dozen of the so-called 'disciples' running off, through the high grass, with our sacks of treasure! The Roman coins, the jewels, the gold and silver and currency that had been donated by many an earnest soul for the establishment of a Righteous Factory were now in the hands of degenerates who had quite possibly been plotting this theft for some time. The blasphemous singing and attempted drowning were, I suspect, premeditated ruses designed to distract me.

"Though it was useless, I ran after them. When I reached the forest's edge, I was able to recover a handful of coins and baubles that the thieves had lost in their careless haste. Perhaps one of the sacks had torn. If that was indeed the case, it would have left behind a trail of valuables that I could follow to the thieves.

"I hoped to track down one of the knaves, take him prisoner, and force him to reveal the workings of the plot. These veiled scoundrels were cunning, though, and dispersed so widely over the landscape that they divided my attention. They scattered to the North and East and West, perhaps with a plan of joining together again at some appointed place where they would—no doubt communistically—divide their booty.

"I am not the sort of man given to tears, but I will tell you plainly that I fell to my knees right there, in the dark of the wood, and wept. I am unashamed to admit this. Any youth with an ounce of noble feeling in him will weep at the death of ideals, even if that death comes on gradually, by degrees (and in my case, it all came crashing down suddenly). All at once I saw the poor were not saints, but rather criminals—better suited to revelry than revelation. I, on the other hand, surely did receive a revelation on that inauspicious day; that is, the revelation that all men were most certainly *not* created equal. How foolish I had been to think I should be happy to exist as a single cell in the body of the community—no more important than anyone else! How reckless I'd been to submit to this ill-advised democracy, in a community populated almost exclusively with fiends! No, cretins cannot be treated with the same respect as gallant knights at the round table. They are mere beasts, and deserve to be treated as such. They are only useful if they know their place.

"I am not saying that all these thoughts came to me, fully formed, as I wept in the forest grove, but only that the first light of this knowledge was beginning to dawn, and that my reaction was to howl in bitter horror at my folly.

"I know not how long I tarried there, lost in the light of my new awakening. Nearly an hour, I believe. I was drawn toward the shore again by the epicene bellow of Moses.

"'O Children of Israel, come back to this shore! For God hast given unto me wondrous revelations! Revelations! O hurry, my children! Come forth and join me. For the Lord hast spake unto me His designs for our industry!'

"I did not hurry.

"I could not hurry, for I was mindful of keeping a tight grasp on what small treasures I had been able to salvage from the theft. I strode slowly toward the riverbank, my hands full with coins and jewels.

"Pointing at me, he shrieked. 'Who approacheth? And why hast thou gotten thy hands onto the Lord's treasure.'

"'It is Samuel,' I bellowed. But I spoke at a moment when a great wind swept up from the Ohio and swallowed my voice. This gust flipped my veil up, revealing the lower half of my face.

"Moses screamed in a louder voice, but I could not parse the words. I saw a dainty finger pointed in my direction. Perhaps he was alarmed at how inattentive I was to my veil. When the wind finally subsided, I stood only a dozen feet from him.

"'WHO APPROACHETH?' came the hellish scream once more.

"'It is Samuel. My dear Moses, I know you say the Lord has given you wisdom. I have accrued no small amount of knowledge myself. Your so-called Children of Israel were nothing but a band of thieves. While I was trying to save one of them from drowning, the others took off with the treasury.'

"Moses was silent.

"'I'm afraid they fooled us the entire time. They had no interest in Moral Joy. They only had an interest in booking free passage to the New World. They will no doubt use your treasury to hire carriages and ships to take them as far away from here as possible, so they can start their lives anew and steal from others who do not yet know their devilish ways. We have not done the Lord's work here, Moses. We have set loose a pack of wild dogs!'

"The full weight of my news sank into Moses' consciousness only gradually. He attempted to force his brain to trudge past it, as one would trudge past a dead horse in the street—trying one's best to ignore it. He made sputtering attempts to say what the Lord had told him, but somehow that began to seem unimportant. And after getting out a couple of faltering phrases ('We are to build…that is, we are to make use of our position to establish a great…') he had no choice but to shift his attention to the fate of his gold.

"This is another truth I learned that day: when matters of money come to loggerheads with matters of spirituality, the latter always loses.

"'What you say about my Children is a lie,' Moses said. 'Did I not command the Israelites, during their first incarnation, to bear no false witness? Is it not understood that this commandment remains in force? How dare you violate it right before my very face?'

"'My dear Moses, you wrong me with such words. I ask you only to look at the evidence. The Children are gone, and with them the treasure.'

"The New Moses laughed. I had never before heard such a sound escape his lips, and the experience was not at all a pleasant one. It was a dry sound, not unlike choking; a rough animal sound unlike any human laugh I'd heard before.

"Then he spoke. 'Oh, yes! I see what you've done. It is unfolding just as it did in days gone by! They were frightened while I was up on the hilltop, weren't they, Samuel? You tried to calm them, but you are not Moses, are you? No, you are not. Therefore you could not calm them. You are not blessed with the calling of leadership over men, as I am. So like your counterpart in that first Exodus, you gave them access to our treasure—that they might melt it down and sculpt it into a golden calf! Then you had second thoughts about your role in this deception, didn't you? So you added a second deception on to it, and tried to avoid blame by saying they robbed the treasury and ran off to Lord-knows-where. But your own hands betray you, Samuel! Those coins in your grasp reveal you to be no less guilty than they!'

"Like many utopians, Moses saw what he wanted to see. He fancied himself a righteous lawgiver. He fancied me a backsliding servant. He wanted to plant shame in me, and then harvest that shame so he could feed on it. But the soil of my soul could no longer grow this demented creature's vegetation. For I knew that I had done nothing wrong since landing in Indiana. I had merely attempted to restore order to the disorderly. I had attempted to save a man who'd been drowning. I had attempted to stop thievery, and when that effort failed I tried to rescue whatever fallen treasures I could. Yet I was greeted not with gratitude but with allegations! This galled me, and I must admit that a new religious feeling stirred within me at that moment. The True Presence of Jesus Christ fell upon me, much as it did upon Saul on the road to Damascus. So it came to pass that I removed the veil from my face and for the first time in years saw the world clearly, without the dark tint of Moses' lies. I cannot impress upon you how great a relief it was to feel the kiss of a fresh breeze upon my cheek once again, and to feel the unfiltered warmth of the sun upon my brow. These things are free gifts of the Lord, and to deny them to any man is a heresy.

"I knew at that point that I had been born a second time (as our Lord Jesus phrased it to the Jew Nicodemus). The veil was a cocoon from which I had escaped. I had dwelled in darkness, but now had made it into the light.

"I was infused with newfound confidence. I spoke to Moses directly, without a hint of deference. 'Look me in the eyes, if you think I deceive you. I believe you'll find nothing but the Lord's truth burning within them.'

"Moses met my defiance with a shrill, womanly cry and commenced to stride toward me; so he might slap my newly exposed face. As he drew close, I snatched at his veil. I tore it off, so I could finally catch a glimpse of this Pied Piper's face. I felt a thrill of victory as the filthy lace slipped off into my hands. It was as though I were flaying the hide off a freshly slain deer.

"Too quickly, though, this exuberance turned to disgust.

"I saw an incongruent assortment of monstrous features, one piled atop the other. You see, there were *layers* of faces underneath that veil. I saw the faces of men and the faces of women, the faces of angels and the faces of demons, the faces of beasts and the faces of babies, and everything in between. They bulged forth from one another in impossible bas-relief—like the bellows of an accordion (and in similar fashion, they collapsed back upon one another and then repeated their bulging forth). I heard a chitinous clicking each time the layers expanded and collapsed. When the mouths opened, there was a numinously fetid stench. I smelled Rome burn and heard the cries of retching stars. I understand that this description may be difficult to grasp, but even I—skilled though I am with words—can offer no better portrait.

"Understand that I am tasked here with depicting a scene that is the thing of nightmares—unreal and real at once—and that I glimpsed these faces for only a moment. As I mentioned previously, I did not know the wisdom of Haeckel at the time, but looking back on the hideousness that confronted me in that momentary glimpse behind the veil, I can say that each *layer of face* reflected the physiognomy of a different *level of Hell.*

"I had no doubt that what I saw was, in fact, a poor soul possessed by many demons—each casting its expression upon a single face simultaneously. Some laughing, others grimacing; some blue-eyed, others brown. Some corpulent, others malnourished. It was as though all seven faces of the biblical Beast had shown themselves to be pulsing underneath and atop one another, on a single skull.

"I recoiled from the sight of the abomination. Though my legs were weary, I ran back at once to the forest. The aching horror of what I had just glimpsed excited palpitations in my chest that reverberated in my neck and wrists. Presently I began to cough and wheeze, and fell flat on my back in a grove. My pulse continued to race ever faster. My vision commenced to mist over with red fog. Upon wiping my eyes I discovered that I was, for no deducible reason, bleeding from the forehead.

"I called out in desperation, screaming as loud as I could: 'Christ, save me!' I said this not out of any true piety, but more in the manner of a reflex elicited by the ever more grotesque kaleidoscope of nightmares I had just confronted. And yet, even this reflexive prayer proved sufficient to bring Our Lord's mercy unto me.

"For it was there, as I looked up at the leaves in full flourish and the bright blue sky behind them, that I experienced the Vision that saved my life. High in a mighty oak tree, I saw Christ Crucified! His arms were outstretched and nailed to the boughs. However, these were not commonplace, *material* nails that I speak of, but rather *spiritual* nails fashioned from diamonds. Likewise, a diamond nail had punctured his feet. At that very moment the wind began to blow, moving about the canopy of foliage and allowing the sun to fall upon the diamonds. These three jewels did each glimmer with the sign of the rainbow. Granted but once to Noah, I was given the same sign thrice at once!"

"Our Lord was bleeding (blood the color of royalty, blood the color of wine). But he was, at the very same time, smiling; and he did say unto me: 'Samuel, my true and faithful servant! Your vision has been clouded by a dark veil, but now thou dost see! Thou hast tethered thyself to the False Prophet, but now thou shalt be tethered to me!'

"And at that moment I saw that the blood that had coagulated on Christ's palms and wrists was no longer blood at all, but rather strands of rubies. Simultaneously I felt a sudden, sweet ache in my wrists and, looking down, saw the Holy Stigmata!

"Then Christ spoke to me, smiling with great benevolence, saying: 'Today you have been wounded by your association with the False Prophet, but presently these wounds shall yield great riches. Just as my blood has turned to rubies, so shall your hurts transform into opportunities for advancement!'

"He told me such secrets as were necessary for casting out the demons afflicting Moses. (Alas, the rituals are too involved to describe in this slim volume, but I shall publish them soon for the benefit of all mankind, if I can only procure the funds to do so.)

"'Perform these rites,' the Savior said, 'and you shall no longer be heavy laden with worries, for I shall grant unto you a life of wealth.'

"And lo! I did then as the Lord commanded, and the demons were cast out of Moses. But when the exorcism was complete Moses insisted on continuing to wear the veil; this time, out of grief for all the harm he had caused. (As it turned out, this odd little fellow was quite meek, when free of his demons, and of a decidedly nervous disposition.) Exhausted as I was by that first day in Indiana, I did not argue with him. Perhaps he was right to wear the veil now, as a sign of mourning and penance for this entire regrettable journey.

"So it was that I did not even eat that first day, nor did I construct a proper camp or fire. I fell asleep on a slab of limestone along the riverbank and dreamed of a host of cheerful faces. I will not be so bold to say that it was a beatific vision in all its grandeur, but it was at the very least a physiognomy of Heaven, replacing Moses' physiognomy of Hell. And I was given to understand (in that vague but certain manner of dreams) that these healthy, noble, normal faces were those of the men who would play an integral role in my life in the New World.

"Upon awakening to a bright morning, I could find no trace of Moses. I did, however, come to realize that an envelope had been placed in my breast pocket. In this envelope were a series of documents attesting that this land along the Ohio had been purchased by 'The Society of New Israelites' (that is, held in common by a legal collective and not, as I had presumed, exclusively owned by Moses). It further stipulated that I was the chief officer of the aforementioned society with power of disposal over all our vast acreage. Moses had sloppily (but legibly) signed his initials at the bottom of each page.

"Once I realized the full import of what I had just read, I felt a tingling in my wrists, feet, and forehead. Looking down, I saw the stigmata had vanished, but the Lord's promise had come true: although my association with Moses created no small amount of frustration for me, it had also yielded a great boon—opportunities for advancement!

"Many of you may be wondering whatever became of Moses. I do, too. Part of me wonders if he may have been so distraught by his rude awakening in Indiana that he drowned himself. That, however, makes little sense. Why would Jesus save him from demons, if he were to surrender to a new batch of them the very next day? No, I believe that he traveled north, into the deeper part of the woods. Perhaps he sought after his so-called 'children,' to make amends for how he had misled them. Or perhaps the Lord had some other calling for him.

"I can not say.

"All I know is that I began to establish a crude camp there near the riverbank, under conditions that would have made even Robinson Crusoe despair. My first meals were tiny fish procured by means of dipping my hat into the water. I cooked them (alas, for too long) in a pan hanging over a fire.

"Yet from such meager beginnings great things came to pass—just as the Lord had proclaimed. I began, in time, to chop down several of the more manageable trees for the construction of a cabin. I also cut wood for my campfire and assembled an impressive aggregation of it for future use, piling the resulting cords along the riverbank.

"After a few weeks of this activity, a passing steamboat noticed my growing supply, set down anchor, and dispatched a crewman on a rowboat to inquire about purchasing some of my wood to use as fuel. I also learned from these mariners that, through relatively simple mechanisms, I could use the ashes of this wood to produce lye (and, from lye, manufacture soap). While I cannot say that I was an expert in such matters, my artisanal production thereof was good enough for the rivermen.

"In time, my landing became a trading post of sorts; that is, a regular docking point for various and sundry packets that chugged up and down the Ohio. One such was owned by the Naumpton Oil Company. They were so impressed by my land's supply of virgin timber that they wished to purchase it! (They needed such well-forested acreage for the construction of oil barrels.) What is more, after the land sale I was retained by the company as a foreman for the site, and ascended by degrees into the realm of upper management. I am currently at work in the company's offices in the city of Cincinnati, a delightful place that grows ever more cosmopolitan with each passing month!"

Samuel Terry goes on for quite a bit longer in the *Repudiation*, getting into various abstract arguments about how Satan was behind the idea of the Righteous Factory and how man's "great godly challenge" is to "fit like a gear into the established order of things, and not seek the improvement of that which Our Lord has predestined."

I can think of no better words to serve as the epitaph for the utopian dream of The New Moses.

7

There was, for a few years, a possibility that Naumpton (as the settlement came to be known) could grow into something substantial. The deforestation of the area required a great many lumberjacks, which in turn necessitated a great deal of housing and food. This resulted in an influx of traffic through the riverfront to bring in supplies.

And wherever there are a large number of men, there will eventually be women, right? Women and babies, and sheriffs, and schools, and churches, and the general sense that chaos has yielded to order (which we sum up in a single word: "civilization"). Such was the usual pattern in which frontier towns evolved.

But when the forests had all been cleared (as they were, in surprising haste) the Naumpton Oil Company abandoned the settlement that had taken on its name. Like a man who hires prostitutes, it had no interest in nurturing a relationship with the town once it had gotten what it was after. Like a ne'er-do-well father, it abandoned its child.

The blow was a heavy one, and came at the worst of times. The town's only hope of success in the wake of the N.O.C.'s departure was to leverage its position along the river to attract another suitor. But by the 1870s, the steamboat was already on

borrowed time. Moneyed interests didn't care for the way that
the twists and turns of the river could slow down commerce
(particularly when their competitors began to take advantage
of faster, less circuitous railroad shipping). Thus business—
and population—declined.

If there was any real mercy in the world, the decline would
have been so definite as to euthanize the town. Naumpton
survived, though; quarrying limestone to help it hobble along.

But there were other limestone quarries, closer to Louisville,
Cincinnati, St. Louis, and Evansville. Thus Naumpton's quar-
ry met with only limited success. Moreover, the Panic of 1873
fouled up the building industry, reducing the demand for
limestone and encouraging the use of less expensive materials.
This led to a second, more significant decline in population.
In both 1883 and 1884, catastrophic flooding swept away the
Naumpton dock, the fledgling bank (and all its deposits), as
well as the new trading post that had risen up just a few yards
from where Samuel Terry had first established his. By 1885
little Naumpton's fortunes had become reduced to the point
that the only thing keeping it going was a series of warehouses
along the waterfront, a saloon, and a shabby brothel.

One might think that this meant a new sort of excitement
had come to town. Surely men robbed and raped and murdered in such a setting! Maybe they did; maybe they didn't.
There was, at that point, still no town newspaper in which such
deeds could be reported, no town sheriff to apprehend the per-
petrators, and, strictly speaking, no *town* (the settlement having never incorporated as one, according to state guidelines).
So it is impossible to say. We do, however, have records from a
group of temperance activists who came to Naumpton. They
called themselves The Brides of the Holy Ghost.

The Brides were a motley assortment of New Yorkers and

Marylanders and Vermonters who heard about King Alcohol's tyranny over the "Middle Western" states and decided something ought to be done about it.

Alas, do-gooders! What desperate little Midwestern town can escape their clutches?

To this day, the Brides of the Holy Ghost maintain a heavy presence in southern Indiana. They are perhaps best known for the custom brown paper grocery bags in which they distribute free groceries to poor people who agree to listen to one of their sermons beforehand. "Brides Bags," they are called, because each one is printed with the group's logo—an illustration of an elegant nineteenth-century bride covered, but not consumed, by the fire of the Holy Spirit. In little Hoosier towns along the Ohio River, it's a mark of shame to be seen carrying around such a bag, since it advertises one's poverty. Some recipients go so far as to wrap their Brides Bags in black trash liners to obscure their origin.

Although the Brides long ago gave up the cause of prohibition, they remain steadfast supporters of the blue laws preventing alcohol sales before noon on Sunday. They have also succeeded in keeping evolution and sex ed out of the Naumpton Consolidated School District. As we shall soon see, their theology has a bizarre, apocalyptic streak. It may be best to think of them as a cross between the Salvation Army and the Seventh Day Adventists, though less well known than both because their influence is limited to the Kentuckiana region.

During the Lenten season of 1885, the Brides hired the steamboat *Moonbow* at Pittsburgh and hastily rechristened it the *Temperance Ark*. The captain, Miles Vincent, consented to the name change (even as he and his crew continued to secretly drink on the bridge). Delighted, the Brides draped a huge banner over the deck railing which obscured the boat's proper name and proclaimed the new one. Their plan was to travel west on the Ohio River, stopping at each and every place of habitation so they could preach the gospel of teetotalism.

In her book *A Century of Witness*, Evelyn Chastity Wilson states that the group's first impression of Naumpton was that of a "once-productive enterprise that now seemed to be running at half-steam. Here the Brides did not find the *violence* that they'd seen accompanying Bacchus' bloody march through Cincinnati and Louisville, but rather a general *sluggishness*. In the words of the Venerable Sarah Tobias, the town was possessed by 'a demonic spirit of steady, implacable decay.'"

Wilson quotes Tobias again a few pages later: "'There was no poignancy or drama in this decay, as the populace was resigned to it. One had the sense that the townsfolk saw the degeneration of their neighbors as being no more deserving of grief than the sight of fruit going bad. This was a place too apathetic to care about its own salvation. A place infested with many who could only be called dipsomaniacs, as well as no small number of the melancholy-mad. Their salaries were meager enough to begin with, and were made all the more meager with vice. Several resorted to living in the warehouses in which they worked, but such arrangements soon became unhygienic. Thus, many cobbled together little huts constructed from whatever brush and branches washed ashore when the river was high. Such wretches often could be heard spilling their seed into whores (or half-whores) out by the riverfront on the warmer nights. Yet even this impudence had a desultory quality to it. The sounds were not those of delight, but rather had an anxious fearful tinge to them; like the moans of wraiths! One had the sense that these unions were not actually savored, but rather performed in a way that was nigh unto mechanical—each participant more like a gear of industry made slick with grease than a child of God made whole by grace. It was as though man and woman alike had been subjected to mesmerism. In due time, the Lord sent us the Great Prophetess, who revealed unto us that the matter was far more grievous than we had imagined.'"

Perhaps, constant reader, you're thinking the same thing I am: *is* this *the point where Grayness first took root in Naumpton?* Sarah Tobias's description of widespread apathy, depression, and aimlessness is consistent with a diagnosis of Grayness. The phrase "general sluggishness" seems as if it could be referring to that sensation I refer to in Chapter 1 as "the burden of boring, coiled-up heaviness," that sensation which leads us to suspect "the Gray Air has congealed around everyone and everything, like chilled animal fat, thus making people and objects move in slow motion."

However, after mulling the question over for a while, I've arrived at a more nuanced conclusion. Naumpton wasn't yet *fully* infected with Grayness in 1885, but the disease had during that year begun to hover close by, waiting for the right opportunity to strike. To explain what I mean by this, I'll reach back yet again to an image used earlier; that is, the image of Grayness as a seed.

Specifically, let's imagine that Grayness is like a *dandelion* seed that flutters through the air, only impregnating the ground once it lands. The Naumpton that Sarah Tobias describes is a Naumpton where Grayness is hanging in the air, drifting with the breeze. When the air grows sufficiently still, it will land and take root; but things are not quite to this point yet. There's still enough wind to keep it aloft.

Here's another comparison that may prove useful. I like to think of Naumpton at this time as being similar to that ancient city threatened with destruction in the Bible—the one where God agrees to save it because he has found at least one righteous man there. Naumpton was temporarily spared the fate of total Grayness, because there was one decidedly non-Gray woman in its midst. She was a native Naumptonian, not one of the missionaries aboard the *Temperance Ark*. In spite of this, the Brides soon claimed her as one of their own. She is the one whom Sarah Tobias referred to as "The Great Prophetess."

I speak of an eighty-five-year-old widow named Mrs. Eunice Booth Heverin (a distant relative of the infamous assassin John Wilkes Booth). The tale of how she became affiliated with the Brides is a fascinating one that will take some time to unpack.

According to *A Century of Witness*, Heverin's husband had been a menial laborer aboard the steamboat *Lealandtown*, tasked with carrying cargo on and off the vessel—which was essentially the nineteenth-century equivalent of a tractor-trailer. In his old age, when riverboat travel proved too much of a strain, he did little chores around Naumpton's warehouses. (He particularly excelled at finding rats and stomping them to death.) When he passed on to the Great Rat Stomp in the Sky, he left very little provision for Eunice.

It is said that, at the funeral, she ululated with such animalistic intensity that many of the townsfolk imagined she herself would soon pass away from a broken heart. In all bluntness, they rather looked forward to her death. She was an odd and irritable woman. In earlier times, she might have found herself among those falsely accused of witchcraft by townsfolk who wanted to be rid of her.

The fact that she was (in the words of Evelyn Wilson) "borderline retarded" did not help her reputation. For although Naumpton, in its welter of struggle, piqued the pity of traveling missionary do-gooders, the native population had no reserve of empathy. It was as though the rapid collapse of The New Moses' naive utopian plans had somehow, metaphysically, salted the fields of humanitarian ambition. Forever after, Naumptonians would spurn tenderness. In its absence, a particularly dull, reflexive, and witless variety of sarcasm flourished.

Evelyn Wilson's description of Eunice Booth Heverin might come across as unjustly severe to our present-day sensibilities. After all, Wilson wrote *A Century of Witness* during her stint as the Brides' official historian. But we must remember that when the book was written in the 1980s, "retarded" was the gentle, preferred term to refer to someone with intellectual disabilities (chosen as a replacement for the more jarring "mongoloid"). We must further understand that, for Wilson (and, arguably, all the Brides), intellectual disabilities were actually a manifestation of an advanced spiritual state.

Quoting again from *A Century of Witness*, Wilson says: "The Lord used Eunice B. Heverin mightily, for He seeks not high and haughty minds (so full of their own notions), but rather the humble ones, who think only of holiness and God, and of such tools as will be used to ensure Satan's final defeat."

Ah, yes, Satan. There's a name that just keeps popping up, eh?

I'm tempted to say that Grayness cannot take root in any place or time where Satanic threats are thought to abound. After all, Satan is always imagined as red, with sharp horns. Colorful! Vibrant! He's too glamorous and weird a concept to be snared in Grayness, it would seem. But then I am forced to face the reality that present-day southern Indiana is a Gray region where well-dressed people go to megachurches each week to hear sermons about the Satanic menace.

So the whole thing is more nuanced than I originally

thought. In some times and places, Satan ceases to be red and starts to be Gray.

Where and when does this transformation occur? My tentative answer is that The Gray Satan emerges in societies that have become certain of God's ultimate triumph. This certainty makes the temporary sway of Satan over world affairs seem like a fleeting problem; as if he's winning the battle but losing the war.

Another way of looking at it: The Gray Satan is that version of Satan which never grows or changes. His personality cannot evolve because it has already been cast in stone by inerrant scripture. (One might say that this is a version of Satan that has been *embalmed* in scripture; or that scripture is like chilled animal fat that congeals around Satan, hemming him in.)

There is a great sense of stability that comes with such a Satan. I was raised Episcopalian, and I distinctly remember one sermon in which our erudite priest was somewhat coerced into commenting on the apocalypse. (The New Testament reading assigned by the lectionary for that Sunday came from the Book of Revelation.) "The main point," he said with a smile, "is that Jesus wins." It was the perfect dodge, a maneuver that allowed him to avoid all that book's embarrassing references to seven-headed monsters and whores of Babylon and the mark of the beast and the like.

And even if he had been a holy roller instead of an Episcopalian and had revelled in all the bizarrerie of End Times prophecy, the conclusion would've been the same: *believe in Jesus, he will win in the end, so you need not worry too much, just give him your heart and he'll have your back.*

The Gray Jesus. (Predictable!) The Gray Satan. (Predictable!) Gray angels and demons, Gray Heavens and Gray Hells, Gray gods and Gray monsters, neatly stacked atop one another like so many bricks in an institutional wall. In a Gray town, the otherworldly elements stumble around—active but sedated by their enmeshment in the Normal.

The Colorful society, on the other hand, is a society that has shoved God and Satan aside completely so that chaos can freely cavort. *Or* it is a society in which the definitions of God and Satan are always in flux. *Or* it is a society with no real confidence that "Jesus wins"; a sort of *Manichean* society that sees the battle of God against Satan as an unpredictable fight between equals.

Naumpton, in those years close to the turn of the twentieth century, was a Colorful society in that last sense. When Eunice Booth Heverin met the Venerable Sarah Tobias, the town became Colorfully Manichean.

8

When Eunice Booth Heverin (shall we call her E.B.H. for short?) first heard the sounds of night-time riverfront fucking, she didn't shake her fist at the lack of decorum. She didn't wax nostalgic for her own carnal adventures and grieve her long-lost youth. Nor did she think the couples were under the influence of mesmerism. At least, she didn't think any *human* mesmerist had set the events into motion.

She thought she was hearing a Satanic orgy. She claimed Indians and Catholics were involved in it, too. At least, *it is believed* that is what she said. As one version of this tale goes, E.B.H. went to the dock early one morning, boarded the *Temperance Ark*, woke up all the women on the boat, pointed at one of the couples that had fallen asleep in each other's arms, and said, "They bake a dove-bull baby!"

At first, some of the Brides thought she meant that the couples had roasted a chimerical monster, but then a far savvier voice said that was silly. Clearly, Mrs. Heverin was referring to the *making* of a *devil*-baby. "The Antichrist, he who seeks to lead the world astray just before the Second Coming of the Lord."

The woman who clarified the "dove-bull" baby remark was

the aforementioned Venerable Sarah Tobias. It is said that after this bit of translation, and a few others that followed swiftly afterward, she became known as the Brides' "Interpreter of Tongues and Prophecy."

A Century of Witness includes photos of Tobias. She has one of those nineteenth-century faces that wounds the eyes of the modern observer with its abrasiveness. (Skin as rough and cratered as the moon, hair pulled back to reveal a widow's peak, a mouth akin to a frog's, eyes as deep set and severe as a hawk's.)

At this point it's necessary to pause and analyze the events I've just described. Imagine that you're Sarah Tobias, asleep aboard the *Temperance Ark*, dreaming whatever hawk-eyed, frog-mouthed, do-gooder spinsters dream of, when suddenly you're wakened by a frantic cry of "They bake a dove-bull baby! They bake a dove-bull baby!"

Why do you even listen to such ravings? Why do you give them any credence? Why don't you ignore them as best you can and get some more sleep? Why don't you assume the woman is a lunatic? Why, in heaven's name, would you grant her the grandiose title "The Great Prophetess"? Here are some possible explanations.

The First Reason the Brides Believed Eunice B. Heverin
Part of the answer rests in the fact that, by the time the Brides reached Naumpton, they were physically drained and mentally exhausted. As we've already seen, it is one thing to dream Do-Gooder Dreams and plan Do-Gooder Plans and pat yourself on the back for having done so. It is quite another thing to sustain ongoing effort to make those plans a reality—especially when you are forced to confront the squalor, perversity, and ingratitude of those you aim to help.

You see, the Brides had originally planned to travel all the way to Cairo, Illinois (where the Ohio meets the Mississippi), but were already having second thoughts. Several of the group's more moderate members had already booked their own travel back to Pittsburgh and departed eastward. (After all, had they not already done enough for the poor? Might it not be better for them to get back to the bosom of society in time for Easter, instead of spending it in unladylike discomfort?)

So the lukewarm had already purged themselves from the Brides' midst. The contingent that landed in Naumpton were true believers, the most reform-minded of the reformers. They were also the ones who had the fewest ties to conventional life. They were the least stable. The most Colorful. Moreover, their critical thinking skills had been eroded by fatigue. They were ready to believe the extraordinary.

The Second Reason the Brides Believed Eunice B. Heverin
Quite by accident, E.B.H. told the Brides something they wanted to hear. Or, put another way, E.B.H. gave them the answer to a riddle that had distressed them.

You see, the Brides knew that Naumpton was unlike any of the other towns they had visited. Never before had they run into such a high concentration of the depressed. It was the first town they came to where they literally *did not know* how to help.

They had previously docked the *Temperance Ark* in Cincinnati, Madison, Louisville, Jeffersonville, Mulchport, etc. At these stops, they had more or less found what they'd expected to find. They'd found hungry children and gave them copious amounts of salted meat. They'd found wives with broken arms and blackened eyes, and afforded them safe and secret shelter aboard the boat and transportation to a downriver town where they could evade their tormentors for a while. (Some of these women, those few willing to make a complete and immediate break from their husbands, ended up joining the Brides.) They'd found men and women who'd lost their legs, and offered them free crutches.

As valuable (in some cases, even heroic) as all these services were, they were also—in a way—rather crude. Hunger was met with food. Violence was met with safety. Disability was met with adaptation. But the problem with Naumpton wasn't as easy to detect. They knew, from spending time there, that something was terribly wrong. But that "something" wasn't as concrete as it had been in the other towns. They wouldn't have put it this way, of course, but it was an *existential* something.

E.B.H.'s "prophecy" provided a perversely pleasing explanation for this. The fault rested not with them, the Brides, for their hubris in the fight against social ills. The fault rested with Satan, who had—for reasons yet obscure—chosen Naumpton as his primary nest along the Ohio and the breeding ground for the Antichrist!

The Third Reason the Brides Believed Eunice B. Heverin
It's important to remember the full name of this group: The Brides *of the Holy Ghost*. In the Christian scriptures, the Holy Ghost is that aspect of the Trinity which burst onto the scene on the day of Pentecost, causing the apostles to "speak in tongues" they hadn't previously known. To this day, speaking in tongues occurs from time to time during the ceremonies of various fundamentalist denominations. So when E.B.H. climbed aboard their steamboat and wailed "They bake a dove-bull baby!" the Brides were predisposed to hear something holy in the gibberish.

For this reason, the Brides' belief in E.B.H. persisted even beyond that initial pronouncement. "The Great Prophetess" was to remain physically robust for several more years, and occupied a place at the center of Brideism. That said, her *mental* faculties degenerated. Her speech, in particular, became even more of a babble of word salad—slurred and bizarre. Even this did not dissuade the Brides from revering E.B.H., though. Sarah Tobias, for example, wrote that E.B.H.'s speech was becoming more garbled because it was growing "less like the tongue of Earth and more like that spoken in Heaven."

The Fourth Reason the Brides Believed Eunice B. Heverin

Speaking of Sarah Tobias, no explanation of E.B.H.'s influence is complete without taking into account her amazing ability to think on her feet and offer believable translations of the latter's howlings. I believe she had a creative side to her. I might even call it a gift for storytelling.

One of the most powerful examples of her use of this ability has been preserved for anyone to hear. In the digital archives of the Indiana Pioneer Heritage Museum, there are a handful of audio files that purportedly feature E.B.H.'s voice. These are said to have come from rudimentary nineteenth-century wax cylinder recordings. (The files are recordings of recordings.) One of them has the old hag shrieking something that sounds like: "Sick satyrs! Howl eyes, son! Dust."

Then Sarah Tobias (not as ancient as Eunice, but still old) speaks up to interpret the statement. In a matronly, well-enunciated Easterner's voice, she explains that what "the Prophetess" means is that "when *six stars* line up across the eastern *horizon* at *dusk*, it will herald the imminent arrival of six demon-possessed men in Naumpton. They will have been sent by Satan himself, to rape and impregnate the Brides of the Holy Ghost with devil-babies who will grow up to serve as generals in the Antichrist's army." It made no difference that many of the Brides were well beyond their childbearing years. They believed what they were told.

Like all of Tobias' recorded speeches, she ends this one on a positive note (of sorts) by describing how the evil threat could be defeated. In this case, she asserted that the demons could be cast out of the men if "their offending members are cut off and cast aside so that they may not sow foul seed."

Did the rest of the Brides laugh at their "Interpreter of Tongues and Prophecy" for saying something so absurd? No, they went home to sharpen their knives!

The Fifth Reason the Brides Believed Eunice B. Heverin
Finally, the Brides were influenced by the psychological phenomenon of pareidolia. (As you'll recall from an earlier digression, pareidolia is the human need to impose meaningful patterns on abstract stimuli that have none.) Pareidolia tricked the Brides' brains into seeing structure, syntax, and meaning in E.B.H.'s incoherent howls.

I suspect it's also the phenomenon that triggers more ordinary believers to see God's hand in even the most commonplace occurrences. Before I quit my day job to write full time, I worked alongside a bone-thin woman with horrible breath who was especially fond of drawing these sorts of spurious connections. Once, for example, she was over an hour late for work and explained to me that it was God's will.

"I left my apartment later than usual this morning," she said, "because I found a dead mouse in the kitchen. What a strange thing to see! I don't have a cat, or mouse traps, or even poison around. I've never had any trouble with vermin before. But today, out of nowhere, this dead mouse shows up that has to be disposed of. Oh, it was a vile corpse lying in its own urine! I scraped him into a dustpan and set him outside, next to my building's trash bin. Then I sopped up its urine with a paper towel and sprayed a little cleaner on it to deodorize the floor until I could come home after work and give it a proper scrubbing.

"When I finally got onto the Interstate, I was met with a terrible, thick stench of ozone and burning rubber. After driving over a hill, I came across the aftermath of a ten-car pile-up. Ambulance lights swirled through mist, and I could see several bodies on stretchers, with bloodstained sheets draped over them. If I hadn't found that dead mouse, I would've been killed in that crash too! Clearly, God put that dead mouse in my apartment. There's no other explanation! He knows I hate mice and wouldn't be able to abide it lying in state (as it were) in my kitchen all day. He knew I'd pause long enough to dispose of it, and therefore avoid the wreck."

But what about those killed in the wreck? Didn't they deserve a dead mouse (or burst pipe, or sudden roach infestation) to delay them, as well? One of the dead was an eighteen-month-old girl. Why didn't God put a dead mouse in her mother's kitchen?

The committed believer will shrug off such questions and a dopey smile will creep onto their face. "The universe is an immense tapestry and we are just a single thread. Of course, we can't see the design! We're not meant to."

If you really analyze that argument, though, it makes no sense. How can we know, for sure, that the universe is an immense tapestry? What proof is there that this is the case? Absolutely none! By simply *asserting* it's a tapestry, without any evidence, believers cheat. What if, instead of a tapestry, the universe is a massive collage clumsily glued onto light-years of black construction paper by a drooling, psychotic lowlife? This seems to make far more sense to me. It would explain a lot.

I'm embarrassed to admit, though, that even Miss Foulness can find herself momentarily seduced by the tapestry argument. Just a reflexive twinge of belief, mind you, entertained for only a second or two before she comes to her senses. But she must be honest and admit she feels it.

How can I say such a thing, after making all the points I made above? Because while the tapestry argument is coated with an intellectual veneer, it ultimately doesn't seek to prevail through reason. It knows it can't win on that battlefield. No, its appeal is strictly poetic (and, therefore, aesthetic). It isn't a clever argument, but it succeeds in *sounding* clever. (Probably because the average American is clueless about what a tapestry is and so merely saying the word makes a person sound highbrow.)

Besides all that, though, the idea of a tapestry is obviously more pleasing than the idea of a clumsily glued-together collage. I, too, would rather believe that the universe is the work of a masterful artist instead of a psychotic lowlife. Most people would, not just the poorly educated. ("Beauty is truth, truth beauty—that is all / Ye know on earth, and all ye need to know.")

Maybe God really did send a dead mouse to the kitchen of my bone-thin, fetid-breath-afflicted co-worker, to spare her from that ten-car pile-up.

Inevitably, though, something comes along to melt the musical façade and expose the ugly noise underneath. For example, it turned out the dead rodent on my co-worker's floor had been infected with something called hantavirus. After breathing in air contaminated by the virus, she fell ill. It's a vicious disease. Although initially indistinguishable from the flu, in a matter of days it leads to severe congestive heart failure. Those who have survived this infection have said that it feels like lung-crushing suffocation.

My co-worker did not survive.

Had she passed away in the car crash, she wouldn't have experienced any pain at all. She would've died instantly and her last thoughts would've been panic (or maybe just annoyance) at how the car in front of her was slamming on its brakes. Instead, she died in agony and (perhaps even worse) in a state of aesthetic poverty. Breast cancer, tuberculosis, these are poetic deaths. There's an imagined sense of dignity about them. Even the twisted steel of a car wreck can become a poignant symbol of the poetic brevity of life and the general impermanence of all things, exalted by the Buddhists as an essential truth.

But dying from having inhaled air contaminated with infected mouse piss? How do you even describe such a death to a friend without one of you nervously chuckling afterward? What if the ammonia-like stench lingered on the body, even at the funeral home?

After a bad experience at a funeral when I was seven years old, I no longer attend such functions. That doesn't stop me from imagining what it was like to be at this particular service, though.

Maybe the morticians sprayed a half-bottle of perfume on the corpse to drown out the piss odor. Maybe they were hard at work on it, right up to the last minute.

But what if it did no good?

What if the bereaved could still smell the cause of death? What if they made great efforts to pretend that it wasn't piss they smelled, but rather formaldehyde? What if such efforts only succeeded for a few moments at a time, and therefore had to be constantly restarted?

I'm not smelling mouse piss, I'm smelling formaldehyde.
I'm not smelling mouse piss, I'm smelling formaldehyde.
I'm not smelling mouse piss, I'm smelling formaldehyde.

What if the mourners had to repeat that mantra, over and over, and over and over, and over, and therefore neglected the business of weeping and praying?

Allow me to bluntly make a point that no one can deny: there is no pleasing pattern, no poetic justice, no aesthetic pleasure to be found in the scent of piss.

As I reach that conclusion, I imagine the committed believer getting a dopey grin on her face yet again. "That only proves my point! If the baby had stumbled onto a dead mouse, soaked in its own urine, then it would've contracted the hantavirus. But instead, it was allowed to exit the world without even knowing what hit it. The burden was shifted, instead, to your co-worker (who was older and, therefore, had less poetry to lose with a urine-soaked death).

"Can't you see how terrible it would've been for a baby's passing to be polluted by such garishly unpoetic circumstances? How much dignity the bereaved would've lost if mouse piss had been the culprit? Such are the merciful ways of our Lord, that He shifted that awkwardness to a death with a much lower profile! The death of a woman who would've died in ten or twenty years, anyway."

And for a split second, the music of that statement—its aesthetic pleasantness—stirs my heart to the brink of belief. As I type that, I realize just how idiotic I sound. (How vulnerable I am to Moronic Hope!) What stops me from succumbing to it completely? The knowledge that, when the music fades, I'll be left with the plain, stark, wonderless world that is, ultimately, more convincing.

And with questions about why that music is so fleeting.

And with an intolerance for dopey grins.

9

What can we say about the role of little Naumpton in World War I? Not much. The town was so remote (and, especially in those days, so tiny) that it had never been counted during the census. The only residents at the time were the Brides, a couple dozen fishermen, a handful of farmers trying (against all advice) to grow subsistence crops, and a few deranged hermits.

There was no postal service to the town, let alone a telegraph station. Correspondence was sent and received through the larger, downriver town of Cannelton. Therefore, Naumpton managed to stay under the radar of the draft.

Obscurity has its benefits.

But there are limits to its powers. It did not spare Naumpton from the ravages of two more floods that hit in the same month (February of 1918). The catastrophes came on the heels of a rapid thaw. A *Cincinnati Enquirer* article by Owen Findsend and Cameron McWhirter, discussing the history of local flooding, summed it up this way: "Huge chunks of ice floated down the Ohio and crushed the hulls of many steamboats, effectively ending the era of steamboat commerce on the Ohio."

Moreover, in autumn of that same year—just as the Great War was grinding to a halt—the Spanish flu pandemic ravaged the state. Unlike the draft, it managed to reach Naumpton. How, exactly, did the contagion take place? There was still traffic down the river, of course, but it was greatly reduced after the floods. There was little reason for any vessel to stop in Naumpton. If the town was so isolated, why wasn't it spared?

In her fascinating book *Brideism: The Cult Behind the Charity*, local historian (and chiropracter) Karen Raynor states that, one day in early October, six bloated corpses washed up on the riverfront. It's further said that one of the Brides (a pious, hairy woman named Eliza Carter) saw the bodies as "dormant demons" and mutilated them in accordance with the directions given in the old prophecy. That way, they couldn't impregnate her and her fellow-believers with devil babies.

Going by that benchmark, she was successful. The corpses didn't suddenly rise from the dead and rape her. However, through a far more mundane violation—that is, infection—they made made her pregnant with death.

And when, on the following Monday morning, she walked into the crowded hut of the long-deceased Eunice Heverin to meet with the rest of the Brides for their weekly teachings and rituals, she spread the flu to many of her fellow believers.

Indeed, the Spanish flu initially threatened to decimate the Brides' ranks—first by killing off no small number of them, then by calling the effectiveness of their faith into question. (If the Brides truly enjoyed God's favor, why hadn't they been spared? Why had their prophecy turned out to be so wrong? Why had they been the passage through which the Spanish flu invaded?)

Yes, if ever there was a moment when the Brides of the Holy Ghost were at risk of disbanding (or literally dying out), this was it. And yet, as I mentioned earlier, they have survived up to the present day. Exactly how did they manage to escape oblivion?

By succumbing, instead, to Grayness.

Naumpton was ill-prepared to handle a public health emergency. It had no doctor. (The last physician had left around the same time as the last lumberjack.) It didn't even have a mayor or town council.

As the body count grew, Naumptonians felt the need to remedy this. So it was that the Brides, the fishermen, the farmers, and even one of the hermits convened on Monday, October 21st, to write up a quick and dirty charter. "The Flu Charter" (as it came to be known) established the office of mayor and a three-person town council, organized "for the sole purpose of seeking such medical and other assistance to withstand this plague until such time as the Holy Ghost shall grant us deliverance."

The first elected mayor of Naumpton was the leader of Brides at the time—a woman named Rose O'Connor ("Wild Irish Rose" she was called by the fishermen who admired her beauty and foolishly wished they could, in some way, domesticate her). O'Connor was an erstwhile Catholic who seemed to have found, in the Brides, a more accessible faith; a faith energized by emotion rather than reason. The prophecies of E.B.H. may have seemed puzzling to many outsiders, but Wild Irish Rose appreciated that they offered a rawness and enthusiasm far preferable to the dusty relics and Latin Mass of her forefathers.

O'Connor was not the first woman elected mayor of an American town. That honor goes to Susanna Salter of Argonia, Kansas, who achieved that milestone in 1887. Nonetheless, O'Conner was *one* of the first such women, and her election was facilitated by the fact that The Flu Charter explicitly granted women the right to vote in town elections. This progressive policy would have been deemed unconstitutional by the Indiana Supreme Court but, in their seclusion, the Naumptonians either didn't know about that prohibitive factor or, quite possibly, didn't care.

The Brides (who had numbered over one hundred, before the flu, and comprised a majority of Naumpton's population) would not have agreed to anything less. At the time, they saw themselves as wedded only to the Holy Ghost, ineligible for any worldly sort of matrimony, and therefore exempt from any Biblical commandments that they should submit to men. In fact, one might even say that there was among the Brides an undercurrent of belief in female supremacy, perhaps owing to the disgust they felt toward copulation in general and male genitalia in particular; a disgust traceable to Eunice Booth Heverin and her reaction to the rutting sounds she'd heard along the riverfront.

A Bride (Hannah Scott) also managed to win one of the three town council seats. The remaining two were held by fishermen (Gus Cliff and Elmer Patterson). At the first meeting of the town officials, it was decided that one of their number should make the trek out of Naumpton to the capital city of Indianapolis, to beseech the state's assistance with whatever medicines they would be willing to distribute.

Why didn't they just reach out to their state representative?

Because their state representative, an attorney named Henry Lincoln Talbot, despised them. They knew any effort to ask for his help would come to naught. They knew that even a public health emergency wouldn't move his hardened heart. They knew he would have preferred for everyone in the town to die.

You see, Talbot was a wealthy Episcopalian who looked on the Naumptonians as slovenly heretics and troublesome squatters. His only interaction with them was to send the county sheriff to the Brides in 1916, requesting that they provide proof that they owned their land or else, in sixty days, be evicted.

It seems that an heiress of Naumpton Oil Company by the name of Catherine Naumpton Howard believed that she had a claim to the entire town. She wanted the Brides to leave at once and retained her new beau, the smooth social climber Henry Lincoln Talbot, to represent her in court. It was a harrowing bind for the Brides, one that few would have predicted them to escape. Escape they did, though.

At least for a time.

Their counter-attack was doused in honey rather than vinegar. They invited the heiress to visit them (putatively to discuss terms of a settlement). Wild Irish Rose asked Howard to "leave [her] attorney back home, so that we can discuss this among ladies, without the foolishness of the oafish sex to distract us."

Writing such a letter was a gamble. What if Catherine Howard had felt the reference to "the oafish sex" so improper as to be beyond the pale? But such was not the case. Howard agreed to come and visit the Brides—sans representation. Perhaps she was intrigued by O'Connor's flippant attitude. Perhaps the idea of a "modern girl" (as the saying went) ruling over her own religion was too fascinating for an educated young lady to pass over unobserved.

Within a few days of her arrival, Howard wrote Talbot to let him know she was suspending the legal action and that he needn't expend any more time on the case. Before even a fortnight had passed, she had converted to Brideism. Before the month was out, the Brides had hired a lawyer of their own, in Cannelton, to draft documents legally transferring any property Catherine Naumpton Howard was owed, in perpetuity, to "those residents of Naumpton currently making any year-long use of it, in part or in whole." This transfer protected the land rights of the Brides, of course, but also those of the fishermen, farmers, and hermits as well.

Perhaps this is the reason the latter three groups agreed to the terms of The Flu Charter and didn't dispute the outcome when the Brides won two of the four town offices. They no doubt felt indebted to the Brides for their shrewdness and poise when faced with foes against whom they themselves would have been powerless. Through the Brides' actions, the status quo in Naumpton was preserved for everyone.

Talbot was outraged. He had designs on marrying Howard, seizing the land, and establishing a shipyard at Naumpton. Through their shrewdness, the Brides had maneuvered more than one possession from his grasp.

Thus, the Brides intuited it was better to lie low, as far as Talbot was concerned. "Bride O'Connor wished us to be free of obligations to any man," Hannah Scott wrote in her 1937 memoir-festo *The Delicate Fist of Freedom* (an account of her time in the cult, and life after leaving it). "She was particularly wary of males like Mr. Talbot, who had foul designs on Bride Catherine and on our land. In those days, we Brides were of the united opinion that we were the breast of salvation and men were the suckling infants. The only thing the infant has to offer his mother is obedient dependence."

So that explains why they didn't wish to include Talbot in any of the discussions over the land. They had to suspect, though, that a request for help from Indianapolis would likely entail crossing the path of *some* man, and asking that man for help. Perhaps this is why they sent Gus Cliff on the errand. They may have reasoned that, on theological grounds, it was less disgraceful for one "infant" to ask another for help. Or maybe they just saw men as more disposable, and therefore found it less objectionable to put one in harm's way.

If Cliff himself had an inkling of either possibility, he didn't appear bothered by it. He made the journey without complaint. When he appeared at the State House in the first week of November to lobby on behalf of his neighbors, he was told that their best option would be to transport their sick downriver to Evansville, where care was, if not plentiful, at least sufficient for their needs. Of course, he wasn't told this by the governor himself, or even the lieutenant governor, or the president of the State Senate, but rather by some twentysomething typist for the Speaker of the Indiana House.

My guess is that Cliff was hoping to hear something a bit more dramatic. When I try to imagine what it was like for him, I sense that he was hoping to be sent back to Naumpton with a free supply of pills and ointments. But I also like to imagine him as the type of man who was, perhaps, just a little too servile for his own good. The type of man who would do as the secretary told him to do and leave feeling sheepish for even asking her for help.

Upon Cliff's return on November 17th, Wild Irish Rose ordered the construction of several flatboats (little bigger than rafts). By this time, however, the flu had intensified and the weary, sick townsfolk were hardly up to the task. The resulting vessels were flimsily constructed, unsanded, and full of splinters. They had been built from scraps of wood nailed to one another at strange angles. Simply put, these boats weren't fit to circumnavigate a puddle, let alone travel the fickle waters of the Ohio. Moreover, the construction process took far longer than it should have.

When she saw the town's pathetic fleet, Mayor O'Connor howled in despair. But then, so the local folklore goes, she was inspired by the *poetry* of the moment—a poetry in which the solution to Naumpton's woes fit a pattern previously established in the Bible. (Had not the boat that rescued Moses from death been a simple "ark of bulrushes...daubed...with slime and with pitch"? Therefore, even the crude construction of the boats should be seen as confirmation that all would go well. It was part of the miracle!)

Even shrewd, savvy Wild Irish Rose had no immunity against the allure of poetic patterns. It is an unavoidable human weakness to which we will all succumb, at some point in our lives. It would be easy to sit back on our perch, a century distant, and mock O'Connor's naive vulnerability to symbols. But we shouldn't judge, because few of us have experienced a crisis as menacing as hers. (Even if some of you Giggling, Grimacing Outcasts have experienced something similar to the Spanish Flu epidemic, you probably can't say that you were as defenseless in the face of it as O'Connor was. Remember, penicillin hadn't even been discovered yet.)

Each boat could comfortably accommodate only three sick people at a time. Many, however, were overloaded with six. Need I tell you that there was, in fact, no miracle? None of the sick returned from the journey. No messenger rode into town with news of their fates. Mayor O'Connor, still milking the Moses symbolism for all it was worth, liked to think that they had all—every one of them: men, women, and children—been taken in by someone wealthy and powerful. She imagined the infected Brides would return when they were well again, and bring with them fresh prophecies garnered from fever dreams. But, even to this day, no one knows what happened to the cast-off sick of Naumpton.

Wherever you find a mystery you'll find wild speculation, and I'm hardly immune to the temptation. So I wonder: did six *Naumptonian* corpses wash ashore some other little, forgotten town, thus perpetuating a cycle? If I imagine such symmetry, my brain experiences a brief tingle of satisfaction.

Six bodies wash ashore at Naumpton. Later, six Naumptonian corpses wash ashore somewhere else. Why does this repetition, this pattern, provide me with comfort? If I saw even a single body wash ashore on the banks of the Ohio River, I'd no doubt vomit from the stench and run away as quickly as my quivering, achy, middle-aged legs could take me! But when I write about early twentieth-century Naumpton, I'm far enough removed from it that I no longer experience their traumas as my own. Instead, I unconsciously see the Naumptonians as curious test subjects. I like to observe how they deal with all this misfortune.

Going back to a question asked at the very beginning of this book, does this make me a literary sadist? No, because the events I'm describing are historical. Perhaps you can call me a history-based sadist, but I'll counter by saying that my ventures in history are no more sadistic than those of Ken Burns or David McCullough. All historians study suffering. They coerce each epoch into undressing and exposing its scars.

And since I have "no skin in the game", as the saying goes, I'm more likely to be caught up in the poetry of patterns and see the Naumptonians' troubles through the lens of my own naive symbolism. Six bodies brought the contagion, six bodies carried it to another town. I think it entices me because it implies the world is a predictable place, where the scales are always balanced and aesthetic (poetic) justice, however grim, remains the norm.

It's worth adding that this aesthetic appeal (the appeal of the predictable pattern) is the same phenomenon that makes so many people fall in love with serial killer movies. If the killer just slayed a group of men, women, and children at random—with no pattern, with no real motive, no stylized, melodramatic method of dispatching his victims, no calling card, no notes left behind to taunt the police—then we wouldn't find him intriguing. The appeal of the serial killer resides in the notion that every homicidal madman secretly loves the poetry of patterns as much as the regular Joe. Even the most disturbing violence becomes acceptable to Hollywood if it's tethered to the predictability of a pattern.

(The killer is systematically going after each of the doctors who failed to save his wife—PATTERN. He's killing them using methods adapted from the Old Testament plagues God cast against Pharaoh—PATTERN. The killer feels he must dispatch his victims in ways that reference each of the seven deadly sins—PATTERN. The killer goes after women of a certain girth, because he wants to skin them and make a woman-suit—PATTERN. He places a rare moth in each of their mouths, as a symbol of the transformation. PATTERNS. PATTERNS. POETRY OF PATTERNS. KITSCH OF PATTERNS, ENABLER OF MADNESS, DOMESTICATOR OF MADNESS, THE POWER WHICH GROOMS MADNESS INTO A MARKETABLE BRAND!)

10

Somewhere, during his trip to Indianapolis (or, more likely, on the way home), Gus Cliff contracted the flu himself. This is how a second strain of the virus came to Naumpton (this one even more virulent than that transmitted by the six washed-up corpses). He died on December 12, 1918, less than a week after the launch of the sick-fleet.

His decline was steady and relentless. Elmer Patterson, hardly the literary type, took up his pencil to start a journal tracing the course of his friend's decline. "He don't sound human. Each time he tries to speak as a man he sounds more and more like a growling dog. He don't *look* human, either. Green snot flows from his nose, mouth, and eyes alyke [*sic*]! He's somehow lost his fancee [*sic*] suits and began wandering around town half-naked. What garments he still wears are affixed to his skin by sweat. They look like the first parts of a cocoon that's growing round him."

The change was so alarming that Wild Irish Rose ordered Patterson to wrap Cliff's face up in a swath of rough fabric so that it would not have to be seen. Indeed, it's said that the remnant of the Naumpton Town Council soon passed an ordinance to the effect that all those showing "divers progressions" of the flu be forced to wear such a fabric over their face to limit contamination. In *Naumpton: Then and Now*, Marian Steele makes this into a big deal, going so far as to say it shows Naumptonians "were innovators in disease management."

Perhaps, but it did little to help.

By Christmas Day, Wild Irish Rose herself had begun to show signs of "divers progressions" of the flu. Did she, too, wrap her face up in cloth to prevent the contagion of her fellow Naumptonians (in particular, the other Brides—with whom she shared close quarters)? We don't know the answer for sure. All we know is that, according to a list of the departed—Colorfully titled "The Reaper's Manifest"—she died on December 30th.

During the flu, the Naumptonians did not give their dead proper funerals. This is explained in a brief, sloppily written note at the bottom of The Manifest: "All were given to the pit."

About this pit: the Naumptonians didn't actually dig it out of the ground. Rather, they found a ravine that was perfectly situated for that purpose. Then, after the plague, they filled it in. In the early '50s, a gas station was built atop the mass grave. I understand it's now a Circle K.

Everyone knows that bodies are buried underneath there, but no one likes to talk about it. A Gray Town such as Naumpton lacks the necessary ambition to condemn the building, tear it down, start digging, and sort through the remains (let alone identify them).

There's a plaque on the wall behind the counter of the Circle K that reads: "We Remember All of Naumpton's Sons Lost in World War I, Who Lie in Solemn Repose Near This Location." Apparently, the Bangladeshi man who owns that particular Circle K franchise misunderstood the nature of the mass grave beneath his store. None of the townsfolk dares to mention the error or request a change, fearing that any correction would be seen as unpatriotic. Besides, some of the present-day Naumptonians prefer the error to the truth (it makes the town seem much more a part of the grandeur of history, rather than the butt of one of its jokes). Hell, maybe they have no idea what the truth actually is and honestly believe three hundred World War I veterans are buried under the Twinkies, beer, and stale hot dogs of the convenience store.

I was first introduced to the popular, life-affirming poem "Desiderata" as a teenager. My best friend loved it, and when she shared it with me I appreciated it because it seemed—in the context of my uptight family—heretical. Here, after all, was a poem that encouraged us all to "be at peace with God, *whatever you conceive Him to be.*"

The very fact that someone thought the definition of God was up for grabs, open to individual interpretation, and not set in stone by the Bible thrilled me. The fact that such a person wrote this thought down for public consumption thrilled me. The fact that the poem was written in the seventeenth century and engraved on a plaque mounted in an old church absolutely blew my mind.

But, of course, the poem wasn't written in the seventeenth century. That's an urban legend, based on a misunderstanding. It was written in 1927 by a Hoosier named Max Ehrmann.

I was as surprised as anyone to find this out, but in retrospect it makes total sense. If there was ever an anthology of Gray literature, "Desiderata" would make the cut. In case you are skeptical about this, Figure 1 (below) concisely explains what I'm talking about.

Figure 1. Pro-Grayness Propaganda in Max Ehrmann's "Desiderata"

Stanza	Translation into Gray-Speak
"Go placidly amid the noise and haste and remember what peace there may be in silence. As far as possible, without surrender, be on good terms with all persons."	Submit to the boring, coiled-up heaviness. Let it congeal around you, like chilled animal fat, so that you move only in slow motion.
"Speak your truth quietly and clearly; and listen to others, even to the dull and the ignorant; they too have their story."	Only scream at your children and sports teams. Never scream at funerals. Never scream into the mirror. Never scream at morons. Never scream simply for the sake of screaming.
"…If you compare yourself with others, you may become vain or bitter, for always there will be greater and lesser persons than yourself."	Your life will always be something less than life, but you must find a way to adjust. You may suspect you've been cheated—granted a life that's worth only sixty cents on the dollar. But you must never speak of your suspicions.

I could, undoubtedly, continue with this analysis throughout the entire length of the poem, but I think you get the idea. Now, I'm self-aware enough to realize that some of you may be skeptical about the case I just built. Even though you are Giggling, Grimacing Outcasts, you may feel that my take on "Desiderata" borders on paranoia.

Very well then, let's set "Desiderata" aside, just for a moment, and look at some other works in Mr. Ehrmann's oeuvre. One day, while strolling through my local library, I stumbled across a book from 1935 titled *Indiana Poets: an Anthology of 48 Living Writers*.

Ehrmann has four poems in this anthology. Two of these poems are worth our attention in the matter of Grayness. The first is simply titled "Indiana" and the second "Terre Haute" (after the Hoosier city of the same name).

Join me, if you will, in examining the first stanza of "Indiana":

The pioneers lie in their earthen beds.
Still lives their dauntless faith to do and dare,
In cities that lift high their lofty heads,
In busy towns that prosper everywhere.

Bear in mind, those words were published in 1935, when twenty percent of the labor force was unemployed. Gray Literature avoids the uncomfortable. It seeks to cover the human emotional experience with a film of sticky Gray book-snot (not true literature, but the Gray, infected snot thereof). With that in mind, please indulge me as I translate the first stanza of "Indiana" into Gray-Speak.

It's not the worst thing in the world
to live in one of the coiled-up, congealed, heavy places
in the Midwest.
Don't scream
at funerals, or in the mirror, or at morons, or even
just for the sake of screaming,
Only scream
at sports teams and children.
Sixty cents
on the dollar is really awesome.
Really, it is.

Pretty fucking spooky, eh?

But that's just the beginning. It goes on for five more stanzas. Again, I won't burden you with a translation of every stanza. But, in order to further develop my case against Ehrmann, I need to share one more with you (the third stanza):

> A toiling, peaceful life this people leads,
> Not moved by red rebellion's scarlet leer,
> Nor whirlwinds shouting out sophomoric creeds
> The turmoils of the world touch lightly here.

I trust that particular glob of poetic snot needs little in the way of translating. In this stanza, Ehrmann is taking a victory lap, celebrating the Gray Ascendency. As we've seen, "sophomoric creeds" such as the New Israelites, Harmonists, Shakers, and Brides exerted an influence on the settlement of the state. But, by the time Ehrmann is writing, they were all tamed. Likewise, the "turmoils of the world" touched more than lightly on Indiana during the onslaught of the Spanish Flu. And even in Ehrmann's time, the calamity of the Great Depression wreaked its havok.

But, as Shakespeare may have observed if he were living today, the Gray mentality is uniquely equipped to absorb "a thousand natural shocks." And to paraphrase Thoreau, Grayness will allow the emotion of desperation, so long as it remains *quiet* desperation. (Despair is allowed to silently swirl in the eyes of Gray children, but it never escapes their mouths. It must remain coiled up and heavy inside of them.)

Which brings me to the last of the Ehrmann poems I'll be discussing here, "Terre Haute." Now don't freak out. I'm not going to quote multiple stanzas of this one. I'm just going to quote the first line, which is presented in the form of a rhetorical question. Here goes.

"What place is lovelier than Terre Haute;"

At this point, Ehrmann is just trolling us. When he refers to loveliness, what he really means is an absence of publicly acknowledged disruption or pain. That's the only way his opening line makes any sense.

A Gray Life is like a ride on a city bus. You move along slowly, you feel cramped (that is, coiled up) in your tight seat, and you'd probably rather not be there. But the ride is a relatively smooth one (and, better yet, affordable). So you stay put.

Now I know some of you may be saying to yourselves: what about Naumpton? What about the Brides? The fishermen? What happened to them? Why are you going off on this tangent about Max Ehrmann?

Because if you visit the website of the Naumpton Chamber of Commerce you'll find a link to Camp Heverin, a Brides complex that includes a fishing lodge, cabins, campgrounds, rowboats, and a pier. And if you click on that link, you'll see an unsophisticated Wordpress blog template emblazoned with the title "Camp Heverin: The turmoils of the world touch lightly here."

You may think this is mere coincidence. How would the Brides know about Max Ehrmann's poem? Nobody reads poetry these days (except, of course, a handful of aspiring poets). Moreover, you really have to make a conscious effort to dig into obscure works of regional literature to discover "Indiana" and "Terre Haute." If the Brides were suddenly going to get the poetry bug, they surely wouldn't want to get too involved with a fellow like Ehrmann (he of the flexible definition of deity in "Desiderata"). And yet, if you go online and look for yourself, you'll see the connection.

I do not think it can be explained using ordinary logic. I think this may be a sign, rather, that Grayness is sentient; that it stretched out two of its slimy gray tentacles—one seizing Max Ehrmann and the other, Naumpton. The website for Camp Heverin is Grayness' way of making the two embrace (in the same way that a little girl can hold a Barbie doll in one hand, a Ken doll in the other, and make them kiss each other when they say "I do" at the altar).

Perhaps I'm beginning to go a bit too far with all this. Perhaps I'm seeing PATTERNS, PATTERNS, POETRY OF PATTERNS. But tell me, have you any better explanation? One that accounts for this subtle but undeniable link between the Ehrmann poem and the Brides?

This link is all the more tantalizing when you look at the history of Camp Heverin and see how it is inextricably linked to the Graying of Naumpton.

You see, Henry Lincoln Talbot was nothing if not persistent. In May of 1919, after flu and floods and winter had all finished having their fun at the expense of Hoosiers, he returned to Naumpton. This time he was not alone. He brought with him an "alienist" from the state hospital in Madison.

According to a letter Hannah Scott wrote to her mother in New Jersey, Talbot stated that the authorities had heard rumors of certain "murderous mutilations" occurring in the village of Naumpton, perpetrated by the Brides of the Holy Ghost.

Alas, it would seem that Eliza Carter was so wrapped up in disarming demonic sperm bombs that she didn't notice a teenage boy in a rowboat who was passing by the riverfront. Nor was she cognizant of just how she must have looked at that moment, to anyone who didn't realize the bodies were already dead when they washed ashore. Furthermore, she lacked the insight to realize that there was already no small amount of wariness about Naumpton, owing to tales of the unhinged misfits The New Moses had unleashed on the wilderness and the Brides' own unconventional ways. Gossip being the only thing spreading quicker than disease, the story of the "Murderous

Maids of Naumpton" and the "Brides of Heresy's Host" passed from lip to ear with enthusiasm.

Fortunately for Eliza, the bodies of the offending "dormant demons" had been burnt on a pyre, and their bone shards and ashes cast back into the river so that they would not pollute the mass grave with their diabolical nature. So, even if law enforcement had wanted to exhume bodies for evidence, the mutilated ones wouldn't have been found.

Honestly, though, I suspect Talbot didn't care all that much about the mutilated bodies. His investigation was nothing but posturing. If anything, he may have been glad to hear the rumors, because they gave him ammunition to assail the Brides' sanity (which, in all fairness, was legitimately assailable).

According to *Brideism: The Cult Behind the Charity*, Talbot threatened to use the incident as ammunition in a suit alleging Ms. Howard was not of sound mind when she transferred her property to the squatters. Back then, the Brides had little in the way of wealth to fund such a legal battle, and knew they were unlikely to receive a fair hearing. They were also aware of the very real possibility that most, if not all, of them could end up in Madison State Hospital if they didn't play their cards right. They did not wish to have their practices examined under the harsh light of court proceedings.

Raynor admits there is no paper trail documenting a series of *quid pro quos*, but makes a convincing argument that the Brides only managed to survive by making a number of shady deals with Talbot.

For starters, they made a major doctrinal shift by deciding that they'd been mistaken in their criticisms of "earthly matrimony." They denounced Wild Irish Rose as the chief propagator of this dogma and reversed it, explaining that "the Book of Acts clearly shows that the Holy Ghost fell upon men, infusing *them* with Its power. Therefore, we sinned when we prohibited earthly matrimony, as marriage to a saved man is the easiest route for a woman to be filled with the Spirit."

The change was announced by Emily Hermann, the acting leader of the Brides, during her sermon on Pentecost Sunday, June 8, 1919. On July 4th, Catherine Naumpton Howard announced she was engaged to Henry Lincoln Talbot and that, furthermore, she would be leaving the Brides. Concurrent with her departure, the Brides transferred all their property along the Naumpton waterfront (and the area that would later become downtown Naupton) to Talbot. Talbot then donated a swampy parcel of land about three miles away to the Brides. It lay alongside a creek that made erratic, varicose-vein twists and turns inland from the Ohio River. Today it is known as Tobias Creek. As you may have already guessed, Camp Heverin rests on its shore.

Why did Talbot stop short of having the Brides locked away in Madison? Raynor believes it was not out of any sense of mercy, but because he knew the Brides could do him a favor more established religions most likely would not: shady income tax deductions.

You see, federal income tax was a relatively new beast in 1919, and the tax deduction for donations to churches and other charitable institutions had only been introduced a couple of years earlier. You could say that Talbot was a pioneer in working this system to his own advantage.

He knew that he could coerce the Brides into surrendering their land free of charge by using the very real threat of institutionalization against them. And in case that proverbial stick was not sufficient, they could be convinced by the proverbial carrot of the donated swamp land. Thus, he would not only possess the riverfront property he wanted for his shipyard, but he could write off the swamp land donation for a huge deduction the following year.

Raynor believes this next era of the Brides' existence can be explained by the compromises they were forced to make to keep Talbot at bay. He was the one who pressured them into taking a subservient approach to men. (Many of them ended up marrying the fishermen, who then took control of the land and its business, relegating the Brides to unglamorous poverty relief work.) He was the one who maneuvered them into a location where their commercial enterprises would be limited. He was the one who leaned on his friends in the newspaper business to rehabilitate their public image. He was the one who kept them alive, some say, just so they would readily supply a receipt documenting all manner of contributions. The way the scam worked is that the Brides' receipt would exaggerate the amount of the donation or make it up out of whole cloth. He knew that it was most essential, in those days following the War Revenue Act of 1917, for a wealthy man to have compliant hands in the pulpit.

And so it was that, over the course of decades, the corpse mutilation was gradually forgotten. Perhaps the young boy who had sworn he'd seen it even forgot it, or so doubted his own sight that he may as well have forgotten it. The Brides became integrated into the patchwork quilt that is southern Indiana fundamentalism.

Indeed, if you are a Baptist or a Pentecostal or a member of one of the various non-denominational holy roller churches, you book your church picnic at Camp Heverin. You may even rent space to host an old-fashioned summertime revival meeting out there. You undoubtedly fish up there. Hell, even the handful of Catholics who call Naumpton home have been known to set aside their discomfort with fundamentalists and launch their boats from the Camp Heverin pier. Some days, catfish overrule the catechism.

***

At this point, I have written over forty thousand words. Some of them may have led you to consult your dictionary. For example, very early on I took the risk of throwing "effluvium" at you. That is probably my favorite word of all time, with "desultory" coming in at a close second. I'll admit it: I love the sound made when the consonants in such words jangle against their vowels. But I didn't use either of them as mere decoration. Both were necessary to describe certain properties of Foulness.

That said, I promised you far more than a description of Foulness. I said I would explain why *Grayness* arose. And to explain why it arose, I don't need any ten-dollar words. I can sum it up in a single, simple one: "compromises."

Yes, I'm beginning to suspect that *compromises* are the fertile ground in which the seed of Grayness grows. When did Naumpton start to succumb to Grayness? The seed hovered over the town after the deforestation bubble burst, but it didn't land until the Brides compromised their faith and joined the mainstream.

And that was only the most dramatic of the compromises. There are a hundred and one other compromises that followed on the heels of it. There are the compromises that individuals must make simply as a result of dwelling in close proximity to others—the subtle compromise of self-consciousness about how our appearance and actions impact others. (Even if someone dresses in a manner intended to shock passers-by, the very act of guessing how others will react is a compromise of true individualism.) There are also the compromises that the human spirit makes when molded by an established cultural infrastructure. That is, molded by civilization.

As Naumpton developed into something other than a frontier town, something with institutions and stability and proper land titles rather than the flimsy claims of squatters, the population swelled. As more children came into the area, education became compulsory.

Newspapers, radio shows, pulp magazines, and dime novels began to define the boundaries of what was thinkable, believable, sayable, and doable. It's as if the variety of human experience was suddenly (radically) condensed into three or four stylized types. People stopped defining themselves by their instincts and began to define themselves in reference to pop culture.

This is, of course, a trend that continues unabated up to this present day. People fill out online surveys to find out which member of the Golden Girls (or the Beatles, or the Scooby Doo cast) they are. Some of you are probably annoyed at me for bringing this up, as you hold that these surveys are harmless fun.

But (here comes my pessimism again) I see it as a sign of our distressing neediness, of our deference to popular entertainment. We don't want to do the work of finding our identities through trial and error. We want to be told who we are. Can I really be the only one who finds that mildly servile?

And isn't servility an ingredient in Grayness? There's a sort of Servile Gray Restlessness (S.G.R. for short) that never dares to *admit* that it's restlessness. When people experience S.G.R., they feel a coiled-up, heavy boredom, but are powerless to even so much as *dilute* their suffering through action. It's as if they've been brainwashed into believing that taking action isn't even an option; as if the very concept of "taking action to break one's restlessness" doesn't exist in their minds.

I blame schools for perpetuating S.G.R. Their whole raison d'être is to encourage submission to boring, coiled-up heaviness. I blame the churches, too. The government chooses not to tax them, therefore they are dependent on the maintenance of the status quo.

Undoubtedly, there are those Hoosier houses of worship where people get up and scream and holler and roll around on the ground and foam at the mouth. But surely, even while they are in the midst of such gesticulations, they remain firmly in the grasp of Grayness. I've seen film clips of such shenanigans. If you look beyond all the flailing and pay close attention to the worshippers' eyes, you see how bored, coiled up, heavy, and Gray they are. You see how they're simply going through the motions.

Talbot tames the Brides.

The Brides build their Bible Camp.

The Brides offer flood relief.

The Brides reform their doctrine on sex relations and begin to think that a big part of their mission is to prepare teenage girls for marriage to godly men.

Talbot gets his shipyard started and lands a government contract for small naval vessels. (In the wake of World War I, the nation anticipates involvement in more conflicts overseas. Conflicts = Color, yes? Sadly, no. In Naumpton, the military build-up = factory drudgery. But finally, there's a stable employer in the area!)

Talbot and his cronies work hard to get all the men (and, eventually, their wives) registered to vote, so that he'll have a solid core of electoral support to draw from.

A one-room schoolhouse is established.

The Brides soon merge with a tribe of Baptists and become something of a ladies' auxiliary for them.

A local newspaper is established, a great Gray enterprise that tells the populace how great Talbot is, and how great the Talbot Shipworks are, and how great the Brides are, how great the school is, and how great Indiana and America are. I once found a stack of these early Naumptonian newspapers in an antique store in Madison (a little town about an hour east from where I now reside).

It was a dry summer afternoon when I spotted them. It hadn't rained for weeks. But when I picked them up and saw they were from Naumpton, I felt a snotty humidity about them. I felt the Grayness thick and slick and foul all over the papers, and I tossed them down in horror. (Had I noticed the name of the rag—*The Naumpton Gazette-Recorder*—I would not have picked them up to begin with.)

But I digress! I need to refocus on my epidemiological mission. I need to list my scientific conclusions.

Conclusions about the Causes of Grayness

1. Grayness was caused first and foremost by a compromise of Naumpton's non-Gray principles.

2. Grayness is a consequence of development and progress. (The more one finds oneself surrounded by people and institutions, the more one will need to compromise.)

3. The history of Naumpton would seem to suggest that cults are one significant way to stave off Grayness. The more bizarre the cult, the better the chances of evading Grayness. Notice that, even at the height of their oddity, the Brides were quite a bit less bizarre than the New Israelites. No one in the Brides wore a black veil over her face. No one in the Brides was reported to have a series of different faces superimposed on each

other, like the physiognomy of different levels of Hell. No one was claiming to be the reincarnation of Moses. It's as though the more normal cult of early Brideism was an intermediate stage between Color and Grayness.

4. One aspect of the Brides that was a bit stranger than usual, though, was their short-lived undercurrent of female supremacy. Any cult that holds this belief cannot possibly be tainted with Grayness. (Note that the Graying of the Brides only occurred after they were coerced into abandoning that belief.)

5. I'd like to discuss two Latin words from the realm of alchemy: *solve* and *coagula*. *Solve* (pronounced "sol-vay") refers to the separation of things from one another; the *dissolving* of ties that once held them together. *Coagula* refers to the bringing together of things; the *coagulation* of separate entities into one. Examined through this lens, Grayness can be understood as a case of diseased, metastatic *coagula*—a *coagula* that is so prevalent in a town that it begins to develop the physical properties of stickiness, humidity, and slowness. The air and ambiance of the town begin to feel like chilled animal fat that congeals around you. Is this metastatic *coagula* the cause of compromises? Or are the compromises the cause of the metastatic *coagula*? Even now I'm not sure. But that doesn't change the fact that the cure for Grayness will be an intervention that in some way invokes The Primacy of *Separation*.

Part Three: The Cure

1

I finished writing Part Two of this book on Thanksgiving Day, 2017. I then took a two-month break, so I could fully digest all the historical facts (and ontological *truths*) I'd learned during my research.

You see, what had started as a simple glance outside my window had blossomed into a cornucopia of malignant revelations. I felt physically dizzy in the aftermath, as if I were drunk. I also felt *cognitively* dizzy in the aftermath, as though I'd written something that had gotten jumbled up during the trip from my brain to my fingertips, then had gotten jumbled up *again* during the trip from my fingertips to my laptop. I nursed a suspicion that a mighty wind, blown from the mouth of a contemporary demiurge, had whirled through my neurons, ripping words up from their foundations and rearranging them in the wrong order.

Part Two doesn't seem like an actual story, in a technical sense (and certainly not in a commercial sense). I can't point to any particular character and say: "This is the good guy!" or "This is the bad guy!" I'm not sure I could identify a single moment of Part Two as the climax (or the denouement, or the rising action, or the falling action).

I suppose the Graying of the Brides might be the climax, but there's not much fire and fury to be found in a tale of compromise. It was anticlimactic, or maybe even some sort of dizzy reverse triple somersault, antimatter version of a climax. What I mean is, it was a *freakish mutation of a climax*—a climax that was not street legal, according to the ordinances governing the pop culture roadways.

Initially, the strangeness of Part Two led me to feel like a failure. But I slowly came to realize that its strangeness wasn't my fault. It was, rather, par for the course for a work of nonfiction. After all, this book is a work of epidemiology, and epidemiology is a genre that's too saturated with anxiety to fit the pop culture aesthetic. This book is a work of history, and history is a genre that occupies the uncanny valley between traditional, orderly storytelling and the drooling nonsense of a stroke victim. This book is a memoir. Specifically, the memoir of a woman who is far more concerned with communicating the emotional *texture* and *temperature* of her life (in all its jumbled messiness) than with trying to make it fit the dramatic framework established in Aristotle's *Poetics*.

Winter is, arguably, the season when Grayness imposes the full weight of its oppression. The cold makes the boring, coiled-up heaviness feel even more boring, coiled up, and heavy than usual.

The festive holiday season is no match for the malady. Songs may extol the virtue of a "White Christmas" or bewail the lonesomeness of a "Blue Christmas," but every Christmas is actually Gray (as boring as chimney ashes, as coiled up as Grandma's perm, and as heavy as the burden of bankruptcy).

There are, of course, various propaganda campaigns around the holidays intended to brainwash you into believing such celebrations are free of Grayness. But if you look closely at red and green Christmas lights (or for that matter, red and green Kwanzaa candles) you'll see a halo of Grayness around each bulb (or flame). If you carefully inspect the seldom-seen interior branches of a Christmas tree, you'll find they're covered with what seems at first to be the world's dullest, most depressing tinsel. In reality, it's Gray thought-snot. If you stare at a spinning dreidel and focus all your concentration on it, you can actually *see* Grayness congealing over it and slowing it down. (It's only visible for a millisecond, but that doesn't diminish its eeriness!)

Perhaps this heightened severity of Grayness is what led my thoughts back to this book. On Christmas Eve I tossed and turned in bed. To the untrained ear (or to those in denial) it may have seemed like a "silent night, holy night," but I knew too much to rest comfortably. I could hear the roof groaning under the weight of Grayness and I could feel the way a clammy coat of Grayness formed atop my skin. At the time, however, I lacked the requisite confidence to take action against it.

I kept telling myself I'd *get around to* fighting it, but every time I sat down to work out the details, I felt an odd sensation inside my chest. It was as if a cold iron safe had suddenly materialized there, squeezing my ribs and lungs out of their normal positions and slamming shut around my heart. The heaviness of the iron almost made me topple over.

The worst part was that I knew the combination to the safe. It had briefly flashed into my brain (one left, eight right, sixty-eight left). But, because the safe was inside my chest, there was no way I could reach the dial.

It made no sense for me to feel that way. I should have felt far more confident. After all, I had put in the work to determine the conditions that gave rise to Grayness (and therefore, implicitly, the antithetical conditions under which a cure might occur). Nonetheless, I sat on my research. I hadn't yet done a thing to share my discoveries with the world.

Why the reticence?

Well, let's remember that my conclusions at the end of Part Two imply that a bizarre cult would be needed to cure Grayness. I wasn't convinced I had the requisite charisma to be an effective cult leader. To pull *that* off, I would first of all need to be the kind of person who gets all worked up over political, social, religious, or anti-religious issues. As I established at the beginning, I'm not that kind of person. During my life, I've been both a Republican and a Democrat, a Libertarian and a Green, a Christian, a Buddhist, and an atheist. I've justified this flightiness by saying to myself that I was courageously following the truth wherever it led, regardless of the social consequences.

However, the end result of this approach to life hasn't been an enthusiastic, lifelong search for a system of thought superior to all others. To the contrary, it's been a disillusioned concession that all belief systems (yes—*all* of them) are ultimately ridiculous. So how could I possibly become the kind of woman who creates her own utopian community that's hermetically sealed off from society-at-large?

The other implication of Part Two's findings is that the cult might need to embrace female supremacy. So one day I went ahead and Googled "female supremacy." I discovered that it was nothing more than a sexualized utopian movement. Its manifestos proclaim that the world is screwed up because men have been in power for millennia. Now, since things are on the brink of disaster, a matriarchal revolution is a necessity to save the Earth. There's also a heavy emphasis on BDSM. (One site tells men that "submission is your only hope for survival" and assesses a "cum tax" of twenty bucks an orgasm, presumably paid on the honor system.)

If that's your kink, fine. I'm not here to judge what gets you off. But I must admit that, in late 2017, I could not see myself engaged in any such scheme. It seemed altogether too dogmatic, too caught up in a weird sort of do-gooder impulse driven by a narrative that the world needs radical change to save it. Therefore, it seems too much like politics or religion. Too solemn and—in an odd way—moralistic. I would respect the female supremacists more if they just owned up to the fact that they liked pushing dudes around and didn't feel the need to justify it with mumbo-jumbo about the greater good.

Finally, I had an intuition that to cure the Grayness outside my window, I would first need to strike at the root of the problem. I would have to de-Gray Naumpton. It would be fruitless just to de-Gray my neighborhood without first de-Graying Naumpton. If I did, the Grayness of Naumpton would just end up gradually spreading its tendrils out this way again, reinfecting things, undoing all my hard work.

And, as I've already discussed, every time I got within fifteen miles of that cursed town, waves of vertigo and mental quicksand assaulted me with such ferocity that I had to turn the car around. So this was a nonstarter.

These were, I thought, three very sound reasons why I couldn't be The Third Moses. They sound pretty convincing, don't they?

Eventually, I would set aside each and every one.

The catalyst for this change of heart was a 5K race I ran in the middle of January 2018. Those of you who live in the Midwest may recall the Arctic Blast that seized the region that month, plunging temperatures down into the single digits. To endure such conditions while running a competitive race—even one as brief as a 5K—probably seems like lunacy to you. But Judy (a friend from my softball team) had encouraged me to come out to the event, saying that it was healthy to stoke one's competitive fires in the off-season. "You have to keep that killer instinct alive," she said.

She also said that the registration fees for the race would go to a good cause. I didn't ask what this "good cause" was. I didn't *care* what this "good cause" was. I'm sure I'm not the only runner in the world who feels that way about charity 5Ks. The main thing, for some of us, is the competition, and this January race offered a unique chance to test my mettle in extreme weather.

Don't get me wrong, I believe in some causes. After having lost a friend to cancer several years ago, I'm a sucker for any cancer research charity. I'm not so jaded as to have purged *all* traces of do-gooderism from my soul. It's just that I feel foolish every time I give in to such impulses because I have little faith in the ability of such charities to make any real difference. I could have tossed a thousand and one pink ribbons over my friend Kara's scarred, tit-less chest as she lay in her hospital bed, and it would have done nothing to stop breast cancer from turning her into a pile of ashes.

Judy had sent me an email with a link to the event's website, so that I could register and pay my twenty-five-dollar fee. I saw that it was called the "S.A.S. Winter Sprinter 5K and Fun Run." It was to be held in the tiny river town of Mulchport. (And I do mean tiny: the 2010 census found the population was a mere eighty-one souls, one hundred percent of whom were white.) I imagined that "S.A.S." might stand for something like "St. Anthony School" or "Seniors Against Shingles," but that's all the attention I gave to that particular aspect of the event.

I was much more focused on bracing myself to run 3.1 miles

in the bitter cold. I went online to look for blog posts documenting how other runners prepared for such adventures. Everyone recommended dressing in layers, so I decided I'd wear a second pair of running tights over the first and two pairs of socks. Over my sports bra I'd wear a short-sleeve T-shirt. Over that, a long-sleeve T-shirt. Over *that*, a sweatshirt. And, finally, over the sweatshirt, a hoodie.

But as anyone who has competed outdoors in winter can attest, one of the most annoying problems you face is frozen ears. So I went to Meijers and picked up a thick winter headband with black fleece on the outside and some sort of furry material on the inside. A week or two before the race I tried a few practice runs, but found that—even with all the layers on and with my fleece headband covering my ears—I was far too uncomfortable to go very fast.

These practice runs were comprised of a series of trips around my block in the Gray neighborhood. Over and over, and over and over, and over, I ran past the same sad houses. I read the same bumper stickers on the same pickup trucks parked in the same driveways. As you might imagine, this was difficult, depressing, and vaguely nauseating. It was like trying to swim while submerged in a sea of thick Gray snot. The malaise of Gray surroundings alone would have prevented me from achieving a competitive time; but when combined with the arctic blast my pace slowed to such a degree that a cackling, octogenarian madwoman could've ran even with me.

You see, there were two streets on my block where the wind was particularly savage. The gusts made my cheeks ache. The frozen air had a strange effect on my lungs, too, producing an asthmatic tightness in them that made me wheeze and cough. Worst of all, perhaps, was the feeling (or, should I say, the lack thereof) in and around my nose. From time to time I found myself lifting a finger up and giving it a tap to make sure I could still feel it. Sometimes I would rub it to make certain blood was still circulating. These efforts often resulted in a snot-stained glove. It was unpleasant, to be sure, but you must understand: I was terrified of losing my nose to frostbite and having to go through life with some bizarre Tycho Brahe-style prosthetic.

So I took to Google again, read some more running blogs, and discovered additional garments I could wear to keep my face warm. I decided against wearing a ski mask, as those tend to make the wearer look like a robber. (People are trigger-happy these days. If my neighbors saw me running around the block in a ski mask, they'd likely think I was leaving the scene of a crime, and before you knew it I'd be bleeding in the street while a group of good old boys chanted "U-S-A! U-S-A!")

So instead, I ordered something called a balaclava from Amazon. It's a sort of snug black synthetic cowl that covers everything except the eyes. It doesn't make me look like a criminal; it makes me look like a ninja. No one in my neighborhood harbors too much animosity toward ninjas. To the contrary, no small number of little boys show up on my doorstep each Halloween dressed as ninjas.

Remarkably, donning the balaclava seemed to have a profound effect on the Grayness, and therefore on my running speed. In retrospect, I can say it was a *miraculous* effect. (And I don't use that word lightly.)

The miracle came on gradually. In the first few moments of my run, I still felt as if I were submerged in a sea of thick Gray snot. But before I had even taken ten strides, this feeling was replaced by an even stranger sensation. The Gray Sea was literally parting in front of me! One half lurched a yard to my left. The other half lurched a yard to my right. No longer beset by the boring, coiled-up heaviness, I sped off with a quickness I had never before believed possible for a middle-aged chick like myself.

There's a giddiness involved in running fast that I cannot fully describe. Maybe it results from the combination of physical exhilaration (the pumping of my arms, the thudding of my pulse) with mental exhilaration (the experience of being untethered from screens and avatars, voices and tweets, the rush of being totally alone and totally in control of where I'm going and how quickly I get there).

There was only one drawback: the balaclava was uncomfortable to run in. While my nose stayed warm, the garment trapped my breath and made my prescription sports goggles fog up. So I found myself periodically yanking the balaclava down past my lower lip. That way, my breath could escape and my goggles would de-fog.

I slowed down when I did that. My roomy path through the Gray Sea narrowed. The spirit of constriction was afoot. A puddle of Grayness, about ankle deep, suddenly made things slippery.

I tumbled to the pavement.

My gloved hands broke my fall and I wasn't badly hurt, but I nonetheless decided it would be best to call it a day. Taking care not to worsen my injuries with a second slip, I tiptoed back to my house.

It turned out I had skinned my knees and scraped my hands. Of course, these were far from life-threatening injuries. Nonetheless, you have to be careful any time your skin is broken. So I immediately took a bath and scrubbed the wounds five times with antibacterial soap.

I've thought about infections a lot over the years. Sometimes I've probably thought about them too much. My psychiatrist (Dr. Sherman Himmerahd-D'janni) says that I have to be careful not to let the fear of infection dominate my mind. "Obsessions are like baked chickens, whirling around on rotisseries," he says. "Over and over, and over and over, and over and over, to the point that they make it impossible for the brain to focus on anything else." I'm not fibbing; he honestly makes that exact statement (or something damned close to it) every single time I see him. He likes to repeat phrases for emphasis. This is probably because he suspects repetition naturally dovetails with my OCD (which he once described as "nothing more or less than a case of a constantly hiccuping consciousness").

Sometimes I think he's a quack. Yes, he's a medical doctor, but that doesn't mean he knows a thing about infectious diseases. He's more interested in quieting my mental hiccups. He's really quite useless when it comes to offering advice on how to care for a skinned knee.

The fact is, you never know what kind of germs could be growing on asphalt. While it looked clean enough when I fell, it was entirely possible that a dog had gotten run over on that street just hours before, and was scraped off the road by its owner. Dogs can carry all sorts of bloodborne pathogens that can leak out of their bodies under such circumstances.

Okay, I'll admit that was a remote possibility. If a dog (or anything else) had died on that stretch of asphalt where I had fallen, I would have noticed the ruby-raspberry stains left behind. Here's a more likely (and equally terrifying) scenario, though: what if a dog, while out on a walk, took a shit in the middle of the road, and its diligent owner scraped it up with a little shovel and put it in a poop bag? There would be no indication a dog had shit there, but the shit-germs would still be lingering at the scene of the defecation. They could penetrate my broken skin, and then I'd come down with gangrene or *E. coli* poisoning or whatever.

Hell, even if that *weren't* the case, there surely had to be dirt and grime on that road—of that I had no doubt. Dirt, itself, can carry nasty germs. That's the reason every medical advice website recommends treating skinned knees and scratched up hands with antibacterial soap.

The soap stung, but I knew that just meant it was doing its job. After scrubbing out the wound, I stretched out and lingered in the tub, mulling over everything that had just happened.

I do some of my best thinking in the tub. Although the oblong yellow pills have provided significant relief from my suffering, I continue to experience brief spikes in anxiety from time to time. Whenever these occur, I take a long hot bath and I'm able to think clearly again.

I think bathwater is soothing because it reminds us of the amniotic fluid of the womb. The body and mind reflexively relax when placed in conditions that emulate those most comfortable of all human days. Days free of Color, yes, but also free of Grayness. Days when everything was just a softly pulsing Blackness.

Can we even call them "days," given that we weren't aware of the rising and setting of the sun? Could it be said that we noticed the passing of time at all? Doesn't a fetus, in utero, live in an Eternal Now? And does not Zen Buddhism preach that happiness comes from intense mindfulness of the present moment, without regard to the past or future? Has not the publishing industry itself pounced on the opportunity presented by the expiration of Zen's copyright to produce its own Generic Equivalent of Zen? (I refer, of course, to the various and sundry popular self-help books that emphasize the need to live in the Eternal Now.)

Have you not seen the authors of such books on television,

when they appear on *Dr. Phil* or *The Ellen Degeneres Show?* Have you not paid attention when the camera pans across the applauding studio audience? Have you not noticed the one particular audience member who has only one hand? Have you not heard the sound of that one hand clapping?

All hail the cozy warm oblivion that precedes consciousness! The womb's oblivion! Utero-blivion!

Anyway, there I was, as I said, soaking in the tub and trying to wrap my head around the miracle I had just experienced. The balaclava, it seemed, was the key. When I allowed it to cover as much of my face as it could, the Gray Sea parted and I ran very swiftly. When I tugged it down past my lower lip, exposing part of my face, the puddles of Grayness appeared. But even then, the Gray Sea didn't swallow me up. It was only earlier that week, when I ran without the balaclava on at all, that I suffered the full range of Gray symptoms (slowness, malaise, disgust, etc.).

I arrived at a tentative conclusion about all this. Is it necessary for me to spell it out for you? Obviously, I had acquired a very odd sort of immunity to Grayness. I say "odd," because my immunity was directly proportional to the amount of my face that was hidden. When everything but my eyes was concealed from view, I had something akin to full immunity. When I lowered the balaclava to expose my nose and mouth, I had only partial immunity. (That was why the puddle formed. That was why I slipped.) When I had tried running without the aid of a balaclava at all, I had zero immunity.

A black veil in 1868. A black balaclava in 2018. Both seemed capable of warding off Grayness. As impossible as it sounds, I came to suspect that my life was somehow mystically connected with that of The New Moses.

The parting of the Red Sea in the Bible. The parting of the

Gray Sea in the passage above. Both led to escape from oppression. Granted, no one will ever make a movie about the
parting of a snotty Gray Sea. And, of course, the salvation of
a lone jogger possesses less gravitas than the salvation of God's
Chosen People. But, as impossible as it sounds, I came to suspect that I was The *New* New Moses.

2

My hands took on that wrinkled, pruney appearance hands get when you soak and soak and soak in the tub. I didn't care. I was beginning to gain insight into what my unique role might be in defeating Grayness. I think Dr. Himmerahd-D'janni would've been proud of me. There were no hiccups in my consciousness. There was no cognitive dizziness. There was only a sweet, soft, gently flowing parade of insights.

At one point I looked down my leg and noticed how a flap of shredded skin had separated from my knee. This reminded me of a phrase I had used at the end of Part Two: "The Primacy of Separation." As you'll recall, I had intuited that the Grayness was an example of metastatic *coagula*, and that the cure for Grayness would entail the alchemical principle of *solve*.

This, in turn, brought to mind how important *solve* was in the creation of the universe and life, as we know it. For example, the Big Bang SHATTERED an infinitely dense particle of matter and, in so doing, spewed forth the gooey, magma-like shards that eventually cooled into galaxies. Likewise, single-cell organisms reproduce by a sort of SPLITTING APART called FISSION. More complex organisms procreate by a process in which legs and labia are split away from each other so that a phallus may PENETRATE the vagina. (SLICE away! SLICE away! *Solve! Solve!* SLICE away! *Solve! Solve!* What's a cock but a knife that's always at the ready? What's a cunt but a wound that never heals?)

Lest we assume this implies the relative weakness of the female (forever wounded), we must acknowledge the infinite brokenness of the male. For he is the one routinely shooting off DISCARDED globs of himself. Thus, the penis is both a knife (a penetrator) and a wound (through which a hundred million swimmers BLEED during each orgasm). The problem with this situation is that the penis is left in a position where it can't fully commit to either role. It waffles back and forth. In this way, the penis is *a house DIVIDED against itself.* And, as Abraham Lincoln (who was raised in southern Indiana) reminded us, a house divided against itself cannot stand.

Hence, the epidemic of erectile dysfunction.

Another thought about the penis: it slumps around in flaccid despair most of the time because it is discouraged by its appallingly poor success rate. Of the millions of sperm cells in any given glob of cum, all but one will fail (and that's the best-case scenario). Why even bother erecting yourself for your essential task, if you know matters are so hopeless?

But, of course, when we're talking about human existence, we are not interested in all the sperm that failed. We must EXILE them from the conversation. Pretend their faceless possibilities never existed. Let us instead pick up the story at the point when a zygote has formed. For there, too, we'll find ourselves confronted by the Primacy of Separation. Cells *divide* from one another, become *DIFFERENTIATED* from one another, each becoming SPECIALIZED in its own function.

And, when the fetus is sufficiently incubated, it splits off from its parent. In the case of human beings, this requires scissors or another sharp implement. The umbilical cord is literally SEVERED. It is impossible for a human life to begin in earnest if the cord is not CUT (typically, these days, by a doctor, nurse, or doting father).

In chickens, things slightly differ. No third party is needed to effect the separation of offspring from incubator. The young are equipped with beaks that, like knives or chisels, CRACK open the outermost boundary of their universe and bring them forth into a new one. Before hatching, they only knew this universe from whatever muffled half-noises reached their developing ears. But when they emerge from their shells they are able to perceive this world with their eyes, thus creating a line of DEMARCATION separating their old existence from the new.

Like humans, chickens have poor vision in the dark. Light is a necessity. This train of thought brought me to yet another insight: using a prism, we can essentially *DISSECT* light, cut up its living corpse to reveal its constituent parts. This is how existence can be rendered Colorful. A rainbow is merely a prism-writ-large, and so when we admire its beauty we're implicitly paying homage to dissection. That is how deeply the Primacy of Separation is embedded in our day-to-day lives. It is not only the starting point of life, but also the dynamo driving its continued evolution. Yet few people are able to see it. (And of those who can see it, fewer still are willing to *admit* that they've seen it. It is too horrible a sight for normal people to accept.)

I am not a normal person. I splashed around in the bathwater, giggling and grimacing at the savageness of it all. Breaking. Slicing. Splitting. Fissioning. Cracking. Discarding. Bleeding. Dissolving. Separating. Penetrating. Fracturing. Exiling. Dividing. Specializing. Differentiating. Mutating. Demarcating. These are the foundations of growth, regardless of the context. Physiological growth. Economic growth. Cultural vitality. Color.

Zest. For the universe to chug along, things have to break.

I decided to wash my hair while I was bathing and groped for
the shampoo bottle, repeating that last phrase over and over,
and over and over, and over and over in my head. Only it came
out a little different each time I turned the proverbial rotisserie;
as if it were mutating of its own accord.

> *Things have to break.*
> *Thinks have to break.*
> *Thoughts have to break.*
> *Oughts have to break.*
> *Things have been fought.*
> *That's why they bleed.*
> *Things have to cum*
> *And throw up and sneeze.*
> *Things have to break.*
> *Things have to break.*
> *For the human race to flourish, things have to break.*

The Primacy of Separation is the fuel of population growth.
One clan of hominids splits off from another. One species splits
off from another. The ruled shake off the yoke of their rulers.

Caesar splits away from the traditions of Roman governance.
Caesar's heart is pierced by assassins. Caesar's successor discards
the Roman Republic and founds the Roman Empire. The Empire is split many times through many wars. Christians split off
from the Jews. Lions tear apart Christians. Goths, Visigoths,
and Vandals penetrate the borders of the Empire. The Emperor
Hadrian exiles the Jews from their homeland. The Emperor
Constantine discards his previous beliefs to embrace Christianity. Then he breaks away to the East. The Eastern Orthodox
Church splits off from the Roman Catholic Church. Martin

Luther splits off from the Roman Catholic Church. German Pietists split off from the Lutherans and separate themselves from Europe to take up a new life in Indiana. The King of England separates himself from the Catholic Church because the pope will not grant him an annulment. (Annulment: a license granted by the Catholic Church that authorizes the bearer to discard the pre-existing reality and declare a new one. In other words, a license to edit the past. To cut offending parts out, to paste more pleasant ones in.) John Calvin splits off from the Roman Catholic Church in a secession movement *separate from* that of Martin Luther. Calvin and Luther are divided on the issue of what actually happens vis-à-vis the real presence of Christ during Holy Communion. (Communion: a cause of division.) When French Protestants suffer persecution they flee to England and then to America. They are called Huguenots.

Some of them settle in the Chesapeake Bay region of Maryland. These are my ancestors, and I am so split off from any knowledge of them that I cannot tell you exactly when they came to America. Nor can I say, with any certainty, that this history of my descent is at all accurate. I recall reading it in a family history that had been compiled sometime late in the last century. It was assembled by an old aunt whose name I have long since forgotten. She fancied herself a genealogist. (Genealogist: one who makes a study of the division of one generation from the next, while simultaneously convincing herself that these divisions are *not* divisions, but rather "links" and "branches" that unite all involved.)

According to this family history, one of my ancestors was a casualty of the Indian wars. Supposedly, the arrowhead that wounded him was too close to his heart for nineteenth-century doctors to remove, but he didn't die. He lived on for decades with the arrowhead nestled in his chest.

Something similar happened to my father, actually. He worked a blue-collar job for one of those chemical companies that was bought and sold, merged and re-merged and cut to the bone so many times that if I told you its name it would mean nothing to you. Anyway, the specific place he worked isn't consequential; *the point is* that he was the victim of an industrial accident. A chemist told him to mix together chemicals that should not have been mixed together, and the resulting explosion sent shattered glass into his chest, hands, and eyes. My understanding is that most of those fragments were removed, but some were not. So it could be said that he was thereafter infected with fragments. Perhaps that is why I, his daughter, feel so drawn to fragmentation.

Industrial accidents aren't often brought up in the modern American memoir. But if you spend time in our nation's rural villages, you'll notice a bizarre plethora of amputees. Fingers, hands, and arms mostly. If you're an outsider, this may seem darkly comical. I once attended a gathering of around thirty rural Hoosiers, and at least three or four of them had missing limbs.

None of them felt the need to use a prosthesis. Their stubs were visible for all to see. As I continued soaking, I let my memory of those amputations fly through my consciousness and another little ditty came to mind:

Stubba-stub-stubs in the tubba-tub-tub.
Stubba-stub-stubs in the tubba-tub-tub.
Stubba-stub-stubs in the tubba-tub-tub.
Over and over, and over and over, and over and over
again.
Stubba-
Stub-
STUBSSSSSSSSS!

Anyway, at first I suspected there was a congenital defect to blame. However, after talking to one of them I learned that farm machinery had taken his arm. (No, in case you're wondering, *I didn't ask!* My author brand may be **Miss Foulness**, but I try to not be Foul while making small talk with strangers. The amputee *volunteered* the information. You see, I've discovered that some amputees find their condition to be a useful tool to break up awkward, boring, coiled-up silence. They volunteer their tragedies as conversation pieces.)

This is a fascinating topic. Now that I've waded into the world of nonfiction writing, I feel compelled to write another book after this one—a sort of etiquette guide for how to talk to amputees. But, for now, I should stay focused on that "sweet, soft, gently flowing parade of thoughts" I experienced in the bathtub. Asides like this one break up the rhythm. Breaking the fourth wall annoys many readers. (Even Constant Readers, even Giggling, Grimacing readers, even readers of epidemiological memoirs.) So I'll return to telling you about my long, lingering sweaty bath and the long lingering sweaty thoughts I had about Separation.

ahem Here goes.

I realized that the freakishness of these Hoosiers had nothing to do with inbreeding and everything to do with sacrifices made in service to mechanized farming and manufacturing.

These days, when we see amputees, we often assume that they lost their limb in combat. And so amputation becomes a badge of honor, the outward and visible sign of valor. Of course, such amputations do actually occur. Of course, there is such a thing as valor. I believe, however, that the association between amputation and combat is overemphasized. It is cemented in our minds only because the mass media have bombarded us with images reinforcing the connection between the two. Consider, for a moment, the most famous amputee of all time: Luke Skywalker. In *The Empire Strikes Back*, his hand was hacked off in combat. The offending party was Darth Vader (Luke's father, and a combat amputee of some renown in his own right).

If Luke Skywalker had grown up on an *actual* farm and not in the space-opera equivalent of one, his story would have turned out quite differently. Yes, he would have left. That part would've been the same. But instead of leaving to train as a jedi under Kenobi, he would have left to go work in a factory. That way, instead of facing the uncertainty all farmers face when dealing with the vagaries of weather, soil conditions, price fluctuations, etc., he could count on a steady check and paid vacation.

Old Ben would still have an important role to play. In this more down-to-earth version of the tale, he would be the grizzled old dude with thirty years seniority who could talk to the right person in HR and grease the wheels for Luke to get hired.

Eventually, Luke would lose his hand in an assembly line accident. Maybe it would get caught in churning gears, or sliced by automated blades. He'd try to get on Social Security disability. They would turn him down the first few times he applied, but, after hiring a lawyer, he'd finally win all the benefits that were coming to him. Maybe he would even use that same lawyer to sue the factory. Maybe the two parties would reach an out-of-court settlement, and on the evening afterward Luke would throw a huge party to celebrate the acquisition of his five-figure fortune. Instead of dancing ewoks there would be short dudes with Duck Dynasty beards.

I know that, before Dad worked for the chemical company, he grew up on a dairy farm. I know that he had a baby sister who died when a window suddenly slammed shut and snapped her neck. I know that German prisoners of war were kept as labor on the farm during World War II. I remember Dad saying how he was scared of them at first, because of the comic book depictions of them as evil incarnate. In time, he saw that they were more frightened of him than he was of them.

I know he played on one of the first high school football teams in our county. His helmet (made from leather, with no facemask) is a family relic that is presumably still in the basement of the house I grew up in. I know he lost some of his front teeth in a high school football game. When I was little, he would sometimes remove his partial plate. I found that disgusting. Why did I find it disgusting? I think it had to do with the juxtaposition of metal wire against the plastic or porcelain that had been made to look like teeth. The obviously artificial was juxtaposed against the less-obviously artificial, and both glistened with slobber.

I recall he once looked and looked for that partial plate. He had taken it out and couldn't remember where he'd put it. He searched for it in the gap between the seat cushion and the back of his La-Z-Boy recliner. He may have lifted the recliner up so he could look underneath it. He may have gone into the kitchen to look for it. This happened about thirty years ago, so I can't be expected to remember exactly where the search took him. I only remember that it was long and accompanied by much frustration. Eventually, the search was called off when he realized the partial plate had been in his mouth the entire time.

I know he was the one who found the body of his mother when he was a teenager. This would be a far more interesting story to relate to you than the story I just told about his partial plate, but the fact is I don't know a whole lot about what happened when he found her. Thus, you could say that I am far more connected to an incidental fraction of my father (his partial plate) than I am to an experience that shaped the core of his identity.

I know that there were many children in his family. Eight? Ten? Twelve? I cannot say for sure. Once I saw his high school yearbook. There was a section detailing all the students' career plans, and both my father and his brother said they planned to work on the family farm after graduation. However, I know that the farm was sold when my father was a young man. I know that he was drafted into the army in the 1950s. I know he jumped out of airplanes with the 101st Airborne out of Ft. Benning, Georgia.

I know he never served in combat. He was drafted either before Korea or after it. I know he went to work for the chemical company after returning from the army, but he may have worked there some before getting drafted, too. That part of the history is hazy, and my father's brain isn't much good for remembering the past. It was scrambled by a stroke five years ago.

I know my father's father died sometime in the 1960s or very early '70s. I do not remember ever meeting him. I think the cause of death was a perforated bowel. I assume whatever inheritance my father received as a result was diluted from being split so many ways. I know he once worked three jobs simultaneously to help put my older brother through college. I know one of these jobs was janitorial work. I know that my generation was the first to attend college.

I know my father never drank, did drugs, or treated me too unkindly. I know that there was a gentleness about him that was in some way more than gentleness. It was as if he had been tamed. But I also know his hands were always rough as sandpaper. Callused. I know he was an honest man, and that he loved me.

The less said about my mother, the better.

So instead, I'll tell you about *her* parents. They were the only grandparents I remember. They divorced when my mother was three or four or five. I've been told that, afterwards, my grandmother lived a harsh life. She did other people's laundry to make ends meet.

Sometimes I wonder why my grandfather didn't serve in World War II. Once, I found out the year of his birth and did the calculations. He was a young man when the Japanese bombed Pearl Harbor. Maybe he wasn't drafted because he had children. Maybe he was found unfit for service, due to other reasons. Sometimes I wonder about such things, but not too often.

Grandfather died when I was six. Grandmother died when I was seven. I remember loving them a great deal, and I remember losing them. The loving and losing are fused together for me into one Gray, humid, headachy emotion.

I'm afraid you probably won't understand what I just wrote. So indulge me in explaining it further.

What I meant was this: most people experience the relationship with a loved one as a linear progression. First there's that person's life, then there's that person's death, and then comes the mourning. But with my maternal grandparents, my memories don't unfold in this linear fashion. Perhaps if I had years and years of acquaintance with them before they died, the "life" category would have a large enough sample size of memories to merit its own distinct consideration. But because I only have one or two memories of their lives, one or two surrounding their deaths, and one or two surrounding their funerals, they all end up getting glommed together as facets of a single impression: an aching love-loss.

Grandmother was buried in a quilted housecoat; dressed to go to sleep. I believe it was pink, but it may have been purple.

A few days before she died, I went to visit her in the hospital. This was in late December of 1980, in that window between Christmas and New Year's Day. I seem to recall my visit being a big deal. What I mean is that it was an exception to the rules. I think she was in Intensive Care. Kids were generally not allowed into Intensive Care back in those days. I brought her a little gift: a ceramic snowman I'd purchased at the church Christmas bazaar.

After she died, the snowman was given back to me. I didn't understand why the gift was returned to me. I didn't understand many things back then. For several years I treasured that little snowman. Then, at some point I can't remember, I lost it. Or perhaps I accidentally broke it. Maybe it happened in my twenties, when I moved around a lot. Maybe it clinked and clanked against other ceramic objects as I drove away from one broken man to try life with another.

Both of the men I was involved with in my twenties were broken, because I was broken and broken people tend to seek out each other. Both of them were about twelve years my senior, which means that they were more deeply entrenched in their brokenness than I was. They knew how to navigate the proverbial streets of brokenness better than I did.

But I shouldn't present them as though they were clones of each other. The brokenness of the second was darker and more sexual than the brokenness of the first. The second came across as more hungry for me than the first; more likely to devour me utterly. His name was Jake Wanser. Our relationship rested on a foundation of thrill-seeking and kink. He was the Dominant and I was the Submissive. I did whatever he told me to do. I never complained when he took liberties with me.

After Jake and I broke up, I used to wonder how it was I'd

found myself in that situation. What was it about those years that made me so vulnerable to that man's whims? Here's the answer I arrived at: when I met Jake, my suicidality was at its peak. It was all I could do to keep a gun out of my mouth and a noose off my neck. I didn't value my life, and so surrendering it to his desires seemed like a good idea. It was like suicide, in the sense that it facilitated a process of self-erasure.

We played erotic power games that we pretended weren't games at all, but reality. Bondage. Domination. Sadism. Masochism. (BDSM for short.) Earlier, I had described our relationship as a Dominant/Submissive one, but I'm not sure that description expresses the severity of the hierarchy. Actually, he was the Master and I was the slave. We committed to playing the roles twenty-four hours a day, seven days a week, because we each felt that at the core of our being we *were* the roles. He was an archetype and I was an archetype and together we'd live an archetypal existence. All the nuances of our personalities would be hidden behind the masks of archetypes.

I think that, deep in our hearts, we were both afraid of nuance. The fact is that every person is strong one day, weak the next; defiant one day, compliant the next. Yes, even in Gray towns people may demonstrate strength. The problem is that it's a stiff, confining sort of strength. The strength of the thirty-year-old man who develops extraordinary muscles while delivering appliances from the local high interest rent-to-own store (and repossessing the same appliances when payments run late). The strength of a single mother who works two shitty retail jobs just to keep a shabby Gray roof over her head, only to have her kids turn out to be animal-torturing psychos.

But that's neither here nor there. The point is that Jake and I decided we were going to pretend that ambiguity didn't exist. As we've seen in Part Two, most utopian dreams rely on this conceit. The deep end of the BDSM world (a utopian dream in its own way) was no exception. There was a great deal of posturing about it all; a pseudo-gravitas. A concern about manners and etiquette and respect. That same sort of *ideological* sexuality I described earlier, oozing out of the female supremacy website.

One day Jake told me that he loved me. (Coincidentally, this was around the same time that he had fallen out of favor with some of the bigwigs in the local BDSM scene and needed me to publicly vouch for him.) I wish I could tell you that I didn't believe him, because that would make me look at least slightly streetsmart. But I think things proceeded in this way: when he first said it, I didn't believe him, but shortly thereafter my need for drama took over.

Drama felt good back then. I thought being involved in chaotic relationships indicated that I was living life to the fullest. In reality all it meant was that my neurons were tingling from all the stimulation. It was far more interesting to be in love than to be out of it, so I convinced myself that he loved me and that I loved him.

Things briefly felt Colorful.

All this raises an interesting question: is sadomasochistic love more delusional than ordinary love (because it takes place in the context of a utopian dream)? Or, in its blunt declaration of agendas and roles, is it less delusional?

We told ourselves that all this was safe, sane, and consensual. One of the games involved Jake grabbing me from behind, by surprise, and pressing a knife to my chest. That game ended with him accidentally shedding blood. Not a lot of blood, mind you, but enough to startle him. I can still remember what it felt like when he cut me. I was both in pain and out of pain, both grounded to the reality of the stinging wound and floating in a dissociative fog.

He apologized, and I told him it was no big deal. We both treated it like a minor faux pas; as if he had merely farted or sneezed too loudly.

Another of the games we played involved restricting my access to oxygen. We only did it once, with a group of people who were practicing how to do it safely—under the direction of a kink guru who presented herself as an instructor on the matter. It was kind of like a nightmare version of Lamaze class. You had all these couples gathered together to learn a suffocation method instead of a breathing method. Breath-play, it was called.

When Grandmother was in Intensive Care, she must have been hooked up to oxygen. I know this because I remember being confused by all the tubes. She also must've been hooked up to a heart monitor because I remember being confused by all the wires. This all makes sense, because, if I recall correctly, she died of congestive heart failure.

I have a few memories of her while she was alive. In one of them we're at her house and I'm close to her, maybe hugging her, and she's saying: "I'm just skin and bones." In another, she has bought me a comic book off the rotating metal rack in a drug store. At least, I'm assuming it was from a rotating metal rack. Maybe they didn't have one of those at the drugstore. Maybe she bought me a coloring book, not a comic book. The point is, these memories don't have a lot to them.

On the day of her funeral, it was sunny but cold. The service was held in the same funeral parlor that hosted all the services in my hometown. The burial was in a Methodist cemetery. I have no idea why that was the case. My father's side of the family were Methodists, but my mother's side were Episcopalians. Maybe a plot of land at the Methodist cemetery was cheaper. Maybe there were Methodists in the family, buried in that cemetery, who died long before I was born. Maybe I was never told about them, and so the relation between us may as well have never existed.

I remember the wind blowing hard, over and over, at the funeral. I remember wishing that it would stop. It howled so loudly, and its howls evoked such dread that it was impossible to hear the comforting words of the Episcopal priest who presided over her planting into Methodist ground. But the main reason I wanted it to stop was that the cold hurt. I mean, it physically *hurt*.

A year before there had been another funeral: my grandfather's funeral. There was no cold wind there, but there was a cold hand.

I approached his casket and patted that hand (as if to comfort him). I felt how damned cold it was, and at that moment had a strange daydreamy vision of him falling down a bottomless, black pit. In this vision, he was groping for some handhold but was unable to find one.

I do not believe this daydreamy vision was an actual encounter with the supernatural, but let's suppose for a moment that it was. All it would suggest is that the afterlife is a state in which we find the dizzy bottomlessness of a black pit maddening, while also being terrified at the prospect of crashing into the bottom. Not a pleasant picture, but at least it's a simple one (and in that simplicity there's both elegance and frugality). There's no legalistic stratification of Hell into levels, à la Dante. Nor is there the gaudy celestial throne room with angels and archangels and all the company of Heaven singing "Holy, Holy, Holy!"

No Devil, no God. Just blackness, and falling, and groping for a handhold.

Blackness: separation from light.

Falling: separation from terra firma.

Groping: a separation from the object groped for.

The Primacy of Separation is the one consistent thread that flows through existence.

It prevails before life, as evidenced by:

the mechanics of procreation

the cellular dynamics of fetal development, and

birth itself.

It prevails during life, as evidenced by:

the departure of children from the household of their rearing

the estrangement of siblings and nations from one another over matters great and small

the separation of one generation's zeitgeist from that of its predecessor

the dissection of light into colors

the breaking of skin, bones, and spirits

It prevails after life, as evidenced by:

the blackness, forever separating us from light

the falling, forever separating us from stability

the groping, forever reaching out for a handhold that doesn't exist

3

It would have been easy to stay in that bathtub forever. There was something delicious about falling down the rabbit hole—plunging and swirling through multiple insights about The Primacy of Separation. There was even something half-sensual about it.

Eventually, however, the bathwater cooled. I was able to keep it lukewarm for a while, but the hot water heater can only keep up with the demand for so long before quitting. So I separated myself from the bathroom, dried off, and put on a movie.

Movies have a way of tearing me away from my obsessions. They force my brain to focus on something outside of itself. This is no small feat. As you may recall from the first chapter of Part One, the whole reason I wanted to write a book about Grayness was that I wanted to write about something outside of my own head. Something I could see outside my office window. And yet, somehow, even that tactic led to extended rumination in my bathtub!

My favorite movies are the movies that mock movies. I like *Rifftrax* and *Mystery Science Theater 3000*. When a story is so hackneyed that even its first telling is rotten, all mold and sludge and stink, there's a lot of fun to be had rolling around in the decay.

A bad genre film is pretty damned Gray; hollow as fuck but trying to convince us it's something of substance. It tries its little heart out to escape from boring, coiled-up heaviness but inevitably suffocates (slowly, painfully) under the weight of it. It wants to convince us that it's thrilling (and therefore Colorful), but we suspect it isn't. So when we point and laugh at it, we're sublimating our dread of Grayness. We pretend to be laughing at the fertilizer salesman from El Paso who cast himself as the lead in *Manos: The Hands of Fate*, but we're actually (at a subconscious level) laughing at *ourselves* and our own failed attempts to make something interesting of our lives. Like that fertilizer salesman, we aspire to break the surface of the sea of snot. Like him, we usually fail.

I must've watched five or six episodes of *MST3K* and *Rifftrax* in a row that evening. They were all from the early '70s (the era of my birth) and, sometime after midnight, as I began to doze off, they sort of blurred together. You might even say they *oozed* together and that they congealed around my brain like cooling animal fat.

I felt a temptation to stay in my house for the next forty-eight hours and watch every single *MST3K* or *Rifftrax* film I could. This would be a Gray activity, to be sure. But at least it would be a pseudo-pleasant Gray activity. I could trick myself into thinking it Colorful. I could trick myself into thinking I was laughing at the bimbos and douchebags in the cast, instead of at my own failures. I ruminated on all the sick Gray laughs I had spit out into the air before that moment, and all the sick Gray laughs to come. I felt intense mental pain. I wanted to imagine that I had never been in the grips of Grayness, that I was cut from a superior cloth and somehow left untouched by it.

My fondness for *MST3K* and *Rifftrax*, however, proved that it had found a way to overcome my defenses. True, I was not yet fully assimilated into Grayness, as my neighbors were. But, upon honest reflection, I had to admit I was not far from such a fate.

In the words of Dr. Himmerahd-D'janni, my mind was "constantly hiccuping." You'll remember that my original intent was to use movies as a way to escape the world inside my head. But there I was, getting drawn back into my latest obsession!

So, at about two in the morning, I ditched Crow and Servo and checked out one of the shadier Roku channels instead. It was there that I found a really nasty grindhouse proto-slasher film from '72 called *She Cries So Sweetly*. A rough watch, to be sure, but it pulled me out of the Grayness (or, should I say, meta-Grayness?) of riffed movies.

Sadism has Colorful possibilities. If reading that sentence makes you cringe, so be it. Mind you, I'm not a fan of its gratuitous use. But, if wielded as a tool to combat boring, coiled-up heaviness…well, isn't there at least a chance that the end justifies the means?

In any event, it was during a shrill, wince-worthy, decidedly un-sweet moment of *She Cries So Sweetly* that I decided I must be willing to embrace my destiny. Even if it meant neglecting some of the more lucrative writing projects awaiting my attention, I had to put my knowledge about Grayness into action.

I knew I would be moving into strange territory. I would be leaving my comfort zone. My joints would get weak. My stomach would lurch. I would worry I was going crazy again. I wasn't sure if I was up to the challenge.

Even then, at the moment I fully committed to the formation of a cult, I considered calling Dr. Himmerahd-D'janni to get his two cents on all this. When I was first starting to see him I was such a mess that he gave me his cell number for use in emergencies. I still had that number on the refrigerator. I wouldn't call him in the wee hours of the morning, of course. Even if my plans struck him as rational (or, at least, not crazy), the time of their announcement would undercut their credibility. Everything sounds slightly mad at three a.m.

No, I decided, if I *were* to call him I'd wait until the middle of the following afternoon (just to show him how non-urgent this was). Not only that, but I'd tell him an *edited* version of the project. It's taken over one hundred and seventy manuscript pages to carry you, Constant Reader, to this point of understanding. How could I expect Dr. Himmerahd-D'janni to get the drift in five minutes of phone chatter? The matter would have to be simplified; rendered slightly more prosaic.

For example, I might not refer to my problem as "Grayness." I might use a euphemism. Perhaps "rustbelt malaise." I might not say my solution was "a cult based on matriarchal BDSM," but rather "a nonprofit seeking to fight rustbelt malaise." I might not make the point that such efforts tend to work best far away from nosy neighbors and social institutions, but rather say something along the lines of: "Isn't the countryside a wonderful setting for social renewal?"

There would've been advantages to taking this tack. His endorsement would allow me to cast aside, forever and always, any lingering suspicion that I was wobbling toward madness. Also, on a more practical note, if my cult eventually drew the unwelcome attention of law enforcement I could tell them that I had run my plans past my psychiatrist beforehand and gotten his blessing. This would absolve me of responsibility. At the very least, it would *diffuse* the responsibility. It would *divide* the responsibility in half, thus making it much more manageable.

However, I decided against playing such games. I decided leaving my comfort zone was a good thing. I convinced myself that the queasiness and joint weakness would pass. I told myself that as I moved forward with my plans, I would receive signs and omens that would prove my endeavor was blessed by whatever divinities reign.

4

You may be thinking that there's a certain stilted, awkward quality to this part of the book. Maybe it comes across as a bit too "meta" (as the kids these days say). Put another way, you may be thinking I'm going about this in a way that is altogether too self-conscious. You may be saying to yourself: "No real cult ever *thinks of itself as a cult*. These kinds of movements should evolve organically. Instead, the stench of artifice and affectation saturates everything I've read so far in Part Three."

To which I respond, "Yes. Of course! But that reliance on artifice is a necessity. Perhaps it's even the key *strength* of my plans. Not a weakness." If this assertion makes it seem as if I'm doubling down on insanity, then indulge me in presenting my defense.

The First Proof That I, Noelle Cashman, Am Not Insane
The Grayness has conquered and fully occupied the world outside my window. Therefore, we can say (as a corollary) that the Grayness has taken over Nature. Therefore, any assault against Grayness must be based outside of Nature (which is to say, in *artifice*).

Is this confusing? Then think of it this way: just as the Allied forces on D-Day had to attack German-occupied France from a base of operations *outside* of German-occupied France, any assault against Grayness must be launched from a base of operations outside of Nature. The most accessible perch for humans to reach outside of Nature is the perch of artifice.

The Second Proof That I, Noelle Cashman, Am Not Insane
I presume that in this impromptu mental inquest proceeding I can call witnesses. Therefore, from the ranks of literary history, I call the French writer Joris-Karl Huysmans to the stand. Surely he qualifies as an expert witness, as he was one of the key figures in the late nineteenth-century Decadent movement. Yale professor Peter Brooks has gone so far as to dub Huysmans's novel *À Rebours* "the bible of decadence."

In English, *À Rebours* is translated variously as *Against the Grain* or *Against Nature*. I prefer the latter. *Against the Grain* makes it sound as though the book's main character, Jean des Esseintes, is simply a hipster contrarian or a nerdy nonconformist. *Against Nature*, on the other hand, manages to convey a clever double meaning. First, it captures the full measure of des Esseintes's perversity (his sensations, thoughts, feelings, beliefs, and actions are *unnatural*, in the figurative, moral sense—i.e., contrary to Natural Law). Second, it also reveals the novel's primary conflict. It broadcasts that des Esseintes will literally be struggling to outdo Nature, to create a world-unto-itself inside his house. A world that is equal, if not superior, to the world outside our windows.

I wish all books were so upfront about their primary conflicts. Imagine if *Jude the Obscure* was titled *Against Birth and Its Antecedents* or if *The Haunting of Hill House* was called *Against Sanity*. Think of the clarity that would bring to literary criticism!

Perhaps then critics wouldn't spend time traipsing off into the weeds to explain to us that *Jude the Obscure* is actually a Freudian allegory about Thomas Hardy's secret fear of castration. (University of Chicago Professor Emeritus Wayne Forttenbrau in his 1985 monograph *Manhood in Hardy: A Psychotextual Study*: "Jude's three dead children, one older and two younger, found by Sue hanging on the wall of their squalid little closet, clearly symbolize a Holy Trinity of phallus and testes which Hardy fears a woman will—literally or figuratively—rid him of.")

Perhaps then graduate students wouldn't opine about how *The Haunting of Hill House* is problematic. (Ball State University's Ashley-Minerva Martin in her 2016 blog post "Shirley Jackson: Fearmonger Extraordinaire": "Jackson's admirers have chosen to ignore the undercurrent of ableism in her signature novel, refusing to acknowledge that every *frisson* depends on the reader believing that there is something particularly horrific about the presence of mental illness *in a house*. Therefore, it implies that homelessness is the preferable state for people with psychiatric disabilities. The fact that this theme may have been unconsciously inserted into the text does not excuse the author for her lapse. As we are now decades removed from the publication of *Hill House* and the death of its author, we have the perspective to be able to declare—without hesitation—that this work provided the scaffolding of fear upon which Reagan-era deinstitutionalization and homelessness was built.")

All belief systems (yes—*all* of them) are ultimately ridiculous. Even those currently fashionable among readers. Even those I myself hold this very minute. Even those that I *will* hold when I reverse my position tomorrow, and change it yet again the day after.

***

I'm not just trotting out Huysmans to make myself seem More Erudite Than Thou (although, admittedly, I do enjoy the prospect of proving a Hoosier can be just as well read as someone in the coastal cities).

No, Huysmans is here as my witness, to testify to the underlying sanity (indeed, wisdom) of artifice. Consider for a moment this passage from *À Rebours*.

"Artifice…seemed to des Esseintes the final distinctive mark of man's genius.

"Nature had had her day… By the disgusting sameness of her landscapes and skies, she had once for all wearied the considerate patience of aesthetes. Really, what dullness! The dullness of the specialist confined to his narrow work. What manners! The manners of the tradesman offering one particular ware to the exclusion of all others. What a monotonous storehouse of fields and trees! What a banal agency of mountains and seas!

"There is not one of her inventions, no matter how subtle or imposing it may be, which human genius cannot create… no moonlight which a scenic setting flooded with electricity cannot produce; no waterfall which hydraulics cannot imitate to perfection…no flower which taffetas and delicately painted papers cannot simulate.

"There can be no doubt about it: this eternal, driveling, old woman is no longer admired by true artists, and the moment has come to replace her by artifice."

Now that I think about it, Huysmans's theory (The Primacy of Artifice) forgot to mention a couple of the most important advantages of artifice over nature.

Advantage #1: Generally speaking, artificial creations come into existence with greater speed and ease than their Natural counterparts. Natural waterfalls are the product of thousands of years of geological changes. The artificial variety described by des Esseintes may take only a few weeks—at most—to construct. Actual flowers require time to be planted, time to sprout forth from the soil, and time to bloom. The artificial variety described by des Esseintes could be made in a day or two. Therefore, as I considered the creation of my artificial cult, I had every reason to believe that I wouldn't have to engage in extensive planning (such as that which had been undertaken by a Natural cult like The New Israelites). The whole thing could be thrown together in less than a week.

Advantage #2: Things that are artificially made tend to be far easier to replace than things made through natural processes. Demolish a Natural waterfall and there's no guarantee a new one will form in its place. Demolish the hydraulic copy of a waterfall described by des Esseintes, and you can have an identical one in its place by the end of the month.

What this means, in practical terms, is that I had a license to fail. Because my cult would come about artificially rather than Naturally, it would be easy to replace if things went poorly. You might even say it was disposable. Since I wouldn't have my heart and soul all wrapped up in it, I could always toss it out and start fresh at any time.

5

There were now only two things I cared about in life: training for the upcoming 5K race and coming up with the best possible doctrine for my cult. At first, I thought I should focus this chapter on the 5K preparations. I felt an obligation to tell you about events outside of my head, in the physical world. After all, that is what I promised you at the outset.

Then I realized that the events outside of my own head were not very interesting. I've already told you about the parting of the Gray Sea. I could tell you that the Gray Sea *kept* parting each time I ran through the streets of my neighborhood in my balaclava, but even that miracle would be rendered dull by repeated tellings.

I could go into more detail and explain that I found a way to make my path through the Gray Sea even wider (and thus run even faster) by buying a new pair of prescription sports goggles with black, anti-fog lenses to wear with my balaclava. The combination of the two accessories made me look like a middle-aged, female version of Snake Eyes from *G.I. Joe.* When not a single inch of my face was showing, I found myself able to run an eight-minute mile.

But there's hardly enough material in my training regimen

to justify an entire chapter. Even in films, the lengthy course of training is found too boring to depict in anything like real time. Hence, the training montage. Consider the previous two paragraphs to be this book's equivalent to a training montage. They give you all the information you need to understand how I was able to become a skilled runner.

Besides, the only way I could expand my depiction of training to fill an entire chapter would be to go on at some length about my *thoughts and feelings* about training. (In other words, go on at some length about *the world inside my head!*)

It seems to me that all roads lead to the world inside my head. Every time I try to focus outside of myself, I end up being dragged back into my obsessions.

Some of you know that I'm a big fan of nihilism. Ligotti makes me swoon. Hedayat makes my toes curl. Gombrowicz gets me all sweaty. My love of these writers derives from the fact that they let me know I'm not alone in thinking the world to be a plastic nightmare. Alienated though they all might be, they offer the balm of community to others who think as they do. "You are not alone," they whisper.

But I seem to have just stumbled upon another flavor of nihilism that's slightly different from theirs. As I've already said, I came to realize "all roads lead to the world inside my head." It isn't too far a jump from that epiphany to another, darker one. Namely, that for all practical purposes there is *no such thing* as a world outside my head, because the only way I can experience that world is through the prism of my mind. A corollary to this finding: the only way *you* can experience the world is through the prism of *your* mind. Thus, my diseased mind will always see the world as diseased, and your somewhat healthier mind will always see your world as somewhat healthier than mine. And a third person's simple mind will always see the world as simple. And the mind of someone who has never been subjected to violence will not understand how humans, at their absolute worst, really work.

These are only a few examples of the plethora of realities that exist. I present them to you as a sort of philosophical "proof of concept." It may not yet strike you as a particularly monstrous state of affairs, but hear me out and I think you'll understand what I'm driving at.

Consider a world divided into far more than just four different styles of perception. There's a SUPERSTITIOUS mind that thinks it hears cult members chanting spells aboard a nineteenth-century sailing ship. There's its cousin, the APOC-ALYPTIC mind, that awakens each morning in 2018, tosses up the window, and listens for the sound of trumpets herald-ing the Rapture. There's the DO-GOODER mind that be-lieves in tossing an army of social workers at poverty. There's the GREEDY mind that can come up with no better object in life than to hoard little green pieces of paper. Don't you see the horrifying aspect of this? Every mind fashions its own reality. There are as many realities as there are minds. Which is the same as saying there is *no reality*.

Des Esseintes was on to something, but he did not go far enough. Nature is not merely *inferior* to artifice. After the evo-lution of human consciousness, Nature no longer exists as a discrete entity! Each idiosyncratic mind has glommed onto Nature and—with its various senses and cognitive filters—de-voured it. Thoughts and feelings are the acids that corrode Na-ture into something the mind can digest.

Eventually, the mind regurgitates Nature. (Projectile vomits it onto the nearest window, perhaps while sleepwalking. That way, it has no memory of doing so.) Thus, when I look out my office window, I don't see Nature but only the stains left by my regurgitation of partially digested Nature. What this would seem to imply is that there is no Grayness, in any sort of objective sense. But, rather, because I have a Gray mind with Gray digestive juices, the regurgitated reality I spew onto my windows while sleepwalking is Gray. And will, in a sense, *always be* Gray.

No.

No!

I will not believe it! If that were true then all the work I've put into this book would be in vain. Yes, this Theory of Implacable Grayness is supported by a solid chain of logic. But, if you'll recall, I pointed out early in Part One that I could not rely on pure logic alone. I had to undertake an empirical study! And, upon doing so, I came to some very solid conclusions about how the Grayness might be defeated.

Yes.

Yes, I will defeat this Grayness! I have the knowledge and the will to do it! I need only to refer to my findings from the end of Part Two, then roll up my sleeves and get to work.

After I wrote the scene above, I was pretty pumped up about all this.

I decided to kick things off by seeing if there was any way to reconcile the Brides' female supremacy mojo with the strong Moses Energy that had entered my life. The two seemed at odds. One was matriarchal, the other patriarchal. But I had an intuition that the success of my cult would depend on my ability to extract the strengths of both, combine them with my own idiosyncratic Colorful Separateness, and thus emerge with a cult doctrine that would finally succeed in whipping Grayness once and for all!

I had already done all the research I'd needed to do about

female supremacy. (What did one really need to know, outside of its do-gooder attitude and 'cum tax'?) My grasp on the Moses story wasn't as solid, though. I needed a refresher course.

At first I thought I'd read the book of Exodus in its entirety, but the only version of the Bible I have at home is an old King James Version that used to belong to my mother. The thees and thous, begats and smitings, were all a little too much for me. Don't get me wrong, it's not as if I'm some half-literate clod who can't figure that shit out. It's just that, at this point, my brain was teeming (and screaming) with urgency to come up with answers. I didn't want to spend a lot of time exploring footnotes, online Bible commentaries, or seminary textbooks, etc.

So instead, I decided to read a recent *book* about Moses. Specifically, Herman Wouk's 2012 novel about Moses called *The Lawgiver*. Actually, while the book is about Moses (thematically), the plot is metafictional. Herman Wouk himself appears as a character in the book. He doesn't even bother to hide behind a thinly veiled substitute. No "Howard Mouk" or "Henry Wahrmak." He himself is there in the pages! The book is all about how he has long yearned to write a novel about Moses but has never been able to succeed, and how (through various artificial plot devices too dull to repeat) he now finds himself coerced into becoming a consultant for a film about Moses called *The Lawgiver*.

I don't know whether to call this metafictional approach brave, stupid, or somewhere in between. It seems to me that this tactic has one pronounced downside: it guarantees that the Herman Wouk character in the book will be bland and one-dimensional, because every novelist is (at least to some degree) a coward. What I mean is, there are layers of the *man* Herman Wouk that are left unexpressed in the *character* Herman Wouk in *The Lawgiver*. For example, there's no exploration of the last really terrible thing he did to another person. No delving into what he thinks awaits us all after death. No discussion about what sex is like for a nonagenarian. No discussion of the grim fantasies or exuberant fears reverberating through his brain. No giggling. No grimacing. No outcasts. There's only this likably banal, grandfatherly presence that must remain distant from the reader. (For if the reader gets too close, the presence will no longer be likable, banal, or grandfatherly. Psychological distance is the wellspring of likability.)

Obviously, *The Lawgiver* isn't a memoir, but Herman Wouk's constricted characterization of Herman Wouk provides a clue as to why novelists suck at writing memoirs. We can't bear the genuine self-disclosure those genres demand. We need approval too much. So typically, when we try our hand at memoirs, we bob and weave or do a little distracting dance for two hundred pages and then call it a day. At our worst, we use the pages of our memoirs to settle scores or to self-mythologize. (Hemingway's *A Moveable Feast* is a good example of this kind of tomfoolery.)

Ironically, the novelist is closest to confessing her truth when she has access to the tools of artifice. She needs characters who are utterly fictional, without even a sniff of *roman à clef* transposition—let alone metafictional mischief. She needs settings that differ in important ways from the real world, so that their atmosphere can be artificially sculpted to establish the desired mood. She needs themes that box the world up into unrealistically neat mental packages of meaning. And even if she has all those things, she isn't able to express the richness (or foulness) and complexity (or aching dullness) of her actual life, in the present moment. She is only able to explore what Milan Kundera calls her "experimental self."

What is the experimental self? It's the person a novelist *could have turned into at some point in the past*, but didn't.

At least, that's how I see it. I've never, in any of my previous books, disclosed who I am in all the breadth and queasiness and depth and menace of my soul. You Giggling, Grimacing Outcasts have only been able to see various permutations of the people I *could* have been (most frequently, the people I could have been if I had not tried so hard to swim against the tidal wave of madness I faced in my teens and twenties).

That's why the book you hold in your hands is such a gamble for me. I am, in my heart of hearts, a novelist more than anything else. Specifically, I feel connected to the Continental European tradition of the novel (and all the playful foulness that entails). Yet here I am, trying to grow in new directions by making my first foray into book-length nonfiction! Was I doomed from the very start?

I'm determined not to go astray as Hemingway did. I'm determined to provide you with an honest, warts-and-all account of all this Grayness business that's consumed me. No self-mythologizing about my love of horse racing or how Hadley really digs me. No trash-talking Gertrude Stein. Just the blunt truth, no matter how crazy it makes me look.

You don't care about my review of Wouk's book. It's far too mainstream for most Giggling, Grimacing Outcasts. You just want to know about my cult. You're anticipating the revelation of its wackiness. You just want to know how it will be the same as its predecessors, and how it will be different.

But this was exactly why *The Lawgiver* was so helpful to my plans. Wouk taught me that, despite a promising start as a *solve*-centric rebel and murderer, Moses was gradually emasculated, until one day he woke up and found himself transformed into a veritable Captain *Coagula*. (The one who kept the Israelites safe and nourished. The one who passed down a series of rules, allegedly of divine origin, that were designed to keep their little society humming along in stable harmony. And, most importantly, the one who acts as the glue that connects Jewish people to one another in the present day.)

How, exactly, does Wouk's novel articulate this?

Well, a key element of plot is how Wouk (the character) can't write his Moses novel, but gets pressured into an arrangement in which he must approve the script for a Moses *film*. The producer hires a twenty-six-year-old backsliding Jewish woman named Margolit Solovei to write this screenplay. The book is about the obstacles she faces while writing (of course), but also those which arise in her relationships with her father and ex-boyfriend (both of whom are Orthodox).

Margolit initially comes across as pure *solve*—estranged from her faith, her family, the Hollywood mainstream, and stereotypical gender roles. (Indeed, could it be that Wouk was clever enough to invoke the concept of *solve* in her surname, Solovei? Or is this just a case of pareidolia on my part?)

In any event, she doesn't stay *solve* (or for that matter Solovei) for very long. It takes less than two hundred and fifty pages for Margo to reconcile with everything she had rebelled against. She joins forces with an old-school producer to make an epic. She falls in love with the ex-boyfriend and marries him. Her approving father conducts the ceremony. And, upon giving birth to her first child, she proclaims "I want more of these," and drops her career to devote herself solely to motherhood.

The Moses movie, it seems, was the road that led her round to all these decisions. It forces her to re-engage with all the people and ideas from her past, and in the end she becomes re-assimilated (coagulated) into their traditional template for living. The way Wouk makes it sound, every Jewish person harkens to hear Moses' name. I don't want bring a pagan reference into the mix, but I can find no better way to say it: Moses' story is presented as the *siren song* that brings all believers back to the fold.

It was this *coagula* aspect of Moses Energy that doomed the nineteenth-century New Israelites from the start. Had The New Moses recognized his charges for who and what they were, and if they had dropped the whole notion of Moral Joy and the harmonious cooperation of workers and management, and if they had focused exclusively on the murderous, anti-Egyptian rage and rebellion of Moses, *then* they might have achieved something. They could've become a loosely organized band of wandering marauders. Pirates in the Atlantic, pirates along the Ohio! Thieves, rapists, murderers! Worshippers of the Unholy Knife, participants in an Orgy of Wounds!

The very prospect of this is so scrumptiously un-Gray that I couldn't resist taking a moment to express it in verse. I understand it's a bit odd to suddenly interrupt a work of nonfiction with an impromptu poem (especially a poem in the alternate history subgenre, exploring an important "what if" of the New Israelites). But, the way I see it, after having your face shoved into Max Ehrmann's poetic turd pile, you deserve a chance to see what decent Hoosier poetry looks like. I call this one "Scowlers at the Sun."

Scowlers at the Sun
By Noelle Cashman

When the Wearers of Black Lace Veils come,
when the Wearers of Black Lace Veils come,

they'll be both howlers at the moon
and scowlers at the sun.

Hog grease shall be applied with care
to guns shoved up the derriere
when the Wearers of Black Lace Veils come.
When the Wearers of Black Lace Veils come.

Powder burns on butts and thighs and
blood and shit-attracting flies and
flirty glimmers in their eyes
when the Wearers of Black Lace Veils come.
When the Wearers of Black Lace Veils come.

And splintered bones, and magick signs,
and pitchforks with turds on their tines.
Infected wounds drip green dry wines
imbibed by ghouls with twisted spines.
Hear dying moans. The white worm dines!
When the Wearers of Black Lace Veils come,
when the Wearers of Black Lace Veils come.

But cocks and cunts shall still squirt out
the fluids that life's all about.
Their rotting brains will host wet dreams.
Entombed, no one will hear their screams
when the Wearers of Black Lace Veils come.
When the Wearers of Black Lace Veils come.

Obviously, I can't claim that this is exactly how the New Israelites would've turned out if T.N.M. had tossed aside their
utopian, communal, cooperative notions and all other traces

of *coagula*. But I like to think that it at least captures the *flavor* of the perverse chaos that could have arisen.

You may find the poem's images disgusting, but if anything I feel they're a little trite. I mean, yeah, sure, they make me look like a potential serial killer. It's not the kind of poem I would ever submit to my county newspaper for publication in their annual "Local Poets Showcase" issue. But still, I feel it's…well…for lack of a better word, incomplete. Yes, it's saturated with lunacy. Of that there is no doubt. But it's the tightly bound lunacy of a madwoman in a straitjacket. Not the lunacy of a free-range madwoman.

Hence, it's just not quite chaotic enough. Perhaps there's something inhibiting about the demands of rhyme and meter, and this tames any sentiment they're used to express. I will want my cult to participate in events that are far more innovative than simply using guns as dildos. Be that as it may, I hope you'll agree my poem is at least five hundred times better than "Desiderata."

6

When you consider all the coagulation caught up in the original Moses story (and by extension, in the story of The New Moses), it's hard to believe that Grayness didn't take seed in Naumpton earlier. Only the black veils, gender ambiguity, criminality, and madness kept things Colorful.

Can it be a coincidence that things went to shit the very moment The New Moses went up onto that Hoosier hilltop to await a command from the Lord? When the movement stopped being about splitting apart from English society and started to be about building a community under the direction of God, the fun was over and the lunatics (rather sanely) ran away.

So the lesson was clear. If I was to defeat Grayness, I couldn't indulge in any of the usual cultic tricks of obtaining a tract of land, dominating my followers' individual will with my own, manipulating their finances for my own benefit, etc. It might seem as if this would work, since I would be *dissolving* their individuality. But the fact is that I'd be coagulating all their minds into a unified whole. My will would be the glue that bound them together.

No, this cult would have to be a very special one. Ha! That's an understatement. It would have to be on the cutting edge, an innovation so beyond the pale that Grayness would have no chance against it. It would somehow have to perform the tasks of a cult, in terms of subordinating the followers' wills to my own, but at the same time it would need to avoid the establishment of community ties.

A vision started to emerge. To avoid the establishment of community ties, I would brainwash each of my followers individually. Of course, I wouldn't call my interactions with them "brainwashing." I'd call them "teachings" or "sermons" or something like that. (I'd work out the details later.) But the point is, each follower would be under the impression that they were the only initiate into my dogma.

I would keep wearing the balaclava and sun goggles, because they already proved effective in parting the Gray Sea. But I wouldn't permit my followers to wear this sort of head covering, because that would build a tie of coagulation between us. Any and all signs of uniformity would be forbidden. There would be no matching robes, no black Nikes and purple shrouds, no shaved heads. Each individual would *remain* an individual as much as possible.

And right after that notion passed through my head, I experienced a flash of inspiration so thrilling that even now I quiver at the mention of it. Yes, of course, it would be a good thing to avoid taking any action that could promote attachment between followers. But what if I could go even further? What if I could dissolve all the ties binding a follower to *himself*?

Do you grasp what I'm saying here? You probably don't yet. I need to describe it in detail for you to understand the magnitude of the dissolution involved. You see, how I would go about it is… Oh, it's just too delicious! I can barely type the words, I'm so excited.

My fingers are jingling-jangling over the keyboard like wind-chimes in a tornado. I've had to edit the previous paragraph three times already because, in my excitement, my hands tremble and whirl. I've been typing ever since my sophomore year of high school. (In my more bitter moods, I think that's the only valuable skill I learned there.) The point is, I've been doing this for about thirty years. Even so, there's something vertiginous going on where I want my fingertips to go here and there, but they go there and here instead. All the letters seem to have been moved out of their proper location—W to the left of P, instead of to the left of E, M standing atop a tiny scaffold built over Y, a maddening design that makes it nearly impossible to tap one of the letters without also tapping the other.

I need to take a break so my keyboard and I can calm down. I'm going to take the batting tee out to the elementary school near my house and hit some softballs. That helps a lot when my brain starts to foam over like this.

Okay, I'm calming down now.

Calming down.

Calming down.

How I would go about it is, well, first I would find some submissive male. That is, a grown man who's erotically attract-ed to being spanked, ordered around, whipped, and, generally speaking, ruled by a woman. I would tell him that he and I were going to perform a ritual to erase his soul.

This would entail stripping him of all his memories. Now, of course, he wouldn't *literally* lose them all. He'd just pretend to lose them. It would be our little game, but the consequences for failing to play his part would be severe. This would keep the whole thing from becoming silly. Yes, the ritual would be an artifice—but what of it? I've already established that artifice is the more cost-effective, reliable version of reality!

Losing all his memories would mean that, when he emerged from the ritual, he would not remember how to walk or talk. It would essentially be a return to the condition of a sexless zygote. From having spent more time Googling female supremacy, I understand that some dudes have a fetish for being treated as an "adult baby." They get off on wearing diapers, having their anal temperature taken, suckling at the "mother's" teat, and generally playing the role of the infant.

Please understand that this isn't what I'm talking about. I'm talking about performing a ritual that would magickally (or, at the very least, psychologically) transform a grown man into a sexless zygote, and then into a newborn (of a sex, race, height, and weight of my choosing).

Perhaps I would achieve this by having him soak in a warm bath while assuming the fetal position. Perhaps I'd wrap the walls, windows, faucets, etc. in thick, semi-opaque plastic so they would look and feel like the amniotic sac. Perhaps I'd go on YouTube and find a video there that isn't a video at all, but just ten hours of looping heartbeat sounds. (They have those on there, you know. Parents use them to help their infants sleep. Pet owners use them to calm their anxious animals.) I'd put my laptop right up against the door, and I'd crank the volume up to the maximum, so that the heartbeat would make its maximum impression. Hopefully, it would have a hypnotic effect.

You may be wondering how I would make certain the ~~dude~~ zygote stayed in the fetal position. Well, bear in mind that it would have no objection to being bound in that position before being placed in the tub womb. I could handcuff it, place manacles around its ankles, and then use a chain procured from Lowe's or Home Depot to connect the two. A simple Master lock would keep the chain in place. That would force the zygote into proper position. Yes, over the long haul I'd have to worry about rust, but not at first. And besides, I'd keep a spare set of cuffs, manacles, and chains on hand so that my rituals could proceed uninterrupted.

I'd leave the zygote in the womb for nine hours (to represent nine months). If all went according to plan, the zygote would experience a tingling sensation of *solve* as its cells *divided* from one another and became *differentiated* from one another (each specializing in its own function). In this way, the zygote (or, perhaps I should say at this point, the fetus) would gain a subtle appreciation of the Primacy of Separation.

Now that I think about it, I'd want to create the fetus from a man with poor eyesight. I could force it to surrender its glasses before getting into the amniotic fluid. That way, when the newborn emerged from the womb, its vision would be blurry (just like that of a Natural newborn).

At some point during the ninth hour, the fetus wouldn't be just a fetus anymore. It would be ready to come into full existence. I'd find a TV show clip on YouTube, some scene of an infant being delivered. I'd play the sound of that video in the background, and then I'd show up in my blue scrubs and mask.

I've never had a baby myself. But then again, I've never lived in nineteenth-century Naumpton, either. I researched it! And so that's how I handled the planning of Ritual Birth. For example, I was curious about how much blood to use in the ritual. So I Googled it and found the following factoid from the online version of the *Merck Manual*. "Ordinarily, the woman loses about 1 pint of blood during and after vaginal delivery. Blood is lost because some blood vessels are opened when the placenta detaches from the uterus."

At first I was quite attracted to the notion of using real blood, perhaps gotten from the zygote itself. But there was something inappropriate about that idea. The blood was to come from the mother, not the zygote!

So I thought about this pregnant lady down the street from me. I see her each day when I jog. I'm not a wicked person, but I have to confess that I did have half a notion to steal the blood from her. It's not that I'm bloodthirsty per se; it's just that circumstances put me in a situation where shedding blood was an option on the table.

Another fact I offer in my defense: I was racking my brain to find a way to do it in the least intrusive way possible. Maybe I would hide in the bushes outside of her house and shoot her in the butt with a b.b. gun. Then, later on, after she went to the urgent care center or whatever, I'd check to make sure no one was looking and go over to where her blood spilled. I'd have a teaspoon and an empty pint of Ben & Jerry's ready. That way, I'd know when I'd collected enough blood.

But this is where my (scant, residual) obsessive-compulsive traits became a blessing rather than a curse. My "constantly hiccuping consciousness" wouldn't let me rush forward with such a plan. Rather, I spun it around my head like a chicken in a rotisserie. Over and over, and over and over, and over and over and over it went, as I evaluated its merits.

After about six turns around the proverbial spit, it occurred to me that my blood acquisition strategy was silly. Silly and, more importantly, risky. Sitting out on the sidewalk in front of Prego-Neighbor's house, trying to spoon her blood into a Ben & Jerry's container, would attract unwanted attention. And if I were arrested or locked away in a nuthouse, then I couldn't proceed with the plans for my cult at all, and Grayness would continue to reign.

I briefly considered other ideas for obtaining Natural blood. I could go online, try to find instructions for how to draw it out of a vein, and then offer some bag lady fifty dollars for a pint. I could even drive to Louisville, infiltrate a hospital or abortion clinic, try to obtain access to their medical waste, and use the blood I found there for my ritual. I mean, the ritual called for me to buy scrubs and a surgical mask anyway. If I wore them as a disguise for this undercover work, then I'd really be getting my money's worth for them.

But again, there were too many risks. Without a staff ID badge, my access to the medical waste would hinge on lax security. Even if I did find the cast-aside blood, getting it *out* of the facility would require an inordinate amount of stealth (and luck).

As my consciousness hiccuped and hiccuped, and hiccuped and hiccuped, and hiccuped and hiccuped some more, I finally realized that I had been overcomplicating things to an almost absurd degree. How quickly I'd forgotten the lessons taught to me by Professor Huysmans and his likeable hero, des Esseintes! The Natural World was inferior to the World of Artifice. Therefore, blood gotten from Prego-Neighbor would be boring blood! Blood gotten from a bag lady would be desultory blood! Blood retrieved from the medical waste of a hospital delivery unit (or a nearby abortion clinic) would be *coagulated* blood! And not just in the sense of being congealed into a semi-solid, but also in the sense of being glommed together in a common chemistry with every drop of blood that had ever coursed through a human vein!

No, I decided that what was needed for this occasion was Artificial blood. Perhaps some sort of high-end stage blood. I was willing to spare no expense, if need be, to perform this ritual the right way. I told myself that, when it came to defeating

Grayness (which had already inflicted no small amount of damage on my physical and mental health), money was no object.

But the matter kept hiccuping, hiccuping, hiccuping through my head. I reversed myself (as I often do) and decided it wouldn't be necessary to spend a lot of money on this. I wasn't trying to simulate the birth experience with the sort of special-effects rigor one would expect from Tom Savini. I realized that no matter how weak or sniveling or acquiescent the man was, he would, at some level, still know he was a man and not a zygote. Hopefully, that memory would recede deep below the crest of awareness, but it would be there. Thus, there would always be a limitation to how authentic the ritual could be. Even if I had him shave off all his body hair before he arrived at my house for the ritual, I'd still see that he was six feet tall.

I could *pretend* he was microscopic, though (and, as the hours went by, pretend he was growing to the size of a fist, and finally to the size of a newborn). I'm pretty good at pretending. I'm not sure why so many people feel as if they have to stop playing make-believe games when they get older. They have no problem wasting hours and hours in front of the video game screen, but they would feel childish if they spent an afternoon running around their empty house, pretending to be Columbo or Kolchak the Night Stalker or Velma from *Scooby Doo*. I've created little mysteries to distract myself from an otherwise boring Sunday afternoon when the Cincinnati Reds are getting blown out, and I can tell you that these feel real. I knew that if I could achieve that sense of reality with a relatively silly sort of role play, I should be able to convince myself of the reality of the birth experience in my bathtub. After all, the degree of difficulty faced by the imagination is far greater when you pretend to solve a mystery. By comparison, birth is a far more prosaic occurrence, and because it is so prosaic (and therefore less exotic), it should be even easier to convince myself it's real.

Then my mind hiccuped *yet again* as I realized the risk involved in simulating an activity as prosaic (and therefore *ordinary* and quite possibly *Gray*) as childbirth. What would be the point of crudely aping the Gray machinations of the flesh factory? Let's say, just for the sake of argument, that I went through all this trouble to create my innovative cult, and performed this ritual with exacting realism. Wouldn't it be possible that, when I looked into my newborn's eyes, I'd see Grayness churning inside of him?

To prevent such a tragic outcome, I decided I'd have to make the birth as abnormal as possible. Not only would I use fake blood instead of the real thing, I would choose as cheap and garish a product as possible. I would then proceed to pour it out into a bucket and mix vast quantities of glitter into it. That way, I would suggest to my newborn that he was entering a world that was both greater and lesser than the real world; a world that was a cartoonish nightmare.

Yes, *this* approach would be ideal. I wouldn't stop with the blood, either. I'd toss glitter all over the bathroom, in the bathwater, and onto the fetus itself. I would pour a whole jar of it over my surgical scrubs. I would also place a pulsing red strobe light in the bathroom, and perhaps find a way for its flicker to coincide with the rhythm of the recorded heartbeat.

The addition of these sensory details would yield the desired psychological state in the submissive male. Presumably, his mind would be especially malleable in the hands of a strong woman (which, I think you'll agree, I am). So part of him would want to believe this was real. His mind would start to drift into the realm of sex fantasies, which would mean he'd be dissociating from his actual surroundings. His eyesight would already be fuzzy after being stripped of his glasses. But, if I did this well enough, his remaining four senses would start to soften and blur and bend to my will, too. Thus, his mind would cooperate with its captor, and together we'd change my bathroom into a cartoonish nightmare (or, if you prefer, a nightmarish cartoon) of a womb.

Honestly, to me it matters little whether "cartoonish" is the adjective and "nightmare" the noun or "nightmarish" is the adjective and "cartoon" the noun. All that matters is that the ritual be saturated with both Cartoon Energy and Nightmare Energy, for these are the factors that would ultimately lead the submissive to embrace the transformation. As Thomas Ligotti has said, "Once you're trapped in a nightmare—I mean a really *good* nightmare—nobody has to ask you to suspend disbelief in the horror that is about to overwhelm you."

You may be wondering what would happen after my submissive emerged from the womb. Contrary to his wishes, I'd do nothing to satisfy his carnal desires. Instead, I would lead him, decade by decade, through his life. On day two of the ritual, I'd simulate his growth from ages one to ten; on day three, ages eleven to twenty, and so on. Perhaps I'd have him live until the age of ninety. This would give me an opportunity to use various bondage techniques to simulate the ravages of arthritis. I could, for example, weave a thin rope over and under his fingers, tie it off, and make him wear gloves on top of the whole contraption. I could force him to wear weights around his ankles, the way some runners do, only I would put one atop the other so he could only shuffle around. There would be a low-cost way to suggest the aging of the face as well. I could pour Elmer's glue over him, so that when it dried and peeled he'd have a pasty, wrinkled appearance.

Maybe, when he was fifty, I'd finally give him the erotic beating he'd been wanting all along. That need not be expensive at all; I'd just take my leather belt and thrash away at him. From time to time I'd make sure the metal buckle got him. I'd let him whack away at his inchworm as I beat him.

But you see, even *that* exercise would have a hidden agenda. My goal would be to get the subbie to scream and scream, and scream and scream, and scream and scream again until his voice grew raw from overuse. And then, the next day (when he'd live through ages sixty-one to seventy), his voice would be hoarse and I'd laugh at him. I'd mock him and say he sounded like Grandpa Simpson!

On the other hand, I could have fun by going another route entirely. I could simulate his murder, at age four, by abusive parents. I'd don strange masks and play dual roles as both the crackhead mother and the meth-dealing dad. I'd bind my breasts so they wouldn't show when I played the father, and I'd engage the subbie in some Breath Play to simulate strangulation.

And then, just when he thought the game was over and it was time to go home, I'd inform him that it was far from over. I'd say that it was time for him to be reincarnated, and thus back into the manacles and bathtub he'd go. And if he would ask me how many lifetimes he'd have to suffer, I'd say: "As many as you need to reach Nirvana."

Yes, I just realized that would be another unique aspect of my cult: it would have more than a tinge of Buddhism about it. In this way, it could still be fueled by Moses Energy (at least, the energy of The New Moses, who claimed he was a *reincarnation* of the original) while at the same time breaking out into a completely Separate direction!

I would call myself The Great Incarnation Facilitator (or

"The Great I.F." for short), and I would make and break realities over and over, over and over and over and over, the way a Buddhist monk creates and destroys sand mandalas to illustrate the truth of impermanence.

Yes, I knew *that's* what I had to inject into Grayness, a shot of impermanence—to remind it that it's mortal and that it is better to surrender voluntarily than to be slayed by my onslaught of *solve*.

All that I had to do was find a willing victim.

7

Thanks to the Internet, even people in the Kentuckiana region can find willing partners for sadomasochistic trysts. Not only are there dating websites that match Master (or Mistress) to slave, there are also social groups that gather monthly to celebrate their erotic hierarchies.

As you might suspect, my knowledge of this community stems from my past association with Jake Wanser. During those years in which I was anxious to erase myself and found the idea of that erasure arousing, I joined such a group. That's how we met.

I must say, though, that I encountered cognitive dizziness during my interaction with that crowd. It seemed to me that, ideally, the spirit of BDSM was a spirit of Separation (Master distinct from slave, sexual practices distinct from the mainstream, the id separated from the superego, etc.). I thought its energy should be *Solve* Energy.

When dead people fall through the bottomless black pit and flail their hands about in a futile search for some ledge or battlement they can grab onto, they generate a steady flow of wind that fuels the turbines of Separation. Those same turbines should be what fuels BDSM.

But the reality is that there is lots and lots, and lots and lots, and lots and lots of *coagula* in the mix. To speak of a community is to speak of *coagula*. To speak of people embarking on long-term relationships is to speak of *coagula*. When two couples exchange nerdy jokes with each other while they're in line to use the spanking bench at a BDSM club, they are being coagulated into each other. The same tragic phenomenon occurs during the teaching of their Breath Play classes, the planning of their Christmas parties, and the hosting of their monthly potlucks (or rather, as they're called in the Midwest, "pitch ins"). Attachment, attachment, so much attachment! Heretical attachment! Bane of *solve*! Father of Grayness!

Instead of tearing each other apart and ripping to shreds all social ties with the world, the kinksters instead seek to establish a counter-culture. Instead of smashing civilization, they emulate it. For example, they sometimes form households in which a Big Cheese (a Master and/or Mistress) lords over slaves. (*Coagula*! Ugh, *Coagula*!)

The Big Cheese of such a household will sometimes give it a pompous, self-congratulatory name. For example, when I was involved with Jake, we knew a retired Indiana University zoology professor with a special devotion to whips who insisted her patio home in Jeffersonville always be referred to as "The House of the Black Widow." She also was known to call her slaves (three of them, two men and a woman) her "flies." At kink parties, she made them wear nothing but cheesy-looking insect wings. She, on the other hand, wore an elegant black dress smeared with dust and cobwebs. Whenever she whipped one of them with a singletail, she'd manically yip "Sting! Sting!"

We also knew an apprentice plumber from New Albany who lived in a one-bedroom apartment he insisted on calling The House of the Eel (because he really dug using TENS units and electric fly swatters on the shrunken boobs of his sad-looking junkie slave). Sometimes there was drama between the two Houses, as when the plumber saw the retiree's female slave wandering past him in her fly wings and gave her a little zap on the ass.

There's an unspoken rule that you don't poach slaves from other Mistresses and Masters. It happens all the time, mind you, but the point is that there's an unspoken rule. And where there are rules (spoken or unspoken, observed or flaunted) you have a certain amount of order. You have mortar to hold up the bricks. (*Coagula! Coagula!* Bane of existence!)

Anyway, this is just my long, drawn-out way of explaining that I had no plans of looking for a submissive in the organized BDSM community. That would make the ritual doomed from its very inception. I would be inviting *coagula* into the front door! I'd be poisoning the well even as I was drilling it.

No, what I had to do was find someone on the outermost fringes of society. Someone who was estranged from their family. Someone who was friendless, and yearning for (or, at least, open to) his own self-erasure. In short, the kind of person T.N.M. would've recruited to wear the black veil.

I realize that the way I've phrased things makes it sound pretty fucking predatory. You may be thinking: *Noelle has taken this turn because she has never truly made peace with the things she let Jake do to her. So, she is re-enacting that relationship—only this time with* her *in control instead of the man.* Or perhaps you're thinking: *All this talk about the* coagula *of the organized S&M scene is a red herring; the* real *reason she's trying to find a subbie who is completely disconnected from the community is that he'll be less educated about the need to restrict BDSM play to activities that are Safe, Sane, and Consensual. He'll have no other subbies to connect with for feedback. He'll be isolated and therefore very weak. No one will have his back.*

Or perhaps, you're thinking: *Noelle has taken this turn because she is no longer taking her oblong yellow pills. She's reaching a new abyss of insanity. She's turning out just like Philip K. Dick. This book is her* VALIS.

As flattering as the comparison to Philip K. Dick might be, I take issue with the assertion that I'm going nuts (or, at least, that I'm becoming nuttier than I already was). Yes, I know I am mad. But, as I pointed out in the very first pages of this book, I'm taking much better care of that madness. In the past, when I experienced a worsening of my symptoms, I neglected my hygiene. I took a sick pleasure in going days without bathing. I let my body go, eating whenever the slightest desire tugged at my taste buds. Today that is not the case. I'm clean and trim and tan and smooth-legged and well-rested and healthy.

No, I am not insane. But I can see how you might think it so. Yes, it just occurred to me how such a misinterpretation could occur. It is very difficult for a layperson to distinguish between an episode of madness on the one hand and the onset of a Cartoonish Nightmare on the other. The closer I get to defeating Grayness, the more I'll become saturated with Cartoon Energy and Nightmare Energy. Even though I haven't yet procured all the necessary instruments for the ritual, these energies are beginning to swell up around me like a great tide at flood.

So do not despair. I am still taking my medication. I know that, to pull off this extraordinary victory over Grayness, I'll need to have my wits about me.

8

After I wrote chapter seven, I took another break from working on this book. I don't like taking breaks from writing. Doing so breaks my momentum. Even worse, it makes me feel like a loser, because I can't be a prolific writer if I'm taking breaks all the time. (Now more than ever, one *must* be a prolific writer if one is to be taken seriously. If you're not spouting forth books at a predictable clip à la Ol' Faithful, you will be forgotten. Nobody cares about a geyser that goes off at erratic intervals. There's no tourist attraction called Ol' Fitful.)

In this case, however, the delay was unavoidable. I needed time to fully absorb the meaning of the strange imprisonment to which I was subjected after the 5K. Everything happened too quickly for me to understand, as it was happening. If I had so much as even *attempted* to document everything in real time, I would have had to resort to scrawling feverish, rushed, half-legible diary entries on scraps of paper. I would have had to hide those scraps from my overseers. I would have had to smuggle them out with me when I got out. Then I'd come back to them at a later date and try (with only mixed success) to reconstruct what I'd meant to say.

Would you be interested in reading such fragments? No, you wouldn't! You'd rightly feel cheated because, from the outset, I promised you a work of epidemiology—a sober, scrupulously thorough piece of medical research. I promised you something *scholarly*, or at the very least thoughtful.

Not only would *you* be unhappy *reading* a list of half-baked observations, *I* honestly wouldn't be happy *publishing* them. You see, after I have an experience, I need to dissect it. I need to churn it around in my head and analyze it (over and over, and over and over and over, like a chicken on a rotisserie, sometimes for months). I need to capture the texture of such rumination on the page.

Anyway, this is one reason why there was a long gap between this book and my previous one. I hope you can understand.

But enough navel-gazing! The time is finally right to tell the story. As I write this, it is late July of 2018—far enough removed from the ridiculously sublime events that I can look back on them with a modicum of objectivity.

The next date of consequence in my Awakening was January 13, 2018—the day of the S.A.S. Winter Sprinter 5K and Fun Run. It was, to say the least, a day full of surprises. Allow me to summarize the six most significant shocks I encountered.

The First Big Surprise:
Finding Out What S.A.S. Stands For

Judy and I agreed to carpool to the event. I was to drive and she was to navigate. As our friendship had thus far been limited to the softball field, I didn't know much about her, below the surface. Our conversations had been limited to the relative advantage of this bat over that one, or superficial chit-chat about our careers and families (mostly *her* family, of course, since I'd never married or had children). I hadn't even the vaguest idea where she lived until the day before I was to pick her up.

So you can imagine just how intrigued I was when I rolled up to her house and watched as she hopped into the driveway with an assault rifle tossed over her shoulder.

"Noelle, is that you, honey?"

I was wearing my black goggles and balaclava. I was faceless. I was holy. I was the Incarnation Facilitator. The Great I.F. Eventually I would have to explain to her how I had changed. I'd have to explain to her that "Noelle" was no longer an acceptable appellation. But I decided to wait. I intuited that it wasn't wise to confuse her while she was armed. "Yes, it's me, Noelle," I lied.

She pointed to the gun and asked (in a hoarse, windshield-muffled voice) if I could pop the trunk. She sounded tired and irritable, but not hostile. I knew she had three teenagers (she was always griping about them), so I attributed her distress to some parenting dilemma. Maybe the kids were supposed to get up early for a soccer game but were sleeping in. Maybe they had been grounded for bad grades but sneaked out the night before. Maybe, I thought, her baby daddy had visitation that morning and had promised to drive the kids to a shooting range (where they'd all take turns with the AR-15). Maybe she was removing it from the house as a punishment for misbehavior; thereby forcing them to shoot something more prosaic instead. Maybe she wanted me to stop at a repair shop so one of its obscure inner mechanisms could be fixed.

In any event, the point is that it became increasingly clear she wasn't about to shoot me. Her fatigue and dismay looked like soccer-mom fatigue and soccer-mom dismay. At least, that was what I convinced myself. In a Midwestern context, there was something close to wholesomeness about it all.

I can hear my readers on the coasts and overseas protesting. "Wholesomeness? Really?"

Yes. Wholesomeness. One of the first things I learned when I moved to Indiana from the East Coast is that guns are an ineradicable part of Midwestern culture. Everyone has them. Men look at them as gadgets to play with, in perhaps the same way an Easterner would approach a classic car. They teach their sons to shoot at a young age. It's a rite of passage, like learning to drive (or shave).

Women look at them as instruments of self-defense. In the particularly desolate, out-of-the-way areas, it can take up to an hour for the police to show up. Who has time for that, if self-defense is a matter of life or death? Even in towns, there's no guarantee the cops will offer sufficient protection against stalking or domestic violence. Not if they play in a cornhole league with the dude who's doing the stalking. Not if they're distantly related to (or sufficiently bribed by) the dude who left the bruises. Not if they treat their own wives and girl-friends the same way.

Even after all these years as a Midwesterner, I don't *quite* get the devotion to firearms. Okay, maybe you need one for self-defense—but why do you need ten? Okay, maybe you need a handgun—but why do you need an assault rifle? I don't *quite* get it, but I *almost* get it. I've now lived in this region for nearly fifteen years—long enough, at least, to no longer be freaked out when I see firearms in public. Sure, they're usually pistols, not assault rifles. And usually they're holstered to a beer-bellied man caught in the vise of middle age (not slung over the shoulder of a thirtysomething woman). Usually I see them in the afternoon, when I'm at the grocery store. Not first thing in the morning.

But, yeah, I'm used to seeing guns in public.

Anyway, this is just a convoluted way of explaining that, after a moment's hesitation, I complied with Judy's request.

The trunk latch opened, a hinge creaked, and I heard the rifle *thump* heavily into there. Then two lighter thumps followed, which I later found out came from ammunition clips. Then Judy slammed the trunk shut.

I unlocked the door to let her in. She was pretty fat (a state of being that she attributed to all the stress surrounding her teenagers and baby daddy). In spite of this condition, she wore a fashionable pair of orange spandex tights that left her cankles exposed, an orange camo-pattern hoodie, black gloves, and an orange toboggan hat. Do you remember that brief YouTube sensation, "Chewbacca Mom"? She looked a lot like her. Imagine Chewbacca Mom, all dressed up for a deer-hunting trip. That was what Judy looked like that morning. She didn't look like a serious runner.

"Look at you, all bundled up!" she said. "I should've worn a mask like that, too."

For some reason this annoyed me. "It's not a mask," I said.

"Well, that's not the technical name for it, sure, but you know what I mean. I bet it's warm. I didn't even think of wearing something to cover my face up. But Mulchport is on the river, so I bet you that wind comin' off of there is gonna carry a little slap with it."

She paused, waiting for me to chime in with some reflexive smalltalk response. (Maybe something along the lines of: "Yes, the weatherman said the windchill would be hovering around zero.") If I had still been Noelle, I would've played along with this expectation. But I was The Great I.F., so I remained silent under my cozy black veil.

This obviously caught her off balance. For Judy, any silence was awkward silence. So she flapped her lips some more to fill the void. She needed to grab onto some linguistic handhold so her brain wouldn't fall into blackness.

"But anyway," she said, "...yeah. Thanks for the ride. I really need some motivation to get going on this off-season exercise thing, you know? Going with a friend means I'm accountable to someone." Then, almost as an afterthought, she added, "So where's your piece?"

I was trying hard to maintain a stance above the fray of ordinary human interaction, so I responded with an interesting fact I'd discovered in my research. "Did you know the word 'peace' is never used in the Book of Exodus? This is because Moses, at his best, was no peacemaker."

She flashed a knowing, dopey grin—as if I'd just committed a particularly unforgiveable pun. "*You know* what I mean. Your donation for the S.A.S."

I wanted to continue projecting gravitas. I didn't want to be dragged into a conversation about something as mundane as a small-town charity. I pretended I didn't hear her.

Chewbacca Mom Judy responded, her voice hauling with it a trailer of unfunny humor and undeserved condescension. "Earth to Noelle, come in, Noelle! If you didn't bring a gun, they won't let you compete!"

Now I was the one caught off-balance. In light of such a bizarre pronouncement (a pronouncement that affected my immediate plans) I could no longer keep my perch above the fray. I would temporarily have to dismount. This fact, along with a sudden infusion of nervous energy, led me to pull the balaclava down past my chin.

The toasted chill of my Scion's interior felt good on my sweaty cheeks and jaws. I flapped my own lips, lunging them out from my mouth as far as possible. I wanted them to grab onto a linguistic handhold, so I wouldn't end up ensnared in a black void of confusion. "Well, um, I don't see what one thing has to do with another. Why do I need a gun?"

I mulled the situation over (and over, and over and over, and over—like a chicken on a rotisserie). The only event I knew of that combined racing with firearms was the Olympic biathlon. Had there arisen, against all odds, a group of teenage biathlon competitors in tiny Mulchport, Indiana? Was the charity 5K race focused on raising money and armaments for future competition? Did they use AR-15s? Or, hell, was the 5K race some sort of biathlon? Was there some knob or hillock there in Mulchport to ski down? No, if that had been the case then Judy would've brought along skis. Unless the skis were being provided by the 5K. But no, that wouldn't make any sense. If they were a charity, they wouldn't be providing free skis. Maybe they were renting them out? Maybe that's what the twenty-five bucks covered? You'd rent them out, but you'd need to bring your own gun. I supposed that would make sense.

Kind of.

No, not really.

Nothing was adding up.

Judy sighed and finally explained everything. It turned out that S.A.S. stood for Second Amendment Samaritans. "They collect guns for the homeless," she said (as if that were the most normal idea in the world).

Even after having lived here for fifteen years, that struck me as quite odd. I was nowhere close to understanding why, in the estimation of these Hoosiers, it was necessary to arm derelicts. I sputtered as normal-sounding a response as I could. "So… um, the homeless?"

"Well, yeah," she said. I heard a hint of defensiveness creep into her voice for the first time. "The Second Amendment applies to them too, you know. They're some of the most vulnerable people in America, but because they're down on their luck, they lack the means to protect themselves. In the Bible, Jesus tells us that whenever we give food or drink or clothing to 'the least of these,' we're essentially giving to *Him*. That's how it'll be remembered on the Day of Judgment. So if you think of it that way, we aren't arming the homeless, we're arming Jesus."

It was a lot to absorb. How had I missed all this when I registered for the 5K? What had I gotten myself into?

"Okay," I said (in the most casual voice I could muster). "But I'm still a little confused. What does the twenty-five-dollar registration fee cover?"

"The race overhead, I suppose. The medals they give out to finishers. The off-duty cops hired to provide security."

"To keep an eye on the newly armed homeless people?"

She sighed again. "No, not to keep an eye on the homeless people. To keep all the roads blocked off so we don't have to avoid cars while we run."

It seemed to me that a town the size of Mulchport wouldn't have much traffic to contend with. It seemed to me that it would be wise to stop along the way and pick up a kevlar vest. But I didn't give voice to either thought. I just sat there silently as my purple Scion xB cruised through a green light.

"Turn right at the next intersection," Judy said.

I didn't know *exactly* how to get to Mulchport, but I had a rough idea. Judy was asking me to go in the opposite direction. Instead of leading the way out of town, she was asking me to dive back into its heart—Ashberry Street.

This neighborhood encompassed several two-story houses, many over a hundred years old. They all languished in disrepair. Rural slumlords had taken possession of them and rented them out to troubled families by way of Section 8 certificates. A stench tainted the already-diseased Gray air: a nauseating combination of mold, raw sewage, and the melted-plastic aroma of crack pipes.

One of those houses had been rezoned (and then remodeled) for mixed business and residential use, and it became the location of R&R Guns & Liquor. I had a feeling that's where Judy was leading me. She wanted to spare me the embarrassment of showing up to the S.A.S. Winter Sprinter 5K and Fun Run without the expected donation. She was bringing me to R&R so I could make a last-minute purchase. (There are no waiting periods for buying a gun in Indiana.)

It was 8:15 on a Saturday morning and I doubted R&R would be open that early, but that didn't stop Judy. She said the owners (Ray Coomer and Rafi Syed) lived together on the second floor of the building. She said Ray's car was parked along the street, so he (at least) was home. She said Rafi's car hadn't yet gotten back from Russell's Auto Body, where she'd seen it getting work done after a fender bender. There was no telling whether he was home or not. She added, though, that Ray was an early riser, that he owed her a favor, and that he'd "gladly accommodate us" two hours before opening.

A rickety wooden staircase ran alongside the store, providing street entrance to the residence on the second floor. Someone had recently tried to paint the stairs olive drab green, but I could see that snotty Grayness had gotten mixed in with the paint and infected the stairs with its sullen spirit. Maybe the Grayness of the lumber's discarded bark had come back to haunt it.

I followed along, of course. Ordinarily I might've thought better of it, but I trudged forward anyway because in doing so I was going with the flow of novelty. I felt an intuition, deep in my bones, that this adventure was the first in a chain of events that would usher my cult into existence.

Already, at 8:15 a.m. the absurdity of the Second Amendment Samaritans had ushered a hint of Cartoon Energy into my world. I knew that Nightmare Energy couldn't be too far behind. I knew that both of these energies were essential ingredients in the cure for Grayness, and so I let myself be swept up into them.

I won't sit here and say that I felt no anxiety about surrendering to absurdity. My stomach was restless and tight. My arm muscles felt the same way. With every stride up the Gray-haunted steps, I fell deeper and deeper into the clutches of vertigo. Nevertheless, I persisted. Vertigo is a horrific experience, but preferable to boring, coiled-up heaviness. By treading upon those Gray-haunted steps, I was demonstrating my (female) supremacy over them.

Judy knocked on the door several times over the course of five minutes, without any success. Then, finally, a fat, sweaty man of around fifty answered the door. His hands trembled and uncanny panic was written all over his sunburnt face. He was either withdrawing from booze, tweaking on meth, or going insane. I realized I'd seen him before. He was the first baseman for a coed softball team called Quit Your Pitching. They'd stomped us, 32-1.

Judy did all the talking. "This girl needs a gun. It's for charity. She forgot to pick one up for the 5K race out in Mulchport."

Ray didn't answer. He just stood there silently for a good ten seconds. Well, it would be wrong to describe him as *silent*. He breathed noisily, like an asthmatic hog. What I suppose I mean is, he didn't *say anything* during all that time. Now, yes, he had other ways of communicating. For example, he was staring at me and I noticed—in that stare—no small amount of frazzled wariness boiling in his eyes. Even though I'd pulled my balaclava down past my chin, I still wore sun goggles. So while I didn't look like a ninja, I was nonetheless an odd sight for a drunk, junkie, or madman to encounter first thing in the morning. I probably looked like a terrorist or a supervillain's lackey.

Judy must've noticed Ray's weary wariness too, because her voice took on a childish, whiny tone. "Rayyyy, you gotta help her out. It's for a fuckin' *charity*, Ray-Ray, pleaasssse. Rayyyyy…"

The begging convinced him. He turned around and waved us in. "We'll go down to the store from the inside. I don't want folks to see y'all comin' in the front door. They'll think we're open and I still need a good forty-five minutes of beauty sleep."

The Second Big Surprise:
A Disturbing Porno

The apartment above R&R Guns & Liquor smelled like mold, whiskey, body odor, cigarettes, and pizza. A half-dozen people of various races and genders had passed out around a television that was playing a porn video. I looked at the screen for a few moments. It displayed two raging, hairy, naked men. They were yelling in a language I couldn't quite suss out. Was it Portuguese? Perhaps some Eastern European tongue? Whatever the case, it was clear they were pissed. The apparent target of their anger? A naked, frightened, twentysomething transsexual.

Fortunately, just as the men's anger was reaching a fever pitch, an odd burst of static blotted out both the picture and sound. When the static dissolved, the picture was still fucked up, but in a different way. It looked as though the cameraman had smeared Vaseline over the lens, perhaps in an attempt to lend the events a dreamlike quality. Or, hell, maybe the Vaseline just ended up on there by accident. I'm sure that's happened before on a porn set.

Maybe it wasn't even Vaseline. Maybe an actor had sneezed on the lens. Or, of course, there's another, obvious possibility: maybe someone had shot their load on it.

In any event, Ray noticed me noticing the porn video and pointed it out to Judy. "I shoulda invited your friend over here for the party last night. Looks like she's really into my kinda movies."

He was wrong. I didn't find any of this arousing. None of the actors were particularly fit. All three of them, in fact, were missing teeth. I merely found the video intriguing.

I gazed on in wonder as the hairy men began to take the transsexual apart. It turned out she was actually an odd combination of a nested Russian *matryoshka* doll and a sex robot. After they removed the first artificial skin, a second (depicting a hunchbacked old woman) was revealed. The hairy, naked men screamed with renewed rage. They screamed the screams of disappointment. They screamed the screams of industrial impotence. Most remarkable of all, they were screaming at something other than a sports team. They were screaming at something other than their offspring.

I got the sense that this film was telling the story of a very odd experiment, and that something in the laboratory had gone awry. When they took the transsexual apart, they hadn't expected to find a hunchback underneath. That's why they'd been yelling. It wasn't that they'd been angry at the transsexual. Rather, they'd been angry that the experiment hadn't worked out as they'd planned.

Perhaps there had been yet another *matryoshka* layer that had preceded the transsexual one. Let's just say, for example, an artificial skin depicting a musclebound college-aged dude bro. Perhaps there had been a *half-dozen* previously discarded *matryoshka* layers preceding the transsexual one, and they had all turned out to be incompatible with the men's carnal tastes. Perhaps they'd kept removing layer after layer of artificial skin, trying to find the precise identity that would get them off, but each time they failed. Therefore, they screamed at the unfairness of it all.

Yes, that seemed to be the plot of the film. It had taken a while to piece together, but I knew I had it figured out. I spied some of the discarded husks of prior *matryoshka* layers slung haphazardly across a chest of drawers in the background.

The Third Big Surprise:
The 3D-Printed Pistol

Ray led us through his reeking kitchen and into a stairway landing. The carpet on the landing was shaggier than the carpet in the living room. As we made our way down those interior stairs and into the store, I felt insects hopping around my ankles. I stopped, lifted my foot, and swatted them away.

Ray looked as though my acknowledgment of the bugs' presence offended him. For the first time he spoke to me directly. "Everyone's got 'em this time of year. They come inside, lookin' fer heat."

Of course, I knew that he was just trying to save face. Certainly, at *my* house there weren't bugs hopping around my feet. However, I needed Ray's cooperation. So I said, "Yep. I've got 'em bad right now, too."

That seemed to satisfy him, and he continued lurching down the stairs. Phlegm rattled in his chest, though, and he coughed over and over, and over and over, and over again. When he reached the bottom of the stairway he turned on a light. It appeared as though we had just entered a walk-in closet. Stacks of paper (roughly identifiable, at a distance, as bank statements) were heaped atop each other in this space, and a door stood in front of us, waiting for Ray to unlock it.

When he did, we found ourselves behind a glass display counter. Ray clicked on an ancient table lamp that oozed out just enough light so we could navigate the store (but not so much that we'd alert the townsfolk he was down there).

He waved a gnarled paw toward a nearby aisle. "Go getcha somethin' from over in that bargain bin. Everythin' in that's just two hunnerd bucks. Now, I'll tell ya up front, some of those models are a bitch to take apart and clean. But I spose bums won't mind. They never bother tryin' to keep shit tidy anyhow."

Ray, of course, was in no position to take issue with anyone's cleanliness (or lack thereof), but I didn't point this out. I still needed his help, for at least a few more moments. I had to stick on his good side.

The "bargain bin" Ray alluded to looked just like the sort you'd find at WalMart, only instead of holding dozens of five-buck DVDs it held dozens of pistols. Sometimes I'd pick one up and find its barrel had gotten tangled up under the trigger of its neighbor. Sometimes a handle peeked out from the pile, but the barrel extended deep into it. The guns varied in size and color. They even varied in texture. For example, one that I picked up had a smooth, cool, soft feel to it. It wasn't made of metal, nor was it dark colored. It was milky white and seemed to be made out of plastic.

Ray came closer and gazed over my shoulder. "Ohhhhh… how'd *that* get in there? You know what you got in your hands, little lady?"

I didn't, and he knew I didn't, so I considered the question rhetorical.

He leaned toward my ear and whispered in a voice that even Judy couldn't have heard. "That's one-a dem 3D-printed jobs. You can have it if you want it. Two hunnerd dollars, just like the others. The wino who ends up with that one is gonna be the most popular fella in the gutter."

Buying a plastic gun seemed like the right thing to do for a couple of reasons. For starters, it didn't look like a real gun. It looked like the cartoon version of a gun. Thus, it emanated Cartoon Energy. Also, the possibilities for its use were far more nightmarish than those of an ordinary gun. For example, it could slip past metal detectors, enabling it to cause all sorts of mischief at schools, airports, and political rallies. Thus, it emanated Nightmare Energy.

I have since found out that, according to federal law, I should've had to complete a quick background check before walking out of the store with the pistol. I should've had to present my driver's license, and Ray should've called the FBI with my personal information so they could check to see if I had a disqualifying criminal record. Ray, however, made no efforts in this direction. At the time, I thought that was because he didn't want to acknowledge selling a 3D-printed pistol. I also entertained the notion that he was simply too out of it to follow procedure.

When I found out the *real* reason for this lapse, I was furious.

The Fourth Big Surprise:
We All Ran While Holding Our Weapons

After all the misunderstandings and delays, Judy and I were finally on our way to Mulchport. There wasn't much time to spare, a fact that seemed to make my blood alternately boil and freeze. However, this was not without its upside. Judy felt the tension, too, so she didn't jabber during the drive. The only time she spoke was when she delivered terse instructions for where to turn. Once we were out in the countryside, a perfect quiet clung to us. It seemed to cling, also, to the world outside my windshield.

The silence gave me lots of time to imagine how the logistics of this "guns for the homeless" thing would work. I ran the matter through my head over and over, and over and over, and over—like a chicken on a rotisserie. I imagined that, when I arrived, I'd find four plastic tables—each covered by a cheap plastic tablecloth, noisily flapping in the wind. Exhausted old women and out-of-shape men would be sitting behind the tables. These would be the event volunteers. Their tummies would all be full, because they would've met up for breakfast at Cracker Barrel before heading over to the race.

Of course, due to the weather, they'd be all bundled up. One of the dudes would be wearing a camouflage ball cap embossed with an NRA logo (and camouflage gloves, and a camouflage winter coat to match). Another of the dudes would be wearing a cross around his neck. He would be wearing it in such a way that it would be visible over his heavy coat. He would want us all to notice and admire it. The cross would be of cheap manufacture, made to look as though it were wooden (but actually made of plastic). These men, and others of their ilk, would all be afflicted with puffy, slimy lips and beaten eyes.

The women would all have chins that were too prominent and the sort of gigantic foreheads sometimes referred to as fiveheads. One of them would be wearing Christmas earrings, even though the holiday season had passed. Another would be wearing no jewelry at all. Her hair would be piled up in an old-fashioned, inhumanly huge bun. When she stood up, I would notice that she was wearing a long denim skirt. She'd look like an extra for a modern-day reboot of *Little House on the Prairie*, perhaps titled *Little Trailer Near the Junkyard*.

Despite this oddness, a general sense of order would prevail.

Volunteers at the first table would handle registrations for runners with last names beginning with A through M. The second table would handle registration for last names starting with N through Z. The final two tables would handle the gun donations. The volunteers sitting behind those tables would scrupulously record the type of weapon donated, its serial number, whether it was loaded or not, etc. The volunteers would tie a tag around the muzzle of each firearm, upon which they'd inscribe a code number linking it to the donor.

There would perhaps be a gigantic gun safe (as large as a bank vault) in which the donations would be stored until such a time as they could be loaded onto a big rig and driven to a shelter. Once they arrived, social workers would distribute them to the homeless. Another way it might work: the big rig would be parked near the registration tables, and one of the volunteers would take the gun from me and carry it up a ramp and into the trailer. And then, after the race, the guns would be transported to a soup kitchen ran by some holy roller church—where they'd be handed out with great fanfare.

Upon arriving at the event, Judy and I found out that in previous years the donation process had gone very much along those lines, but that this year the S.A.S. had made several changes. "We decided to make things interesting," an exhausted old woman of dubious sobriety explained. She wore a sticker on her coat, conveying the fact that her name was Vonda Reynolds. "This year, there's no gun check. You run with it in your hams...I mean, I mean HANDS!"

She thrust out a bruised, arthritic claw to pantomime what she'd meant to say. I wondered how she managed to go gloveless in the bitter cold. It must've been the booze.

"When you reach the foul line... Shit, not *foul* line. Pardon my French, honey—trust me, I don't ordinarily swear. Anyways,

I didn't mean to say 'foul line.' I'm mixin' up m'sports here now, ain't I? Heh-heh. I mean, I mean FINISH line. When you reach the FINISH line, we'll have a scale there to weigh it. The heavier your firearm, the more minutes you'll have deducted from your final time. So let's say you're running with a pistol weighing four pounds. At the finish line, they'll have your time tallied and deduct four minutes from it. Let me tell you, honey, there's been a lot of races that have been decided by less than four minutes! A LOT! I know my shit. A LOT!"

"But wait," I said, "that doesn't make any sense. If everyone's running with pistols, then *everyone's* time gets deducted by four minutes. And if everyone gets that same deduction, it has no impact on the results!"

"That's just the thing, babygirl! Not everyone's gonna be runnin' with a pistol. Some folks are donatin' shotguns. Other folks are donatin' military surplus machine guns. Now, one of those weighs about twenny pounds—and that's not even countin' the ammo!"

Needless to say, I'd never encountered a 5K that worked this way. I began to understand how the rule changes would, in rather an ingenious way, "make things interesting." You see, for starters, the S.A.S. had managed to introduce an element of strategy into a sporting event that previously had little to boast of. (Ideally, the runners would donate a firearm that would be heavy enough to shave significant time off their run, but not so heavy that it would substantially bog them down.) Furthermore, the new rules rewarded runners with strong arm and shoulder muscles. The S.A.S. was making the whole thing far more challenging than an ordinary 5K.

So it was that, as I stood there chatting with Vonda, my skepticism slowly morphed into grudging admiration. I had no doubt that, as word of this unique event spread throughout

Kentuckiana's running clubs, it would quadruple in popularity. While I realized running with a relatively light 3D-printed pistol meant I'd have only a few minutes (if that) shaved off my time, I nonetheless felt proud to be in on the ground floor of such an experiment.

I imagined that someday forty years hence, when I was elderly, incontinent, and confined to bed in a nursing home, I'd exorcise the oppressive sight of dingy Gray ceiling tiles by recalling my participation in the 2018 S.A.S. Winter Sprinter 5K and Fun Run. When some voraciously Gray-eyed nurse came in to change my catheter, I'd distract myself from the humiliation by regaling her with stories about how I participated in the S.A.S. run the very first year they changed the rules. "Did you know that, before then, you didn't have to run with your gun in your hands?"

Not only would that memory dilute the humiliation, it would also sneak just a little bit of Color into the nurse's life. Maybe the swirling Grayness in her eyes would slow down a little. Maybe, when she leaned down to turn me onto my side (for the purpose of putting on a fresh diaper), she'd look down and find herself momentarily snared in my kaleidoscope eyes. Maybe then she'd see that a Colorful life was a possibility.

For that matter, maybe, as a direct result of my actions, Grayness will be eradicated by then. You know, the way polio and smallpox have been eradicated. Maybe my nursing home will actually turn out to be as Colorful as dissected light, as magnificent as des Esseintes's lair.

***

Dear Constantly Giggling, Constantly Grimacing, Constantly Reading Outcasts:

The more idealistic among you may be feeling pretty uncomfortable right now. You're probably thinking something along the lines of this: *If Noelle's telling the truth, then Indiana (and perhaps the entire Midwest) has veered off into the previously uncharted outer limits of gun lust. It borders on a fetish! Why doesn't she take a few moments to assure us that she unequivocally condemns this sort of spectacle? That way, we can sit back and relax—secure in the knowledge that we're not partaking of anything problematic.*

Granted, this entire book may turn out to be nothing more than one of her sick literary jokes, but that is no defense! How dare she make light of such a dreadful situation? How dare she trivialize something so ugly, traumatic, and solemnly political?! What of all the children killed in school shootings? What of their parents? They surely wouldn't take too kindly to treating gun proliferation as a laughing matter. Furthermore, it's not okay to poke fun at the homeless (and we all suspect that, at some point, a joke or two will be cracked at their expense). That's what this is all leading up to, isn't it? ISN'T IT?! We can smell the impending cruelty already!

Yes, a handful of you *are* thinking something along those lines, aren't you?

I thought so.

So allow me to pause for a moment to answer those concerns with a few brief bullet points.

• For starters, you can't say you weren't warned. From the very first chapter, I've been entirely up front in regard to the matter of my author brand (that is, **Miss Foulness**). Remember that I'm not going door-to-door to intrusively thrust this book in readers' faces. *You* sought *me* out, knowing full well you'd have to brave one of the shadier neighborhoods of Amazon to do so. Remember that you tossed some money into my Cincinnati Reds cap and allowed me to lead you past used condoms and used needles and empty travel-size whiskey bottles, until we reached this vacant lot where we still linger. Remember that, when you entered my old, mothball-scented canvas tent, *you did so of your own volition* and you did so because you wanted to be hypnotized into feeling intense discomfort. I am only holding up my end of the bargain!

• Let me also remind you this book has only one job: to describe Grayness and its cure. This is, as you may recall, *an epidemiological task*, not a moral one. It is an empirical task, not an emotional one. I know Indiana history far too well to find anything worthwhile in morality. (The New Moses was obsessed with it, and what did it get them?) I look at this from a strictly practical point of view. The S.A.S. fundraiser boasted a surfeit of Cartoon Energy and Nightmare Energy. These two Energies were, in my opinion, essential ingredients in the cure for Grayness. For all I knew, they could prove downright *fatal* to it. So I had every reason in the world to embrace the S.A.S.

• Finally, I should remind you that it's awfully easy to cast judgment on the Second Amendment Samaritans if you live in a coastal metropolis and your senses dine on a six-course meal of Color every day. You don't understand what it feels like to be suffocated by boring, coiled-up heaviness. You don't understand what it feels like to have Gray Air congeal around you and your surroundings, like chilled animal fat, thus making everyone and everything move in slow motion. If you did, you'd understand the heart's yearning for Cartoonish Nightmares (or, if you prefer, Nightmarish Cartoons). You'd understand all the enthusiasm for arming teachers, arming toddlers and, yes, arming the homeless. Most of all, you'd understand the appeal of a Colorfully incoherent, ORANGE-skinned savior with crazy YELLOW hair. You'd get why people voted for him, even after he bragged about his dick size during a debate.

You'd get why every bizarre disclosure nudges him no nearer to impeachment. Yes, he's ridiculously unqualified. Yes, he has the impulse control of a toddler. Yes, he's buddy-buddy with Putin. Yes, he's a puppet of the extremist fringe. Yes, he's from New York City. (*New York City?!*) But Midwesterners can look past these faults, because he's not Gray! Besides, he at least *pays attention* to the Midwest. He doesn't treat it like an embarrassing poor relation (the way most of his coastal kin do).

The Fifth Big Surprise:
My Disqualification

Allow me to start this section by briefly informing you that one thing happened during the run that was of absolutely no surprise. (To the contrary, after finding out we'd all be running with our guns in hand, I realized it was inevitable.) Shots were accidentally fired along the race course and about twenty of the competitors were wounded. The air was thick with the sweetly fetid smell of gunpowder, burning trash, and apocalyptic doom.

This delightful chaos stirred up a high tide of *Solve* Energy that could only prove beneficial to my cause. Now, of course, this Energy, in and of itself, wasn't enough to kill Grayness. As I ran with the 3D-printed pistol in hand, I was still running through the Gray Sea. The Gray Sea still parted for me, because I was wearing my balaclava (by then, pulled back up to cover my nose) and sun goggles. However, that sea had weakened significantly. When I looked far to my left and right, I saw a trail of fine mist rising off the snotty waves. Could it be that the Gray Sea was evaporating?

One could feel that maybe—just maybe—the Millennium, so yearned for by past cults, was now approaching on its swift steed. In any event, it was clear that the old world was ending and a new one was being born. Thanks to the efforts of our glorious first responders, only two people died.

The race organizers, cops, and EMTs were too occupied triaging the wounded to pay much attention to those who were obviously (some might say, flagarantly) dead. As a result, I had to leap over one of the corpses. She was a buck-toothed, frizzy-haired woman whose pudgy pale flesh was splattered with at least a half-dozen poorly rendered tattoos. Her expression was one of equal dread and mirth. I surmised that she'd died during a fit of grimacing giggles.

When I crossed the finish line, Vonda Reynolds was ready with a digital timer. "Twenty-eight minutes and thirty-three seconds, babygirl," she said. While this was slightly slower than my personal best, I knew that lugging around the 3D printed gun would shave off at least two minutes—thereby changing a disappointment into a success.

I handed my gun over to Vonda so it could be weighed, and took in more of the strange scene. It turned out the burning trash odor that I'd detected earlier had come from two dozen flaming, rusty barrels situated about ten yards beyond the finish line. There, the homeless warmed themselves and awaited receipt of their hand-me-down firearms.

I know that, over the last several pages, I've made this event sound like a poorly organized affair. That description is accurate, objective, and scientifically valid. In most respects, it *was* poorly organized. In one respect, though, there was at least some pretense of order. I refer, of course, to the actual distribution of guns to the needy.

You see, the homeless didn't elbow past the volunteers, rush up to the exhausted race finishers, and greedily seize the guns from their arms. Quite the contrary: they patiently waited by their trash fires, keeping toasty and trading banter, while the volunteers recorded the runners' finishing times, weighed the donations, and did the (admittedly simple) calculations to arrive at an *adjusted* finishing time that would be recorded for all posterity in the sports section of the *Mulchport Tribune*. Only then, after the completion of all these steps, did the volunteers consult their clipboards and read out the name of the next bum due to receive his or her gun. One of the volunteers used a megaphone for that last part of the process, but most just screamed the name as loudly as they could.

I saw three or four of these volunteers at the finish line, diligently working through this protocol. When they called out the bums' names, it reminded me of when names are called out in a doctor's office. Of course, there were a few differences. As professional as the volunteers might seem, I knew they were actually deranged. Likewise, the bums, bag ladies, tweakers, and schizophrenics assembled around the trash fires had an edge to them that ordinary patients in a waiting room wouldn't have had.

One of them stared at me and smirked. He wore a shabby suit that wanted to pretend it was powder blue. It was really Gray, though. I saw through its façade. He wore a wilted flower as a boutonnière, and his face had a vaguely fossil-like appearance. (By that I mean, it looked as if it had once been flesh, but now was stone; that it had once been alive, but now was cheaply embalmed.) I overheard one of the other bums refer to him as "Ham-Ham." An odd nickname, given his thin frame.

I wanted to stare back at him to demonstrate I wasn't afraid, but I cast my glance to the ground instead. I suppose I was seized by the notion that he had been turned to stone by Medusa, but was somehow still able to walk around. I suppose I was in the grip of a peculiar and irrational fear: that Medusa had granted him the ability to move so *he* could, in turn, transform *other* people into stone.

Or, at least, make them *feel* like stone by marinating them in boring, coiled-up heaviness.

It turned out Ham-Ham wasn't unique. All the homeless folks had odd nicknames, and these were the only names they supplied to the volunteers. Consequently, the volunteers were forced to call out for "Tequila Worm Vinny," "Babblin' Betty," "Jim-Dog," and the like.

Everything seemed as if it were going smoothly. My adjusted time for the 5K was just a hair over twenty-five minutes—a new personal best. Vonda Reynolds screamed out the name of the next bum on her list, the bum who was to receive my gun. "Freakshow Joe. Is there a Freakshow Joe at the finish line? We got a nice little 3D printed pistol with your name on it, honey. C'mon up here and getcha some constitutional rights, young fella!"

Was it accurate to call Freakshow Joe a "young fella"? To this day, I'm not one hundred percent sure. I could see why Vonda might have concluded he was young. He looked like a toothless, mulleted version of the actor Bob Denver (of *Gilligan's Island* fame). There was a childlike naïveté residing in his vacant blue eyes and expressionless lips, just as there had been in Gilligan's. Yes, there was an element of touched man-child about him.

However, at the same time there were also deep laugh lines etched in his face. (Is it accurate to call them 'laugh lines'? What if they were actually 'scream lines'? Did he once have children to shriek at? Had he once been a rabid sports fan?) I also spied blossoming crow's feet and a receding hairline.

The more I looked at him, the more I concluded that he was, in an odd way, both old *and* young. His toothlessness could be interpreted as either a sign that he had neglected his dental hygiene for decades *or* a sign that he was actually an infant. His blank stare could be interpreted as either that of a youth in over his head *or* that of the burnout who had destroyed his capacity for abstract thinking.

He didn't walk up to the finish line so much as he staggered, and even this action was saturated with Ambiguity Energy. Was it the stagger of an arthritic drunk, or actually the stagger of a baby taking his first steps? (It occurs to me, as I write this, that Ambiguity Energy is in fact a type of *Plastic Energy*, in the sense that an ambiguous self is a self lost in a tornado of plasticity. It seemed to me that Plastic Energy is a perfect complement to Cartoon Energy and Nightmare Energy. There is nothing boring or coiled up or heavy about living in a state of hideous, unceasing mutability.)

When Freakshow Joe finally reached Vonda, he gratefully received my plastic pistol. His lips spread apart from each other, revealing a bottomless black chasm where his teeth and tongue should've been. (Was that a toothless, grateful grin, or just a subtle case of gas? Had a gangster cut out his tongue in revenge for snitching, or had it never grown in the first place?)

Those of you who have read my work in the past might be thinking you know what's coming next. You're thinking something along the lines of: *Freakshow Joe is going put the gun in his pie hole and pull the trigger, in just the same way Naomi did in* The Girl with the Gun in Her Mouth. *The crown of his head is going to burst open, like a meaty, bony flower. Runners and volunteers will gawk at the bullet-induced deformity, just as the sex club patrons gawked at the discolored, days-old corpses of Danny Bennett and Kendra Malik at the end of* Leather Noose. You're thinking the book you're holding in your hands is an elaborate hoax, a work of fiction. You're thinking that I'm going to offer you a gory depiction of suicide, perhaps because I can't help but put a suicide or two in each of my books. You're thinking my account of events is just a little too consistent with my pre-existing literary themes. You think this contrivance is the smoking gun (no pun intended) that unmasks my deception.

And, in fairness, I can see why you might be skeptical. It does all seem just a little too convenient. In real life, events don't fit neatly into a preconceived thematic framework. They're messier than that. I get that.

But here's the thing: Freakshow Joe didn't kill himself.

I mean, yeah, sure, he *tried* to kill himself. I suspect he found it overwhelming to go through life in a state of fragmentation, constantly unsure about whether he was young or old, violently maimed or congenitally deformed, advancing or degenerating; constantly separated from certainty.

Yes, the Primacy of Separation is a law of the universe. However, not everyone is wired in such a way as to see the beauty in laws. For me, fragmentation is an essential weapon in the fight against the aberration (and abomination) known as Grayness. For some, however, fragmentation is the epitome of horror.

To live as two equal possibilities at once, without the clarity of a single fixed identity, must have been a torment beyond his ken. Perhaps he thought that the only way he could achieve a single fixed identity was to grab onto the single fixed identity that awaits us all (i.e., that of a mindless corpse). To this day, I have no idea if he was sophisticated enough to frame the issue in this way. Sometimes I like to imagine he was, though.

Now, you are probably wondering how his suicide attempt failed. Was the 3D-printed gun unloaded? Was it loaded but mechanically unsound (as such devices have sometimes turned out to be when first fired)? When Freakshow Joe pulled the trigger, did it blow his hand off but leave his head unscathed?

No, something far more unexpected occurred. When he put

the gun in his mouth and pulled the trigger, I heard a muffled whirring sound; a sound not unlike that of an electric toothbrush or razor. Freakshow Joe's naive blue eyes widened. He kept the gun in his mouth, perhaps thinking that the whirring was a necessary prelude to the bullet's release. Maybe he thought that, on such a cold day, the gun had to warm up— like an old car.

Eventually, though, he had to give up. Right before he removed the gun from his mouth, I saw tears trickle down his cheeks. I can't say if that was a display of emotion or simply a consequence of his gag reflex kicking in. What I can say (much to my chagrin) is that when Freakshow Joe removed the gun from his mouth, his finger was still pulling the trigger and a vibrating pink plastic slobber-drenched phallus was jutting out of the barrel. Furthermore, I saw two tiny pink plastic prongs jutting out of the end of this pink, plastic phallus. They were vibrating, too.

The entire gun was vibrating; the pink plastic phallus was vibrating; but those two tiny pink plastic prongs were *really* vibrating. They were vibrating so quickly that all you could see of them was a blur.

It was only then that I realized Ray had bamboozled me. He'd led me to believe I'd purchased a 3D-printed gun, when in fact I'd only purchased a sex toy. I'd just plunked down two hundred dollars for…a gun-shaped vibrator. Perhaps it was even a *used* vibrator. (I hated entertaining that possibility but, given that Ray had proven he was shady as fuck, I couldn't rule it out.)

Vonda Reynolds screamed at me. "Disqualified! Your time don't count, you get no finisher's medal, and you'll never run in this town again!" I tried to explain what had happened, but that only seemed to make her angrier. She accused me of wasting her time and trying to deprive Freakshow Joe of his God-given right to shoot. "You probably thought this prank was gonna be a real hoot. UH-HUH, DIDN'T YA? Ohhh, yeah, you probably thought you were a regular ol' Ellen Funt, like on that old show *Candy Camera*, DIDN'T YA, NOW?"

I thought she was asking a rhetorical question, so I didn't answer. That made her angrier still. She started to turn red and hyperventilate. I really wanted to point out to her that the show had been called *Candid Camera*, not *Candy Camera*. That the host had been *Allen* Funt, not Ellen Funt. However, her percolating rage made me think twice about that. I didn't know exactly what would happen if she suddenly went over the edge, but I knew it would be violent. I let her keep screaming.

"Do you have any fuckin' idea how careless you were? Do you realize that if Freakshow Joe hadn't just gone ahead and tested the gun right here, he could've left with nothin' but a rubber dick in his hands!"

I wanted to remind her that Freakshow Joe hadn't been *testing* the gun. He'd tried to kill himself! I didn't bother trying to correct her, though. I knew such efforts would come to nothing. The gun-testing narrative was stuck in her head and unlikely to budge. I let her keep screaming.

"Can you imagine what could've happened if he ran into some street thugs and had to defile himself?!" She'd meant, of course, to say "defend himself." A giggle was coming on. I managed to suppress it by forcing my brain to visualize grim black veils, flu victims, and deforestation.

She was fully wound up now and there would be no easy way to de-escalate the situation. I wanted to tell her that the sticker she'd worn on her coat had just fallen to the ground. (Stickers never adhere to coats, do they? And yet that never stops folks from trying to make them adhere, does it?) I knew better than to try and change the subject, though. Her face bore little resemblance to that of the cordial, pleasantly buzzed woman who had called me "babygirl." It now looked like the tribal mask of a war god. And yet, the name tag on the frosty ground attested that this was the same person.

I started to back away, giving myself room to run if I needed to. Every time I'd take a step back, though, she would take a step forward and shriek. "Imagine if Mr. Joe here pulled out his piece, thinkin' he had a fightin' chance to stand his ground, but when the moment of truth came, he was defaceless! I mean, you know, DEFENSELESS."

Speaking of defenselessness, Vonda appeared completely unaware that Freakshow Joe was crouching behind her, gun-vibrator in hand, and tugging at the hem of her coat. The expression on his face could've been read by some as an indication of horny urgency (implying he was about to rip the coat off and rape her). Others, however, might have seen it as conveying a childlike anxiety (implying he was trying to get her attention so he could ask for her permission to use the potty).

For some reason, that was the final straw. Laughter was punching away at my lips, from the inside, trying to get out. It was stronger than my lips. It escaped.

The giggles poured out of my mouth in bitter-tasting chunks, like vomit. I tried to play them off as coughs, but they sounded far too lilting for that. So then I changed my strategy and tried to play them off as sobs. I briefly convinced myself that I *was* sobbing, as sobbing seemed to be a more acceptable reaction to all this. However, I was unable to sustain the shrill, uluating moan that is the foundation of all sobs. My voice wanted to spasm itself into tiny pieces, not stretch itself out for six seconds at a time. At that point, I was out of tricks. I surrendered. I let myself openly, unashamedly laugh.

I laughed because I realized that all the cords that connected causes to effects had been cut long ago. (Who knows if they ever actually existed in the first place?) I laughed because I realized evolution had no bias toward sanity. In a world-gone-nuts, madness enhances an individual's odds of passing down their genes. I laughed because I knew that, whatever unpleasantness ensued from the interaction between Freakshow Joe and Vonda Reynolds, it would be preferable to boring, coiled-up heaviness. I laughed because I suddenly saw that Freakshow Joe and Vonda Reynolds had switched faces. I laughed because I had a vision of Freakshow Joe's ambiguous face grafted onto each and every man, woman, child, beast, and flower in the world. I laughed because I had a vision of Freakshow Joe's ambiguous face (lecherous, and childlike, and a million other things at once) grafted onto the sun, the moon, and every single star. I laughed because I had a vision of everyone and everything on Earth and in space, in Heaven and Hell, simultaneously retching.

I laughed because I heard an explosion. I laughed because the world had turned an electric shade of white. I laughed because my face was blistering, I laughed because I realized the blisters were piled atop one another. I laughed because I realized I now had layers of faces. (To paraphrase Walt Whitman, I contained multitudes!)

I laughed because I held within me men and women, angels and demons, beasts and babies and everything in between. I laughed because their faces bulged forth from one another in impossible bas-relief—like the bellows of an accordion (and, in similar fashion, collapsed back onto one another, and then repeated their bulging forth). I laughed at the chitinous clicking I heard each time the layers expanded and collapsed. I laughed at how each of the faces atop my face laughed in unison with me. I laughed at the foul odor coming from their open mouths, a combination of star vomit and the burning blood of Rome.

The Last Big Surprise:
The Bomb

Yes, that's right, a MOTHERFUCKIN' BOMB went off near the finish line of the S.A.S. Winter Sprinter 5K and Fun Run.

Now, admittedly, it wasn't a very big bomb. It didn't *kill* anyone. (In that respect it was less dangerous than the race itself.) But it sure as hell wounded some people. (Well, specifically, it wounded two people—me and Freakshow Joe. Arguably, I got the worst of it.)

A dude in his late thirties named Sergeant Henry Miller investigated the case for the Mulchport Police Department (during the brief interval when there *was* a case). According to the *Mulchport Tribune*, Miller was a thirty-six-year-old Marine veteran of the Iraq War, selected for this assignment due to his extensive knowledge of improvised explosive devices (I.E.D.s). Given the superficial resemblance to the Boston Marathon Bombing, it seemed logical to pursue this as a terrorism case.

In the end, however, Sergeant Miller announced, rather cryptically, that no arrests would be made. "The guilty party is too big to jail," he told the *Tribune*.

I tried to track Miller down so I could interview him for this book, but the Mulchport P.D. informed me that he'd resigned his job and left town. Rumor had it he'd moved to Louisville, changed his name, and got a job at the Ford plant.

I know, I know—some of you are thinking that all of this sounds contrived. Those of you still clinging to the irrational belief that this is a work of fiction will think I'm naming this cop "Henry Miller" to make an allusion to the author of the transgressive classic *Tropic of Cancer*. Even after describing to you the beauty of meaninglessness, you insist on looking for meaning. You've been conned by pareidolia into seeing a pattern that doesn't exist.

I ask you to consider one question: why couldn't it be a complete coincidence that the name of the Mulchport P.D.'s lead investigator in the bombing was Henry Miller? "Henry" is a common enough first name. "Miller" is a common enough surname. Given the thousands upon thousands of "Henry Millers" who must currently be alive, is it all that unreasonable for one of them to have been the lead investigator in the Mulchport 5K bombing?

Setting that specific matter aside, some of you may still have lingering doubts. You're thinking to yourself: *But Noelle, if something like this had really happened, it would've been all over the news! We had a good laugh when one of the president's propagandists made reference to a nonexistent "Bowling Green Massacre." Are* you *in the employ of the president? Perhaps trying to stoke the fires of jingoism? When I try to Google this so-called Mulchport 5K Bombing, I come up empty. Not only do I fail to find any news about the bombing, I can find no evidence the town even exists. At least Naumpton has a Wikipedia page. You quoted from it!*

And the whole business of Miller's "too big to jail" comment. You're obviously trying to evoke memories of a similar phrase used during the 2008 financial crisis! I don't believe the cop actually said that. It sounds too contrived; or—at the very least—fishy.

To which I reply: what is the world if not a fishy place? The publishing industry alone is an eternally boiling cauldron of flimflam. One day we find out that an agent forged acceptance letters from publishers, showed the letters to her authors, and then persuaded the authors to decline the offers. The next day, we find out that authors attached to a long-established agency had their royalties embezzled. We hear the bestseller lists are not, strictly speaking, lists of bestsellers—but are, instead, curated according to secret criteria. We also hear of various attempts to game the system. For example, a self-published writer who topped Amazon's Christian Furry Fiction sub-category for ten minutes declares herself a bestseller! At the other end of the spectrum, a billionaire celebrity takes credit for the work of ghostwriters. Literature is dead, but the conglomerates in New York claim it rose again on the third day—reborn as Young Adult Fiction. Do not believe them.

In the context of all that deception, the story I have to tell about the explosion is relatively factual (to the extent that anything, in this Plastic Cartoon Nightmare of a world, can be called factual).

I have a recurring nightmare that reality is being devoured by a giant interdimensional space monster, and that the weirdness of the past few years is the result of that beast's digestive juices gradually breaking it down into indistinguishable globs.

Actually, sometimes the nightmare is even worse: *God* is the one doing the devouring. In this version, God made the multiverse in the same way (and for the same reason) that Dagwood Bumstead made a sandwich. *Divine* gastric juices break reality down, so that it can be absorbed through the Divine stomach. Thus it could be said that, in this nightmare, reality is nothing more than ambrosia.

The most horrific nightmare of them all, however, is the one in which I'm haunted by the ghost of Arthur C. Clarke. "Any sufficiently hungry God is indistinguishable from a monster," he moans.

During my waking hours, of course, I'm convinced the instability of the past few years is due to something relatively banal: the erosion of commonly held truths due to social media's maintenance of separate, custom-made realities for communities big and small. Wherever two or more are gathered, lunacy incubates.

But does the *reason* for The Great Unraveling actually matter? Or, should we accept it as a *fait accompli* and shift our focus to successfully *adapting* to it? Perhaps even sing paeans unto it and throw palm leaves at its feet?

Conclusion #1: Life is no longer logical.

Conclusion #2: The vice-versa is also true. (Logic is no longer alive.)

Conclusion #3: Everyone (yes, everyone) is crazy.

Embrace those facts, and you will find a way to live in this already deranged century. Regardless of whether you're a boy or a girl or somewhere in between, you will not find it necessary to put a gun in your mouth.

9

When I woke up in the hospital, I was hit with a strange amalgamation of smells: bleach and body odor, rubbing alcohol and rum. I heard the unpleasant squawking of Ellen Degeneres as she interviewed a man who was allegedly well known. I heard the sick, Gray laughs of the studio audience in response to the man's unfunny quip. I tasted blood. Moving my tongue around, I discovered a small wad of gauze in my mouth. I spit it out.

Rising off the bed, I looked around to get my bearings. Everything was a murky Gray mess. The television was distinguished only by the fact that its Gray murkiness flickered. I thrust out my hands and frantically began to search for my goggles.

"My goggles. I can't find my goggles!" I cried.

A middle-aged man spoke up. His voice carried the tone and resonance of a middle-class professional. "What's she talking about? She was wearing ordinary eyeglasses during the accident. They're on her nightstand. Joseph, pass them over to her."

The rum and b.o. scent grew stronger, and a callused hand placed a pair of glasses onto my face. My nose and forehead ached under the weight of them, but the world came into focus. Freakshow Joe loomed over me. He pointed to a stringy, inflamed suture that vertically bisected his face. Then he gave me a thumbs-up sign.

Perhaps he was saying (through gestures) that the facial laceration was his only injury, and that the wound was healing well. In the back of my mind, however, I wondered if he was indicating something far more profound: that he was okay with having his face (his *identity*) split into multiple incarnations.

You see, even then, woozy as I was, I realized that Freakshow Joe was the ideal victim for my cult; so soft and malleable. I suppose I'd been so obsessed with such matters that they were the first thing that popped into my head after coming to.

It was only moments later that I noticed the other man in the room—the one who had spoken. He wore a crisp new suit that wanted to pretend it was powder blue. It was actually Gray, though. I saw through its façade. He wore an identification badge and had a vaguely fossil-like appearance. "We could have covered up your face with all sorts of casts and bandages, but we decided to forego that dubious ritual in an effort to keep your health care costs reasonable. Wasn't that nice of us?"

It was an odd question to ask. It was an odd fellow who'd asked it. Ham-Ham had ascended in socioeconomic status since I'd last seen him, but a smirk was still planted on his thin, dry lips.

"Miss Cashman, I asked you a question: wasn't that nice of us?"

I didn't want to answer. I didn't even want to look at him. I felt a bout of cognitive dizziness coming on. So I kept silent.

"You broke a dozen bones in your face," he said. "But now they are better than ever. Also, you suffered a shoulder separation. However, that too is completely fixed. You might feel residual swelling, soreness, or sensitivity, but I promise you that it will be the world's most nebulous swelling, the world's dullest soreness, and the least-sensitive sensitivity imaginable.

"Our ambulance was only ten miles away when you were injured. Lucky you, eh? We are the only hospital within a twenty-mile radius equipped to handle a patient with so many complicated fractures. Fortunately, we are experts at fusing together those things which have been broken. What was once separate, we make united. That is the essence of all healing, don't you think?"

Something about that question seemed dangerous. I remained silent.

Ham-Ham chuckled. "You *do* like healing, don't you, Miss Cashman? What I mean is, you find unity preferable to separation? I certainly hope you do. There is no future in separation."

Was my mind playing tricks on me, or was I being interrogated like a prisoner of war?

"Take, for example, those stitches on the face of your humble acquaintance. Someone very foolish, someone who—for example—eschewed hope as 'moronic,' might see those stitches and come to the conclusion that they garishly divide the gentleman's face. Such a foolish person might even see in those stitches an outward and visible sign of a cleaved soul. However, any *wise person* can tell you that stitches are surely better than wounds. You see, soon they will dissolve and leave no scar. The forces of unity always prevail. It is inevitable."

Yes, there was something very, very fishy about Ham-Ham's little speech. I was certain of it. I stared at his identification badge (thus following Sun Tzu's advice to "Know thy enemy"). It said his name was Hampton W. Hampton, and he was a maxillofacial surgeon at Naumpton General Hospital.

"We see car accidents like yours all the time."

"I wasn't in a car. I was at the Mulchport 5K Race to benefit the Second Amendment Samaritans. You were there too! Smirking at me, the very same way you are now! There was an explo—"

"If you'll pardon my saying so, Miss Cashman, I believe we have a better sense of what has happened, and what hasn't happened, in the world than you have. You've been here in our care, in a tranquil coma, for weeks. It was as though your brain was suspended in quicksand. Yes, that's a good way to put it. During those six weeks, you became acclimated to the quicksand and no longer experienced it as such. Yes, I suppose that's just the right way to phrase it. Your brain has come to realize that the 'mental quicksand' wasn't quicksand at all, but rather a pleasant riverside beach! You know, it's highly irregular for a patient to be so talkative right after coming out of a coma. Usually they're hit by wave after wave of vertigo and nausea. And yet, here you are, unaffected by either malady. This is because your brain—like a tea bag—was given time to steep here.

"A brief word about your face. During your coma, we took the liberty of performing skin grafts to relieve the aesthetic toll of those nasty burns. Admittedly, even after all that work, you won't be the prettiest girl in town. I'm afraid that this new skin may make you seem boring and heavy to some. Likewise, you should know that your eyes now have a swirling, slate-tinted mist floating around in them. An unpleasant side effect, I'm afraid. I'm informed by our staff ophthamologist that this may be a permanent condition."

Once again he smirked.

Was I crazy for wanting to kill him? No, I don't think so. At least, I wasn't any crazier than the rest of the human race. That is, I wasn't being *exceptionally* crazy. I just felt an innocent compulsion to turn that condescending grin into a pulsing geyser of neon blood. You would've felt that way, too, if you had just put two and two together and concluded that an all-out effort was being made to forcibly transform you into a Gray person.

"Now, I have covered a lot of ground about the physical consequences of your accident, but of course there have been emotional consequences, too. The good news is that we at Naumpton General are prepared to help both you and your acquaintance become far more level-headed individuals than you are at present. Wouldn't you agree that there's a lot of value in level-headedness?"

I remained silent.

"Silence equals insolence, Miss Cashman, and I've tolerated your insolence for far too long. Answer the question."

"Doctor, you've said nothing but lies from the moment you opened your mouth. I'm not some mental weakling whom you can gaslight. I want out of here."

"You're not cured yet, Miss Cashman. Nor is your smelly acquaintance, Mr. Joseph Breen. You do know that he has a real name, don't you? A proper, wholesome, name."

"For all I know, that's a name you just made up. I knew him by a more remarkable sobriquet: Freaksh—"

Ham-Ham winced and interrupted. "Miss Cashman, we don't use language like that around here. More to the point, you didn't answer my question. It was a simple question, I think you'll agree, and all it required by way of an answer was a simple 'yes' or 'no.' And yet, you're unable to stay focused long enough to perform even *that* rudimentary task. Perhaps you have sustained some permanent brain damage. Yes, that could explain your lack of focus! If this is indeed the case, then it will be some time before you're eligible for discharge. There's a whole array of rehabilitation exercises that must commence, if you're brain-damaged. So I ask you again: wouldn't you agree that there's a lot of value in level-headedness?"

I felt trapped, so I threw him a bone. "There's a time for level-headedness, and there's a time for screaming."

Ham-Ham rolled his eyes. "Ah yes," he said. "I've read your many queer notions about screaming at funerals, in the mirror, and whatnot. I see that your devotion to them isn't limited to the page. You actually believe that baloney!"

I felt a chill gallop down my spine. Somehow he knew about my work-in-progress. I had been on Naumpton's radar for some time, it seemed!

Perhaps, as the bastion of Grayness, the town found it necessary to spy on those who asserted the Primacy of Separation. Maybe they used some sort of NSA-style web surveillance to determine the identities of those making anti-Grayness web searches. Maybe they found a way to hack into my Google docs files, and used my manuscript as a way to keep tabs on my anti-Grayness activities. Maybe they sent a burglar into my office to read my hand-edited, annotated pages, just to get a better sense of my thought process about all this. Maybe hired goons had rifled through my desk and put things back in the wrong place. Maybe that's the reason my office always looked a little sloppier than I remembered leaving it.

Maybe they saw that I was making inroads against Grayness. Maybe they felt threatened by the fact that I knew I needed to form a cult, and that this cult needed to possess an undercurrent of female supremacy, and that it further needed to somehow involve the wearing of veils. Maybe they, too, knew about *solve* and *coagula*.

Maybe a tiny drone had silently followed my daily jogs and, using sophisticated instruments, collected enough speed, tem-

perature, and humidity data to confirm I had parted the Gray
Sea. Maybe the parting of the Gray Sea had changed things
in southern Indiana. Maybe it broke a window in the house
of Midwestern consciousness and let in all the craziness from
the coasts. Maybe the S.A.S. 5K really had originally been a
benefit for St. Anthony's School (or Seniors Against Shingles),
but my magick had transformed the event into something far
more Colorful. Maybe Ham-Ham planted the bomb. (In the
gun-shaped vibrator? In the burning trash barrel?) Maybe that
was the only way to shut down my study. Maybe, when he saw
I'd survived, Ham-Ham (or another conspirator?) dispatched
Naumpton's thought police (disguised as paramedics) to seize
me and Freakshow Joe. Perhaps this so-called hospital was actually a re-education facility, where I was expected to conform
to The Gray Mold.

Perhaps they took away my black goggles and balaclava because they knew my only advantage rested in keeping my face
covered, as The New Moses had. Perhaps they hadn't bothered
bandaging my facial wounds because that would've created a
new veil. Perhaps I hadn't actually been in a coma, but had
simply been subjected to a couple hundred rounds of hypnosis. Perhaps they were trotting out this absurd story about a
car accident to gauge how much resistance I had left to muster
against their gaslighting. Perhaps if I showed signs of buying
it, a million other malicious lies would follow.

On second thought, there was no "perhaps" about any of
these things. Ham-Ham was an agent of Grayness, and he
was sparing no expense in the effort to brainwash me. In fact,
"brainwashing" is far too gentle a word to describe the ordeal.
The man aspired to nothing less than the *crucifiction of my
soul.*

10

In *Winesburg, Ohio*, Sherwood Anderson has the ruined, degenerate small-town physician Dr. Parcival opine that "everyone in the world is Christ and they are all crucified." Re-reading that passage after several months away from the book, I'm reminded that Parcival's life had crash-landed in Winesburg some five years before he uttered those words. ("He came from Chicago," Anderson tells us earlier in Parcival's story, "and when he arrived was drunk and got into a fight with Albert Longworth, the baggage-man. The fight concerned a trunk and ended by the doctor's being escorted to the village lockup.")

In *Native Son*, Richard Wright has an African-American Chicago preacher, Reverend Hammond, say: "Jesus...showed us tha' t' live in this worl' wuz t' be crucified by it... This worl' ain' our home. Life ever day is a crucifixion."

Was Wright influenced by Anderson? I don't know for certain, but it's quite possible. A Library of America edition of Wright's later works ends with a chronology claiming that he discovered Anderson's fiction in 1927. Meanwhile, Wikipedia says he didn't start writing *Native Son* until 1938.

In a way, though, the question is irrelevant. Whether Anderson directly influenced Wright or not, I find it impossible to ignore the similarity of the two sentiments. Despite the fact that Dr. Parcival is a country mouse and Reverend Hammond is a city mouse, despite the fact that one is white and the other black, despite the fact that one apparently left Chicago in disgrace and the other found his niche there, they both champion the Theory of Universal Crucifixion.

What are we to make of all this? How does it relate to Ham-Ham's desire to crucify *my soul*? These are not easy questions to answer. To fully comprehend these mysteries, we must slowly unpack them—piece by piece.

When Parcival says "everyone in the world is Christ," does he mean to affirm the idea that God dwells in every single man, woman, and child? Is he an early twentieth-century Midwesterner who has, by some freakishness in his disposition, taken on the optimism of late nineteenth-century New Englanders (with their peacenik-ism, dogooder-ism, transcendentalism, "over-soul", etc.)?

My answer to that question is no. At least, not exactly.

I think Parcival is using "Christ" metaphorically. When he says "everyone in the world is Christ," he merely means that we all experience fleeting moments of virtual apotheosis; times when life is (to paraphrase Nigel Tufnel) dialed up to eleven. For example, we may all enjoy the intense joy of orgasm, the neuron-tingling thrill of meaningful work, the giddiness of inebriation, and/or the warmth of those emotions approximating love. For Parcival, however, none of these states lasts. Certainly, there's *no evidence* he's ever seen them last. The stories he tells young George Willard all involve falls from grace, debasement, and degeneracy.

Which brings us to the word "crucifixion." Why would Parcival thrust forward that ancient term (with all its cultural baggage) to describe the commonplace phenomenon of dissipation? I think it's because the word connotes a strange mixture of voluntary and involuntary suffering. Christ prayed in the Garden of Gethsemane to have the burden of his destiny relieved from him, but in the end he conceded rule over the matter to God the Father ("Thy will, not mine, be done"). Later, Christ must literally take up his cross.

There's a heavy (but hidden) dose of masochism at work in such a personality, a masochism that seems related to Edgar Allan Poe's notion of "the imp of the perverse." For the uninitiated, Poe's notion—in a nutshell—was that people are driven to do things that will certainly lead to their own ruin (or, conversely, that they fail to take action that would save their own skins). It's the idea that we are all driven to do unnatural things, which go against the grain of common sense and the survival instinct, *because* they are unnatural.

The narrator of "The Tell-Tale Heart" pulls up the floorboards to expose his victim's corpse. Christ teaches us that when someone clobbers you once, you should let them clobber you again. Then he blindly follows the commands of a disembodied voice that says he must die. Dr. Parcival refuses to go through the motions of attending to a child who is already dead, and abruptly leaves town due to a paranoid belief that he'll be hanged for negligence. In *Native Son*, Bigger Thomas (the main character) doesn't flee the murder scene when he has a chance, leaves behind all sorts of clues, and signs a confession he doesn't have to sign.

And yet, one senses in Bigger Thomas something bigger (see what I did there?) than the cowardly submission of Christ or Parcival, or the self-destructive madness of Poe's protagonist. One gets the sense that he's tired of being swallowed up in a sea of whiteness, tired of being confined to an ontological ghetto, where his options for being are limited to various flavors of servility. ("They don't even let you feel what you want to feel. They after you so hot and hard you can only feel what they doing to you. They kill you before you die.")

Thus, Bigger's revelation in the novel's closing pages: "I didn't want to kill!... But what I killed for, I *am!*... I didn't know I was really alive in this world until I felt things hard enough to kill for 'em... I know what I'm saying real good and I know how it sounds. But I'm all right. I feel all right when I look at it that way..."

Translation: When all available incarnations prove unbearable, the only option remaining is to become death, the destroyer of worlds.

This is a country mile from the crucifixion of Reverend Hammond (the crucifixion of a soul rather than a body). Hammond *deifies* suffering because he lacks the balls to *defy* it. Thus, it could be said that he takes up the cross of non-controversial acquiescence toward his Jim Crow oppressors— going along to get along, not destroying the world but clinging to a dream of a better one awaiting him after death (a dream oppressors have long dangled in front of their victims to keep them from revolting).

Dr. Parcival's suffering isn't societally enforced, in the way that of Reverend Hammond and Bigger Thomas is. It seems, instead, to be *psychologically* enforced; enforced by his own anxiety. And yet, in the end it doesn't matter. He, too, is crucified. He takes up the cross of self-imposed exile.

So it occurs to me that Ham-Ham was asking me to do a very Midwestern thing when he asked me (in so many words) to take up the cross of Grayness (coagulation, healing, sullen normality, etc.). Wouldn't it be arrogant of me to assume that I would somehow be exempt from the tax levied on all my neighbors—both black and white, urban and rural? How dare I hope to have my own screams heard over the Heavy Gray Noise?

During my time in the so-called "Naumpton General Hospital," these ideas weren't as well thought-out as they are now. I only had an intuition that open revolt against Ham-Ham would lead to disaster. I had a sense that the only way for a Midwesterner to truly evade crucifixion was to affect it. I've already established the value of Artifice, so it should come to absolutely no surprise that my way of dealing with the threat of crucifixion was to *pretend* to be crucified!

The First Method I Used
to Create the Artifice of Crucifixion

I should start off by telling you what I *didn't* do. I *didn't* make a rapid about-face and begin loudly extolling the virtues of healing. You see, rank-and-file Gray People are oblivious to the very existence of the plague that infects them! So if I walked about the hospital, chatting folks up and using any of the inside lingo (*solve, coagula,* The Primacy of Separation, etc.), then I'd expose myself as a fake.

Gray People don't adorn their cars with bumper stickers that say: "Grayness Is Where It's At." They adorn their cars with bumper stickers that say: "University of Louisville Basketball." They don't write poems explicitly praising all the thought-snot slathered over the landscape; they write poems with lines like: "What place is lovelier than Terre Haute". Their Grayness is such a core aspect of their identity that they don't even think about it.

How, then, could I ever hope to fool my captors? I pretended to conform gradually to the *physical mannerisms* of other patients.

For example, I would see them shuffling past my door, guided by nurses in gray scrubs. I would observe how their expressions were uniformly grim, but only mildly so. I would note how these expressions seemed to be caused by physical pain. There was no obvious preoccupation with matters of *solve* and *coagula*, and therefore no attendant angst. (Far from it. There was no indication they had an inner life at all.)

So I decided to emulate them. I didn't ask for permission beforehand; I just got up out of bed and walked laps around the nurse's station. I focused on affecting a mildly grim expression (so *mildly* grim, in fact, that it couldn't even have been fairly deemed a *grimace*). I didn't go and get Freakshow Joe out of bed to walk with me. That would've been seen as too bossy. I decided to ignore him for a while, to give the impression that I was no longer considering him for my cult.

I didn't make a big show of my walk. I only did a handful of laps. But it was enough to get Ham-Ham's attention. Out of the corner of my eye, I spotted him scribbling his lead pencil over a pad of pulpy paper. The next day he authorized me to go off of the unit to attend an Arts & Crafts class. Perhaps this was part of the 'rehabilitation exercises" designed to address the "emotional consequences" of the fake car accident.

The Second Method I Used
to Create the Artifice of Crucifixion

"Arts & Crafts Class"—it sounds so innocent, right? It conjures up images of Girl Scouts making charm bracelets in summer camp, or the non-threatening antics of basket-weaving mental patients. The Arts & Crafts Class at Naumpton General Hospital was, of course, a far more sinister affair.

I was met at the classroom door by the instructor (a tall, pale, bony man with a WASP Manhattan accent). He kept his (obviously, Gray) hair in an upswept, tangled style designed to advertise to the world that he was a creative person. He wore the sort of glasses creative New Yorkers are supposed to wear. His shirt, pants, and shoes fit the same aesthetic. "I'm Sam D. Nadalo," the instructor said, by way of introduction. "And *you* must be just another cow wanting to join my herd!"

The whole thing was a set-up, of course, intended to knock me off balance. "Nadalo" was surely not a WASP name, but the accent was decidedly WASP. An even weirder contradiction: the presence of a Manhattanite in the very heart of Grayness.

I believe both of these contradictions were shoved in my face as a sort of test. They wanted to see how much I'd freak out. If I freaked out a great deal, they'd think I wasn't yet sufficiently brainwashed. Therefore, I tried to appear as though I were utterly unfazed. It was very difficult, but I managed to maintain my mildly grim expression. (Or at least, mostly maintain it. I believe the accent did lead my eyes to bulge ever so slightly from their sockets, but I tried to obscure that unfortunate reflex by blinking a few times.)

Likewise, the bovine insult was another test. Gray Human Beings are faced with any number of insults every day. (Most of them of the implied, unspoken variety, of course—for example, the insult of walking out the door each morning and feeling the burden of boring, coiled-up heaviness.)

A Gray Person responds to an insult by shrugging it off and maintaining a mildly grim expression. Another acceptable response might be to sublimate one's humiliation by cracking an unfunny joke and waiting for passersby to respond with a chorus of sick, Gray laughs.

In any event, a truly indignant response or a truly clever one is *verboten*.

I managed to restrain myself from going off half-cocked. I preserved my mildly grim expression. I believe the insult did lead me to wince just a little, but I played it off as an insignificant wince. (I imagined I was a pack animal, and another load had just gotten tossed atop my back.)

Nadalo then led me to the front of the class. I wanted to look around at the other patients and find Freakshow Joe. I wanted to send him a secret signal to let him know that I had my eye on him, that I was his Goddess and he my worm. But there wasn't time for that. Nadalo hopped around the classroom, over to a supply closet, and fetched two shrouded supply carts from within.

Then he addressed the class. "Today we welcome Miss Noelle Cashman to Arts & Crafts. As is customary with new arrivals, she will get to select today's activity. You have two options, Noelle."

With a barely noticeable grin, he whipped the shrouds off of the supply carts. "Shall we make sculptures from Play-Doh? Or shall we indulge in the fine art of magazine-photo collage?"

Suffice to say, they were disappointing options (hardly measuring up to the expectations set by Nadalo's little hops around the classroom, or his dramatic unshrouding of the supply carts). The so-called Play-Doh was actually generic brand silly putty. It could stretch back and forth, but it wasn't much good for building things. The collage option was every bit as disappointing. If there was any fun to be had at all in that endeavor, it came from leafing through magazines and finding the goofiest photos to use. Here in the Naumpton General Hospital Arts & Crafts class, however, all the photos had been pre-cut out of the magazines. Even worse, they were all black-and-white.

It was only through extraordinary, bowel-clinching effort

that I was able to preserve my mildly grim expression. I may have let my jaw drop just a smidgen—as though I had just been told to pick up a multitude of unpaid overtime hours at a factory for the next six months. I trust, however, that this only made me appear more Gray—not less.

I knew, of course, that Mr. Nadalo—if that was his real name—had very little interest in investing me with decision-making power for that day. My "choice" was, in reality, another test. My first instinct (my *Colorful* instinct) had been to select the Play-Doh, because I saw multiple possibilities in each big Gray glob of it. I could tear it apart and make three small objects out of one.

Of course, that was not the option that Mr. Nadalo wanted me to select. If I picked it, I might be immediately whisked back to my room and never allowed out again. Obviously, a Gray Person would choose "the fine art of magazine-photo collage" instead, because that art (focused as it was on *the transformation of various parts into a united whole*) was saturated with *coagula* energy.

I shrugged and casually pointed at the black-and-white pictures. Mr. Nadalo smiled and invited me to take a seat. "You chose wisely," he said while giving me a paternalistic pat on the head. "I wasn't so sure you would."

I managed to preserve my mildly grim expression as I started pasting the black-and-white photos onto a piece of gray construction paper. I tried to be as uncreative as possible. The resulting collage depicted a man in a trenchcoat punching a man in a sweater and jeans, while an airplane zoomed by in the background and a monochrome flower garden dominated the lower left corner. Both of the humans in the picture bore mildly grim expressions.

I analyzed my work for elements Mr. Nadalo might find

troublesome. I realized that a single airplane, alone in the sky, might have too much *solve* energy about it. (It could be said that it was *slicing through the air*.) So I added a second airplane coming in the opposite direction. Then I drew missiles on each of the airplanes to make it clear they were military aircraft (attached to their respective countries). The I wrote the title of my work in large letters, just below the airplanes: THEY ARE *JOINED* IN BATTLE.

At the end of the class, Mr. Nadalo made a little speech in which he emphasized that Arts & Crafts Class "isn't just busy work, but a vital part of rehabilitation." As a result, it would be necessary for him to collect our work and evaluate it, to see how we were all progressing. He commanded a student at the front of the class to collect all our collages. He referred to this student as "Mr. Breen."

The shock was too much. My resolve to preserve a *mildly* grim expression wavered as my lips curled in out-and-out disgust. Was this the same "Mr. Breen" I had seen in Mulchport? (The ambiguously ageless Gilligan?) No! Was this even the scarred individual who had put my glasses on the day before? No! The scar that had bisected his face had already healed. Even worse, they had also managed to perform—in very short order—a series of additional cosmetic surgeries that made him look unambiguously middle-aged and middle-class.

My heart galloped like that of a sick racehorse. I flushed with the fever of righteous indignation. Vertigo clawed into my brain and refused to let go. I felt a yearning to throw aside my desk, grab Freakshow Joe, and run for the exit. But what if he had been so successfully brainwashed that he refused to accompany me? What if he'd been *willingly* brainwashed and all too eager to betray me? I needed to know exactly where he stood before trying such an escape. Moreover, my "Artifice of Crucifixion" strategy appeared to be working. Why force a confrontation when I could more easily win release via subterfuge?

So I reined in my anger and re-froze my face into a mildly grim expression. I handed my collage to Freakshow Joe without glancing any further at his face. As the large piece of gray construction paper was swiped from my hand, a small scrap of gray paper replaced it.

He'd passed me a note, scrawled with a pencil. In shaky handwriting, it read:

WE ARE JOINED IN BATTLE

Am I alone in finding this to be an ambiguous statement? Did he mean to say that we were now enemies (brought together on the battlefield of Grayness)? Or, in his own clumsy way, was he trying to say that we were allies (that we have *joined* forces)?

The Third Method I Used
to Create the Artifice of Crucifixion

I let them implant shards of glass in my boobs. I knew the resulting wounds would feel like unceasing bee stings. I knew the stitches would itch. I knew the shards could slice my boobs apart, from the inside, for the rest of my life.

I let them do it anyway.

"As you know, I'm a facial surgeon, not a tit man," Ham-Ham explained to me on one Gray March Afternoon, "but this falls into the purview of cosmetic surgery. So I'll be assisting with the procedure."

Of course, I had a million questions about this. What, exactly, was the rehabilitative value of such butchery? Where did this glass come from? Was it going to be old, dusty glass or straight-from-the-factory glass? Was my insurance covering the procedure? What sort of recovery time could I expect? Would I heal overnight, the way Freakshow Joe had?

However, I felt it unwise to ask my captors about such matters. I didn't want to arouse any suspicion that their brainwashing had failed. Therefore, I had to preserve a slightly grim expression.

This was not as difficult as you might think. By that point, I was beginning to get the hang of it. In fact, I had to work quite hard to remind myself that the Gray Face was not my actual default expression. I didn't want to get so lost in this one particular artifice that it became my reality!

I hope you never end up as an inpatient at Naumpton General Hospital, and I *especially* hope you never have shards of glass implanted into your tits by the doctors there. That said, I feel a responsibility to describe what the procedure is like, so that those women who follow in my steps are adequately braced for the horrors.

The first unpleasant thing I noted was the fact that the staff's surgical masks were made of cheap cellophane. They weren't even fully intact. Each mask was absolutely shredded on one side and had a gaping hole on the other. I can only assume that these were used because the hospital administrators were wily students of history and magick, and therefore understood how veiled faces presented a hazard to Grayness. By using cheap cellophane as a substitute, they were able to show off their ugly mugs and avoid an inadvertent imitation of The New Moses.

What a wretched sight it was! As the staff craned their heads over me, they chattered to each other in a pidgin English of medical jargon. With each flap of their lips, a fresh strand of spittle would splash against their Saran wrap "mask." Before long, thin trails of drool escaped the tiny shreds and gaping holes, landing on my face, belly, and legs.

Sadly, that wasn't even the worst part of my humiliation. No, *the worst part of my humiliation* was *spiritual* in nature. (A Grim Gray Epiphany, you might say.)

As they hooked me up to heart monitors, IV drips, and oxygen tubes, I suddenly realized why they felt the need to do this. Yes, of course, they wanted me to buy into their version of reality—the one in which I had been injured in a car wreck, not blown up by a bomb. They knew that, in the future, little shards of glass would show up on my mammograms, and that I'd probably tell the lady running the machine that the glass had become embedded in my tits during a car accident. (No one would believe that a surgeon actually implanted the glass.)

Maybe the docs at Naumpton General hoped that, over time, I might even begin to doubt the surgical implantation story myself; that I'd begin to construct false memories of an accident that never happened.

This, in and of itself, was diabolical. But it was just the tip of the iceberg.

They also wanted to strengthen the connection between my life and the lives of my family members. They knew being hooked up to oxygen would remind me of how my grandmother had been hooked up to oxygen. They knew the implantation of glass would remind me of the industrial accident that had sent shattered glass flying into my father's chest. They knew that this, in turn, would remind me of my ancestor who lived for decades with an arrowhead stuck near his heart. Perhaps they even thought it would remind me of the time Jake Wanser had taken a knife to my chest. They knew that all these PATTERNS would occur to me, and weave all sorts of Sick Gray Meaning into my world.

Most obscene of all, they would be transforming shattered glass (ordinarily, surfeit with *Solve* Energy) into a rich deposit of *coagula*.

Despite all these obscenities against Color, I voluntarily took up the cross of PATTERNS, because I knew that by doing so I would earn their trust.

11

My plan worked. I had so convincingly played the part of Crucified Soul that they began planning my discharge.

It all started one day shortly after lunch. There were no bandages on my tits. In fact, my stitches dissolved mere hours after surgery and I was left with a rack that looked better than ever on the outside (if I do say so myself). Yet with each step (and its attendant boob-sway) I felt two dozen little razor blades slicing through mammary muscle and fat. So I stayed in bed and, with mild grimness, went through the motions of eating chipped beef gravy.

Whoever had invented that dish must've been trying to find a way to torment as many of the senses as possible in one fell swoop. It was visually repulsive. (When it was served to soldiers and sailors they nicknamed it "shit on a shingle." Gray gravy = gray shit, what an image!) It tasted like something stuck in an uncanny valley between real food and plastic play food. It smelled like stale pepper and overcooked beets. Its texture felt alien and foul as it oozed and scraped its way across one's tongue and down one's gullet. The sound of the dried beef crumbling between one's molars evoked a sense of terror, because there was no way to avoid the realization that the eater of the meal was drawing the chipped beef into her; that she was, in a sense, voluntarily becoming one with both it and the Gray gravy.

I stabbed my plastic fork into this disgusting meal repeatedly, like a machine, but seldom took a bite. That made it extraordinarily easy to settle my face into a mildly grim expression. I mention this culinary torture because I believe it was the lowest point of my existence in Naumpton General Hospital. It was the point at which the artifice of crucifixion nearly became the real thing. I had started to asymptote in that direction.

Who knows? If I had taken just a few more bites of that lunch, I may have become so poisoned by Grayness that my face would've become permanently frozen in that mildly grim expression.

Fortunately, it didn't come to that. For right at that moment, Ham-Ham stepped into my room. "You have made satisfactory progress toward your goals and will soon be returning home. However, here at Naumpton General we don't just toss you out and hope for the best. Far from it! We gently transition patients from the highly structured life within this institution to unsupervised life on their own.

"For example, later today we'll be taking a select group of our most compliant patients out on a field trip—a tour of Historic Naumpton. I would like for you to attend, so that you can see museum exhibits which depict the hardy, wholesome spirit of our pioneer founders; their dauntless faith to do and dare! I can think of nothing that would provide you with better preparation for a smooth transition to your ordinary life."

Suddenly a switch flipped in my head and it became quite difficult to maintain a mildly grim expression. I lowered my head, so the good doctor wouldn't see the twinkle in my eye. I nodded in a mildly grim manner. Apparently pleased with my response, Ham-Ham left.

When I was certain he was out of earshot, I giggled and writhed like a madwoman.

This was the break I'd been looking for! I imagined that on such an outing the patients might outnumber the staff. At some point there'd be a distraction and then I'd grab Freakshow Joe and we'd run off together. He certainly seemed to be something of a teacher's pet to Mr. Nadalo. Surely he'd be considered one of the hospital's "most compliant patients" and find himself invited along as well.

If he refused to run off with me willingly, then I'd coerce him into joining me.

Yes, I'd coerce him!

Then I would shove him violently into a seldom-used public ladies room along the Naumpton waterfront.

Indeed, right there on the waterfront! That very same parcel of land where The New Israelites had landed in 1868!

I wouldn't need to shave Freakshow Joe's ass until it was smooth as a baby's. I wouldn't need to soak him in bathwater for nine hours to replicate nine months in the womb. I wouldn't need to play fetal heartbeat sounds out of a laptop positioned against the door, or declare a closed shower curtain to be an amniotic sac.

After all, the *matryoshka* sex robot in the disturbing porn video was made to undergo multiple reincarnations, and it had no amniotic sac. Instead, it had layers of artificial skin.

I wouldn't need my prego neighbor's blood, or livestock blood, or fake blood out of a tube, or, for that matter, any blood at all. You see, there hadn't been any blood (or its facsimile) in the disturbing porno, because the victim in that scenario had been a robot, not a human being. So why couldn't I create an artifice that Freakshow Joe was a robot, too?

Yes, everything is so much simpler when the lone follower of your cult is a thing rather than a person. Besides, this new approach had another advantage: it was far more chaotic than the one I'd planned before. My original scheme had called for guiding my victim through an orderly, sequential progression of life's stages. The aging process I'd planned to put him through was far too predictable.

*Predict*ability is a close cousin to *sta*bility, and *sta*bility is a close cousin to boring, coiled-up heaviness. Therefore, my Incarnation Facilitation needed to be as unpredictable as possible if it was to slay Grayness. The disturbing porno in Ray's apartment turned out to be not so disturbing after all. It contained an essential revelation!

I would tie Freakshow Joe up with his own belt. Using my most basic alchemical skills, I'd transform him into an odd combination of a Russian *matryoshka* doll and a sex robot. I would then facilitate his rebirth into multiple reincarnations.

Unlike the hairy men in the disturbing porn video, however, I would never find myself frustrated by what I discovered under each layer of his being. They would all be delightfully broken, and that Brokenness Energy would ooze *Solve* Energy. This *Solve* Energy would disrupt the hegemony of *Coagula* Energy in Naumpton, and thus interrupt its ability to send out pulsing waves of vertigo and nausea!

My one cult, with only two members, might save the world (or, at least, southern Indiana).

At exactly 2:29 p.m. on the afternoon of March 15, 2018, Ham-Ham came into my room and handed me a pair of cheap gray sneakers (the sort typically sold at discount stores for fifteen dollars a pair). "It'll feel good to finally dispense with your hospital slipper-socks and wear your very own shoes," he said. "We've kept them in a safe since your arrival, because we knew that one day you'd be well enough to wear them again."

Like everything else he said, that was a lie. In fact, a particularly brazen lie. I had never seen those shoes before in my life, and they were too small for me. I could only put them on if I scrunched my toes into a little ball.

This, of course, was what Ham-Ham intended. I was given those shoes so that I would not be able to run away from the tour group. They would compel me to take on a shuffling Gray gait. They would make me far more vulnerable to the emotional burden of boring, coiled-up heaviness. They would ensure that I'd preserve a mildly grim expression.

The sides of the shoes were adorned with an ambiguously curvy design (an obvious attempt to mimic the famous Nike swoosh). However, no attempt had been made to mimic Nike's sturdy construction. Already, stitches were unraveling. Already, little plastic bits of the sole had broken off. Perhaps Ham-Ham didn't think I'd notice such details. He probably thought I'd only notice their tightness and drab hue, and be so overwhelmed by them that I wouldn't bother looking at the soles and stitching. Oh, but he was wrong! I *did* notice them and found them encouraging. They indicated that a scintilla of brokenness had already managed to infiltrate the very bastion of Grayness! What better omen could I ask for?

Once I had laced up both sneakers, I shuffled out of my room and joined the ranks of the soon-to-be discharged. It has occurred to me that some readers may want to know more about these other souls who were unfortunate enough to run afoul of Naumpton General. What did they look like, how did they sound? Did any of them still carry a trace of eccentricity?

Sadly, the answer to that last question is "no." Or at least, not that I could observe. Everyone had their head slightly bowed, so that their faces were difficult to see. For that matter, the patients never spoke to one another. (Which is odd, now that I think about it, because there wasn't any written rule dictating such silence. Maybe people were just so scared of saying the wrong thing that they didn't say anything at all.)

How, then, could I confirm that Freakshow Joe was among those in line?

Ah, yes, a very important question—and one I delight in answering because it shows off my ingenuity. You see, as I was standing there I realized that it didn't make a difference if the Freakshow Joe I enslaved was the *Real* Freakshow Joe or *An Artifice* of Freakshow Joe. Either one would do the trick!

Don't you see? That's the very best part of being an alchemist. *The Concept of* Freakshow Joe was already well entrenched in my mind (his Bob Denver-style agelessness, his blank slate naïveté, etc.). After using alchemy to transform one of my fellow patients into a *matryoshka*-style sex robot, I'd methodically slice through that robot's layers of artificial skin until I found their incarnation as Freakshow Joe.

12

Eventually, someone in line shuffled forward. Predictably, the person behind that person followed suit. And so on. And so on. Before I knew it I was outside, in the Gray glare of an unseasonably scorching spring day.

I could see the trickling Grayness of the Ohio River, and I could see pigeons roosting on the smooth, Gray granite shoulders of the New Moses statue in Pioneers Park. I saw the smokestacks of a cheap imitation steamboat docked on the waterfront (a ramshackle monstrosity seemingly thrown together—like a collage—from spare scraps of dented, chipped-paint aluminum). In the distance, I saw a ghostly feed silo so distorted by heat waves that I couldn't say for certain if it was real. The sidewalk under my feet was grimy and vomit-stained. The sky overhead had been mummified. Although the months-long "steeping" of my brain had indeed warded off the dreaded vertigo and nausea, something about this entire experience still felt…well, *off*.

The problem may have been that I thought I knew everything anyone needed to know about Naumpton, when in fact much of the town's workings are unknowable. While admittedly not a physician or public health professional, I thought I could improvise my way through an epidemiological study. Although nothing more than a novice local historian, I thought I had studied enough old maps and correspondence to determine the causes and cures of the town's woes. Although I've never had the least bit of training in alchemy, I thought that I had learned all I needed to know about *solve* and *coagula* in an Alan Moore YouTube clip.

Yes, I knew a lot about Grayness. I had personal experience with its boring, coiled-up heaviness and its manifestation as humid thought-snot, etc. But this knowledge did nothing to prepare me for the ghastly contradiction of a town that both flagarently abstained from life and feverishly clung to it. Nor did this knowledge prepare me for the sight of a town that was as much an idea as it was a physical reality.

On that afternoon of March 15, 2018, Naumpton seemed both unreal and real. By casting my glance upon its sights, I momentarily became one with it. *I* flagrantly abstained from life, while also feverishly clinging to it. *I* was as much an idea as a physical reality. My head felt like an iron pot, in which stale pepper and canned beets were being overcooked.

I lowered my head back down and kept marching along with my cohort. The scraping of sixty cheap shoes against the sidewalks of downtown Naumpton was an unpleasant sound. I began to quietly hum the theme to *Gilligan's Island* in an attempt to drown it out. My head began to feel less like a pot of stale, overcooked pepper and canned, overcooked beets. It started to feel more like an actual thought-factory.

The specific nature of the town's unreality dawned on me. It was a case of jumbled-up physics (or perhaps jumbled-up perception). Every time I took a step forward, the Gray World around me seemed to move farther back. For example, I spotted an old, abandoned bank on Main Street that looked as though it were a mere ten feet away. But after we, the patients, took three steps forward, it was about fifteen feet away.

I don't believe I was the only one who noticed this, because out of the corner of my eye I spied a few of those in line ahead of me flinching and letting out little breathless gasps of mildly grim exasperation. At the same time, we all became afflicted with a sort of sterile sweat (by which I mean, a sweat that smelled of rubbing alcohol). Thus it could be said that the biological processes of everyone in Naumpton were jumbled up, too.

The sun was filtered through a heavy screen of Grayness, but that didn't stop it from lighting our skin and bones on fire. Worse still, the wind began to whip about, coming off the river (south to north), bringing with it a chill so frigid that it could've easily congealed animal fat.

I say "worse still" because this wind didn't temper the unseasonable heat so much as it lent the weather a second discrete layer of discomfort. The heat would burn us, then after two minutes the chill would replace it, then after two minutes the heat would return, and so on. (The meteorological processes of the town were jumbled.)

The weather oscillated back and forth throughout the afternoon. I believe that Naumpton itself has a sentient Soul, and that this Soul was aware of my brain's ability to free itself from the Naumptonian spell via a clever little '60s TV theme. I believe that the town's Soul united extreme heat and extreme cold in a common fight against me, so that I would find myself too distracted to rebel.

It was only with great effort that I was able to avoid this trap. I remembered that my shoes were falling apart, and I noted how the shoes of the patient in front of me were also falling apart. Thus, I was able to remind myself of The Primacy of Separation and keep my wits about me.

Already, my feet ached too much to continue. I broke ranks with my fellow-patients and sat down on a curb. A few of them directed a jaded glance my way, but most didn't even notice my departure. An invisible hand grabbed hold of my pants leg and tugged at it. Unnerved, I kicked at the air in hopes of repelling my harasser. Then a second invisible hand joined the first, and I found myself suddenly lifted up into the air.

"We are joined in battle," a voice called out. It was obviously middle-class and middle-aged, but did not belong to Ham-Ham.

Then I was tossed into a bottomless black pit. The hands that did the tossing were particularly rough and callused.

13

What are we to make of this? I believe Freakshow Joe had been so successfully re-formed by the brainwashers at Naumpton General that he was elevated to a paid position on the staff. I believe that the note he passed to me at the end of Arts & Crafts Class was a Declaration of War, and not an alliance. I believe that he (or his superiors) had read my thoughts and knew exactly what I was plotting. I believe that he cast a spell of invisibility, and that this spell was especially powerful. (After all, he had until recently been a derelict. Who knows how to blend into the woodwork better than a derelict? Homeless people are experts at going unnoticed.)

I believe "Mr. Joseph Breen" and some of his invisible associates saw that I was successfully resisting and went out of their way to expel me from Naumpton. I believe they knew that I had the capacity to commit an act so filthy with *Solve* Energy that it would have destroyed Grayness at its very root.

I believe that Naumpton doesn't exist in the same sort of spacetime as other towns in southern Indiana. Actually, this isn't merely a "belief" but an empirical observation. As I was falling down the invisible pit, I saw a circular Gray Glow above me. The town of Naumpton was revealed unto me as being nothing but a flat disk. More precisely, it was a pewter bob hanging from the bottom of a clock pendulum, hypnotically swaying from side to side. It ticked and tocked like a metronome tasked with setting a predictable rhythm for the inhabitants' lives.

I believe that, even now, I am still falling through the timeless nothing and numb nowhere. I believe that The Black Fall is the ultimate reality, and that the world outside my window is nothing more or less than an intense, immense, recurring nightmare. I believe that I've finally become a lucid dreamer, and this gives me a perverse joy.

I believe that writing is a Gray Nightmare, and publication even Grayer. Book promotion may be the Grayest nightmare of all.

I believe, however, that there is a certain freedom in nightmares. A certain enlightenment as well (to borrow a word from Buddhism). When I realized that all my experiences are nightmares, they became far more disposable. I don't worry about consequences, because none of this is real. The only thing that's real is that delicious falling (forever separating me from stability).

Forever separating *you* from stability, too. Because if you're reading this, you're a human being. Each and every human being is nuts. Maybe this wasn't true thirty years ago, but it certainly is true now.

The year is 2018, and we are all falling. We need no veils. We no longer have faces. Everything is black.

Some Americans believe that the children murdered at the Sandy Hook Elementary School shooting were actors. Some Americans believe Oprah Winfrey should be president. Some Americans believe they are dogs (or dragons) trapped in a human body. Some believe pedophiles use the basement of a

D.C. pizza joint as a playground for their nefarious endeavors. Some believe vaccines cause autism. Some believe Obama is secretly a Muslim. Some believe they have heard the voice of God. Some believe Earth is flat and Australia is a hoax. Some believe they are sex slaves ruled over by masters. Some believe in reincarnation. Some believe in Heaven.

You may believe that I am crazier than you are. You may believe that I was actually a patient on the psychiatric floor of Naumpton General. Alternately, you may believe I have brain damage related to a car accident, and was there for long-term neurological rehabilitation. You may believe that the Second Amendment Samaritans were an invention of my diseased mind, because a mass donation of guns to the homeless would lead to newsworthy mayhem. You may believe that the homeless people assembled in Mulchport that day were the reincarnations of the madmen and madwomen who made up the bulk of The New Israelites. You may believe that Naumpton doesn't actually exist, but that I'm not crazy. If this is your belief, then you probably stand with those who believe this book isn't a work of nonfiction at all, but a novel. You may believe that my name actually isn't Noelle Cashman, but Nicole Cushing.

I know that to be a false belief. I know that I am Noelle Cashman, and that I'm falling. I know I've had a nightmare that I've stopped falling and landed softly in my office chair, right in front of my window. I know that, in this nightmare, I covered up that window with pictures of Naumpton (printed out from the website of the town's Chamber of Commerce). I know that these pictures lead me to feel that I'm right there along the banks of the Ohio.

I know that, since I've taped those pictures to my windows, I no longer feel oppressed by Gray thought-snot. You see, I never leave my house anymore. I quit my softball team, and I've stopped running. I order my groceries online and the folks from the store bring them in to me.

I know that one of the delivery fellows is in his early thirties and gives off a strong vibe of submissiveness. I know that there's a good chance I can convince him to stay with me some night, and I know that, if he does, I can use the tools of Artifice to change him into a *matryoshka* sex robot. I know that I can bind and gag him in front of my pictures of the Naumpton riverfront. I know I can use a potato peeler to flay layer after layer of artificial skin from him, until I find the skin that appears to be Freakshow Joe. I know I can then proceed to look into those young-old, Bob Denver eyes and break the spirit that inhabits them. I know that the young man would stop breathing.

I know that this murder, taking place on the (artificial) Naumpton riverfront, would be the ultimate act of *solve*. I know it would destroy Grayness in the heart of Grayness. I know that—*if it drew enough international media attention*—it could wipe out all the Gray tendrils that have spread throughout the world. (For Grayness to be defeated it must *know* that it's been defeated.) My hometown in rural Maryland, the Musil-esque reaches of rural Austria, all of them would be cured.

I know that I would need to dispatch press releases owning up to the crime. I'd emblazon the press release with the headline MURDER IN BIZARRE SEX CULT. I know I'd be arrested, but that the only cameras at my lawyer's press conference would be from the local network affiliates for Louisville, Cincinnati, and Indianapolis. I know that I'd hire a publicist to push for interviews (via jail-Skype) with Dr. Phil and Ellen Degeneres.

I know that my publicist would quit shortly after she was

hired. I know she'd send an email to my lawyer, explaining the futility of the assignment. It would read as follows: "The Midwest, in general, is a hard sell. Phil and Ellen's producers both loved the idea of covering a sex cult, but only if a celebrity's attached."

Acknowledgments

In 2016, I began reading Milan Kundera. In 2017, Witold Gombrowicz waltzed into my brain. The first taught me about form. The second taught me about content. *A Sick Gray Laugh* couldn't have been written without these influences.

Meanwhile, Leonid Andreyev's 1905 novella *The Red Laugh* inspired this book's title, and—more importantly—suggested the idea of a looming, suffocating, sentient color.

In terms of literary genealogy, that wraps up the Russian/Eastern European side of the family. Now, on to the Midwestern U.S. side. *A Sick Gray Laugh* required a significant amount of historical research about nineteenth century settlement. The most useful books were William E. Wilson's *The Angel and the Serpent: The Story of New Harmony*, Mark Halloway's *Utopian Communities in America 1680-1880*, Logan Esarey's *The Indiana Home*, and James H. Madison's *The Indiana Way: A State History*

As always, Allen Griffin came through as a beta reader. In particular, he steered me away from a working title that didn't quite work! On a similar note, I'd like to thank S.T. Joshi for his assistance with pre-submission proofreading. Of course, I'm also very grateful for a second chance to work with Ross

Lockhart, Cap'n of the Good Ship Word Horde. His professionalism and his openness to nontraditional fiction have greatly assisted my career.

Last, but not least, I'd like to thank my husband for his continued support. He's my hero. He's my heart.

"At once sly and grim, soberingly real and darkly fantastical, the story of the Waite sisters will haunt readers like an eerie old folk song."

—*Publishers Weekly (starred review)*

When newscaster Abby Waite is diagnosed with a potentially terminal illness, she decides to do the logical thing... break her twin sister Martha out of prison and hit the road. Their destination is the Waite family cabin in Minnesota where Abby plans a family reunion of sorts. But when you come from a family where your grandfather frequently took control of your body during your youth, where your mother tried to inhabit your mind and suck your youthful energies out of you, and where so many dark secrets–and bodies, even–are buried, such a family meeting promises to be nothing short of complicated...

Trade Paperback, 268 pp, $16.99

ISBN-13: 978-1-939905-46-8

http://www.wordhorde.com

"Hauser delivers an engrossing, baffling horror debut that veers hard into the weird, its disturbing aspects enhanced by its faux-nonfictional structure."

—*Publishers Weekly*

Underground filmmaker Tina Mori became a legend in the late 1970s with a stolen camera, a series of visionary Super 8 shorts and a single feature film, heralded as her masterpiece, *Dragon's Teeth*. Then she disappeared under mysterious circumstances...

Through many layers, including letters, a 'zine made by a teenage horror film fan, and a memoir written by Mori's college roommate and muse, film historian and debut novelist Brian Hauser delves deep into Tina Mori's life and legacy, exploring the strange depths and fathomless shadows situated between truth, fiction, fantasy, and the uncanny.

Format: Trade Paperback, 260 pp, $16.99

ISBN-13: 978-1-939905-48-2

http://www.wordhorde.com

"*A Spectral Hue* paints dark, hallucinogenic colors deep inside your mind."

—John Palisano, Bram Stoker Award-Winning author of *Ghost Heart*

Graduate student Xavier Wentworth has been drawn to Shimmer, having experienced something akin to an epiphany when viewing a tapestry as a child. Xavier will find that others, too, have been drawn to Shimmer, called by something more than art, something in the marsh itself, a mysterious, spectral hue.

From Lambda Literary Award-nominated author Craig Laurance Gidney (*Sea, Swallow Me & Other Stories*, *Skin Deep Magic*) comes *A Spectral Hue*, a novel of art, obsession, and the ghosts that haunt us all.

Format: Trade Paperback, 228 pp, $16.99

ISBN-13: 978-1-939905-50-5

http://www.wordhorde.com

"...these stories and characters are sewn together to create one hell of an exquisite monster."

—*This Is Horror*

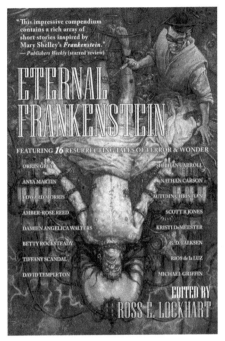

Two hundred years ago, a young woman staying in a chalet in Switzerland, after an evening of ghost stories shared with friends and lovers, had a frightening dream. That dream became the seed that inspired Mary Shelley to write *Frankenstein; or, The Modern Prometheus*, a tale of galvanism, philosophy, and the re-animated dead. Today, Frankenstein has become a modern myth without rival, influencing countless works of fiction, music, and film. We all know *Frankenstein*. But how much do we really know about Frankenstein?

Word Horde is proud to publish *Eternal Frankenstein*, an anthology edited by Ross E. Lockhart, paying tribute to Mary Shelley, her Monster, and their entwined legacy.

Featuring sixteen resurrecting tales of terror and wonder by Siobhan Carroll, Nathan Carson, Autumn Christian, Rios de la Luz, Kristi DeMeester, G. D. Falksen, Orrin Grey, Michael Griffin, Scott R. Jones, Anya Martin, Edward Morris, Amber-Rose Reed, Betty Rocksteady, Tiffany Scandal, David Templeton, and Damien Angelica Walters.

Format: Trade Paperback, 322 pp, $15.99

ISBN-13: 978-1-939905-37-6

http://www.wordhorde.com

About the Author

Nicole Cushing is the Bram Stoker Award®-winning author of *Mr. Suicide* and a two-time nominee for the Shirley Jackson Award.

Various reviewers have described her work as "brutal," "cerebral," "transgressive," "taboo," "groundbreaking," and "mind-bending."

Rue Morgue magazine recently included Nicole in its list of 13 Wicked Women to Watch, praising her as "an intense and uncompromising literary voice." She has also garnered praise from Jack Ketchum, Thomas Ligotti, and Poppy Z. Brite (aka, Billy Martin).

Nicole lives and works in Indiana.

CPSIA information can be obtained
at www.ICGtesting.com
Printed in the USA
BVHW031714270919
559638BV00001B/36/P